LEAST OF EVILS

Recent Titles by J. M. Gregson from Severn House

Detective Inspector Peach Mysteries

DUSTY DEATH
TO KILL A WIFE
THE LANCASHIRE LEOPARD
A LITTLE LEARNING
LEAST OF EVILS
MERELY PLAYERS
MISSING, PRESUMED DEAD
MURDER AT THE LODGE
ONLY A GAME
PASTURES NEW
REMAINS TO BE SEEN
A TURBULENT PRIEST
THE WAGES OF SIN
WHO SAW HIM DIE?
WITCH'S SABBATH
WILD JUSTICE

Lambert and Hook Mysteries

AN ACADEMIC DEATH
CLOSE CALL
DARKNESS VISIBLE
DEATH ON THE ELEVENTH HOLE
DIE HAPPY
GIRL GONE MISSING
A GOOD WALK SPOILED
IN VINO VERITAS
JUST DESSERTS
MORTAL TASTE
SOMETHING IS ROTTEN
TOO MUCH OF WATER
AN UNSUITABLE DEATH

LEAST OF EVILS

A Percy Peach Mystery

J. M. Gregson

This first world edition published 2012
in Great Britain and in the USA by
SEVERN HOUSE PUBLISHERS LTD of
9–15 High Street, Sutton, Surrey, England, SM1 1DF.
Trade paperback edition first published
in Great Britain and the USA 2012 by
SEVERN HOUSE PUBLISHERS LTD.

British Library Cataloguing in Publication Data

Gregson, J. M.
    Least of evils. – (DCI Percy Peach mystery)
    1. Peach, Percy (Fictitious character) – Fiction.
    2. Police – England – Lancashire – Fiction. 3. Detective
    and mystery stories.
    I. Title II. Series
    823.9'14-dc23

ISBN-13: 978-0-7278-8143-4 (cased)
ISBN-13: 978-1-84751-415-8 (trade paper)

To Pat Ross,
who has supported me ever since I began
this strange exercise forty books ago.

All Severn House titles are printed on acid-free paper.

Severn House Publishers support The Forest Stewardship Council [FSC],
the leading international forest certification organisation. All our titles that
are printed on Greenpeace-approved FSC-certified paper carry the FSC logo.

Typeset by Palimpsest Book Production Ltd.,
Falkirk, Stirlingshire, Scotland.
Printed and bound in Great Britain by
MPG Books Ltd., Bodmin, Cornwall.

'I have often thought upon death,
and I find it the least of all evils.'

Francis Bacon, *An Essay on Death*

ONE

The man stood looking at the wall in the cold winter twilight. He tried to enjoy this last moment of stillness. This was the point where you gathered your resources for what lay ahead. It was the last moment when you could turn back, if you chose to do that. But he knew that he wasn't going to turn away from this. He'd put in too much preparation. Research, he'd heard it called – but research was far too pretentious a term for a practical man like him.

It gave you a feeling of power, the knowledge you had. And also the knowledge that others didn't have, about you. No one knew he was here. No one knew what he was going to do. The people who dwelt beyond this wall might have all the resources in the world, but at this moment they didn't know that he was here, or what he proposed to do.

The wall was much older than most of the buildings it surrounded. It had been here for a hundred and seventy years, protecting the solid home and the extensive estate of the cotton magnate who had built it. Cotton was king in Lancashire in those days, had remained king for another century and more. Then, after Hitler's war and the end of empire, cotton had sickened and died. The hundred chimneys which had stood like grimy sentinels over the town had fallen one by one.

The man beside the wall knew this. They had told him about it at school, in the days when he had still attended and listened. They had shown him pictures of the old Brunton, with men in cloth caps and women in shawls and clogs looking obediently and stolidly at the camera outside the gates of the mills.

They were well into the twenty-first century now, and the great mansion of the man who had controlled the destiny of these people and made a fortune from their labours had fallen too. A dreadful thing, the local people said, that such a massive and dignified Victorian residence should be demolished and a brash modern palace erected in its stead. But you were only replacing an inefficient residence with a more modern one, the architect argued; what looked raw and ugly now would merge happily into the landscape after twenty years or so.

The planning committee could find nothing against the change and an impoverished council was anxious to bring new money into the town, no matter how it had been gathered. The immediate neighbours of the estate were relieved to see it preserved in its entirety, when they had feared it might have been developed as new housing, which would stretch to their borders and destroy their privacy. And few people got more than a glimpse through high wrought-iron gates at the new property, because the old wall around the estate had been preserved.

The man studied that wall now. He breathed deeply and regularly, gathering his resources for what he was to do, relishing the knowledge that no one inside the place knew of his presence here. Knowledge was power. And ignorance was not always bliss. Then he realized that he was putting off the moment when he would test his nerve and venture into danger. It was time to act.

The wall had been renovated when the huge new house was built. New money demanded privacy, at whatever cost. But the man in the deserted lane outside the wall knew that privacy meant that you had things to hide from curious eyes. Valuable things. From a distance, the repaired wall looked a solid obstacle. But there were a few crevices in the old mortar between the bricks. That was inevitable. It was also very welcome, to a bold and resourceful predator like him.

They had a security system in the big house, of course. A sophisticated one, as you would expect in a place like this. Entry would be impossible during the hours of darkness. Any unauthorized intruder would be arrested, or worse. Perhaps much worse, if you believed the rumours which circulated in the murky underworld where he gathered his information. No one knew quite how the man who had built this new castle had acquired his money, but everyone agreed he was ruthless.

But the system was switched off during the daylight hours, when the outside staff needed to maintain this modern tzardom came and went. No one expected that anyone would be bold enough to attack during daylight. Research again; and the power of original thought on which he prided himself. When you lived by your wits, it was best to keep them sharply honed. He took a final deep breath, looked swiftly up and down the lane, and set the toe of his trainer into the tiny gap in the mortar.

He was on the top of the wall in a second, his slim body tight against the coping stones to be as inconspicuous as possible. Then he dropped swiftly down on the other side, a twig cracking like a rifle shot beneath his foot. It wasn't really so loud, it was just his heightened senses that made it seem so, he told himself. He crouched for a full half-minute beneath the cypress tree where he had landed. Instant concealment; he congratulated himself again on his careful pre-planning.

The winter twilight was dropping in fast on this sunless day. There were lights on already in the house, as he had known there would be. But not in every room. That was the cleverness of it; that was what you gleaned from careful preparation.

The old wing of the early Victorian house had been preserved as part of the planning bargaining. Here there were no lights visible. The man made for this section, gliding swiftly from bush to bush with swift, simian movements. Crouching beneath the last big rhododendron, he paused and glanced at his watch, nerving himself for the real challenge which lay ahead.

Ten past four: exactly the time he had planned to be here. The accuracy of that pleased him.

The temperature was dropping rapidly now, but he wasn't cold. There might well be a frost overnight, if the skies cleared towards morning as the weathermen promised. But he would be away long before then. The whiteness would cover his tracks, not reveal them. He slid his hand within his close-fitting fleece top and closed his fingers on the jemmy. The old tools were the best, when they suited a job so admirably.

The wood in the side strut of the old sash window yielded to the jemmy quietly, almost noiselessly. Thank heaven for listed buildings, imperfect wood, and the opportunities they offered to the resourceful burglar. It was the first time he had allowed himself to use that word. A burglar he was indeed, but a superior one. Not one of those childish opportunists who pinched tellies and computers and stray bits of cash from ordinary folk, but an altogether more sophisticated class of felon. A man who planned and executed his coups expertly. Hadn't his teachers always said he was a bright lad? It was one of the few things those buggers had got right. He levered open the window and eased his slim frame into the building.

This had been the library in the days of the old house, the woman had told him. He glanced up at the high ceiling and its elaborate cornice, letting his eyes grow accustomed to the dim light. He had a torch in the pocket of his fleece, but he wouldn't use it until it was absolutely necessary. There were easy chairs spread in a semi-circle around a big desk, and paintings which he could not distinguish upon the walls. No books here now. Bloody philistines! Typical of the new wealth which had taken over the country. It made it easier to rob them with a clear conscience.

He moved softly to the door, opened it cautiously, and slid noiselessly on to the wide corridor outside. There was a narrow flight of stairs to his right, which must have been a servants' staircase in the great days of the house. It led him to a landing which was thickly carpeted. He flicked his torch on briefly, illuminated the three wide modern doors opposite him, and moved quickly to the furthest one of these, which adjoined the spot where the completely new part of the building met the Victorian wing.

The door opened readily to his touch. He crept into the big room, flashed his torch beam over the door to the en-suite bathroom, then slid it round the room until it located the item he wanted. The dressing table had three drawers on each side of a large mirror. He slid open the bottom-right one of these, found it contained what he had expected, gasped nevertheless at the myriad facets which glittered and winked under the close light of his torch.

The information had been good. Careful preparation again: the basis of success in this dangerous game. There were velvet-lined boxes which should have contained most of the pieces, but the owner had neglected to put her jewellery away when she took it off. Sloppy cow! Serve her right if she lost it – when she lost it. She'd probably inflate her claim when she contacted the insurance people. These people did that. They made bloody sure they didn't lose, even when they were robbed, people like this.

He fought hard to control his excitement as he pocketed a diamond necklace, matching earrings, some sort of tiara with what he thought must be emeralds. There were five rings; diamonds again, plus sapphires and rubies. A double string of pearls and another necklace, which flashed bright-green emeralds as he laid it across his wrist. Should be in a safe, not lying loose in a drawer, these things – more money than sense, some people. There were silver hairbrushes on the surface of the dressing table, but he resisted them: too clumsy to carry and not worth a fraction of what he already had weighing down his pockets.

His torch caught two enamelled miniatures on the surface above the drawers. He hesitated a moment, then slid both of them swiftly into his pocket on top of the jewellery. He'd no idea whether they were worth thousands or worth peanuts, but they were things of exquisite beauty and he coveted them. He knew even as he did it that he was being self-indulgent. Successful thieves weren't swayed by aesthetic impulses, which got in the way of efficiency.

His hyperactive ear caught the first noise he had heard since he had entered the mansion. It was small and a long way away; several rooms at least, his experience told him. But it was a reminder that he should not linger here; he wouldn't wait for a second one. He shut the drawer carefully; you could delay the moment of discovery by several hours, by a whole day if you were lucky, so long as you took care to cover your traces.

He kept his torch on now as he moved to the landing, located the top of the narrow staircase, and left by the route he had chosen so carefully to climb to his killing. It was good information the woman had given him. Perhaps he'd give her a little extra, when he'd disposed of the stuff. He'd see what he got for it first.

There was a moment of panic when he located what he thought was the door to the old library and found himself peering into a much smaller room. He felt his heart pounding, realized how much on edge he was. No bad thing, that. You needed to be hypersensitive to danger when you were bringing off jobs like this. He was in the big league now.

He found the big room at the second attempt. He kept his torch turned downwards upon the carpet and moved carefully past the desk and the armchairs. He was controlling the urge to rush headlong into the near-darkness beyond the window. That was always the urge when you'd almost completed a job. But haste could lead to mistakes; you had to keep your brain working steadily; you were like a car cruising easily in top gear but with bends still to negotiate.

He had pulled the damaged window roughly shut after his work with the jemmy had allowed his entry. He had a moment of panic now, when the shattered wood seemed to have set itself firmly against the undamaged timber of the frame and trapped him within the house. But when he tried pulling from a different angle, the wood eased upwards with the straining groan of a wounded animal. It left a foot of space, through which the cool air flowed into the room as a refreshing draught. His lithe, small-boned body was through the gap in an instant, where bulkier men would have needed more space and made more noise. He was built for this game, body as well as mind.

It was perhaps that moment of fear and the relief which followed hard upon it which upset his concentration now. As he slid horizontally through the aperture and into the cold-ness outside, he looked back into the house whence he had come, instead of into the new challenge of the wider world outside it.

There was very little light left now. But it was enough to undermine him. He had scarcely registered the cold of the January night when a harsh challenge rang out and chilled his blood. Fifty yards away to his left, from the long shadows beneath the new part of the house.

For a split second, his limbs seemed to be frozen with fright. Then he was away, feet flying over the route he had trodden so carefully twenty minutes earlier. Past the rhododendrons, past the tall firs which had provided such welcome cover as he had crept cautiously towards the house. No caution now, yet the wall he had scaled to enter seemed suddenly impossibly far away.

There were shouts from behind him, a torrent of oaths as he was bidden to stop. But all from one voice, he thought; that must be his comfort. Yet the human brain rarely operates as its owner thinks it should. It now thrust the totally irrelevant thought into the felon's head that it was as well he had left all the bulky items behind in that bedroom, when he should have been thinking only of the route to freedom. He tried to keep the vegetation between him and retribution as he ran.

The wall came at last into welcome view as he rounded the final fir. His very impetus was a help. He had no time to search for crevices in the mortar, but he flung himself upwards with a thrust born of desperation. His hands clutched the top of the wall, his scrambling trainers caught a minimal gap between the bricks. It was all he needed. He thrust with a mighty effort to reach the point of balance atop the wall, then flung one leg over it. Now gravity would ensure that his slight frame dropped clear and triumphant on to the ground outside and the lane which led to freedom.

It was at that point that the first bullet came. He felt the sharp pain against his shin before his ears registered the noise of the shot. For a moment, he thought he had been hit. Then he realized that the bullet had hit the wall beneath him, flinging a fragment of shattered brick against him, but nothing worse.

He hit the ground more heavily in his haste than he had intended, landing with his face in the mould of rotting leaves, forcing the breath from his lungs with the impact. But with the knowledge that the pursuer was armed, fear thrust down every other sensation and took over his being. He scrambled to his feet and was away, his feet beating swiftly upon the welcome tarmac of the lane. He could outrun all pursuit. For no reason at all, he saw the unseen presence behind him as heavier and slower than he was.

The feeling was reinforced by another outburst of obscenities as the man scaled the wall behind him. The odds were with the intruder now. He could surely outdistance this toiling and breathless opponent.

Except that the invisible enemy was armed.

The intruder did not look back, did not see the heavy figure drop on to one knee and take aim at his flying target. The first shot hit the road beside him sparking unnaturally bright with the impact, flinging grit into his panting face. The second hit his arm, but he scarcely felt pain through his fear.

He was sprinting flat out now. And he was right, he was quicker than his pursuer. Without the weapon, he would have escaped. But the third bullet hit his thigh and brought him down. His right leg was useless, even as the left tried to race on with a momentum of its own. He fell in a crumbling heap upon the road, the sudden agony of the flesh tearing from his palm even fiercer than that of the greater wound beneath him.

Things slowed down abruptly. He was groaning when the man with the firearm arrived, his leg clutched to his chest, the blood flooding through his fingers from the ragged hole in his jeans. The man stood breathing heavily above him for a moment, then began to kick his ribs and his head methodically.

Neither victim or attacker was sure of the moment when the figure on the road became unconscious.

TWO

It was a hard winter in East Lancashire, the second in succession. There had been snow on the top of Pendle Hill and the higher mountains of Ingleborough and Pen-y-Ghent to the north of Brunton for seven weeks now. The golf course fairways where former cricketer Detective Chief Inspector 'Percy' Peach now took his exercise had been frozen hard for the whole of January.

It was the last day of that month and it had been a sunny one. But DCI Peach, climbing the staircase to the penthouse office of Chief Superintendent Thomas Bulstrode Tucker, could see no grounds for optimism. Another clear night to come, another hard frost. And before that, another fruitless meeting with the beacon of inefficiency known throughout the Brunton CID section as Tommy Bloody Tucker.

He pressed the button beside the 'Head of CID' sign and watched a succession of lights beside it flash before a despairing voice barked, 'Come!'

Tucker's desk was uncharacteristically strewn with sheets of paper. 'I can come back later if you're busy, sir,' said Percy hopefully.

'No need for that, Percy,' said Tucker affably.

Peach noted the use of his first name: always the warning of some Tucker scheme. 'But I can see you're weighed down with the cares and responsibility of office, sir.' Peach gestured with a wide sweep of his arm at the sheets on the huge desk.

'Nothing that can't be set aside for my Chief Inspector. Do please take a seat, Percy.'

Something shitty was plainly in the offing. Percy lowered his buttocks to the seat in front of the desk as gingerly as a virgin in a rugby club. 'Thank you, sir.'

'And how is the world treating you, Percy? How is married life treating my favourite protégé?'

It seemed to have finally been stored in Tucker's elusive

memory bank that Peach had married his former detective sergeant, Lucy Blake, an event which had brought alongside connubial bliss the unwelcome fact that they could no longer work together. 'Married life suits me down to the ground, sir. I find I am now enjoying a more balanced diet, as well as the multiple and varied delights of the bedroom.' Percy allowed a euphoric smile to accompany his dreamy stare into the middle distance.

'Yes. Yes, I see. Well it's early days yet, isn't it?' Tucker appeared to find the idea of happiness in marriage a difficult concept to handle, which was hardly surprising in view of his own spouse, the formidable battleaxe Peach had christened Brunnhilde Barbara.

'Not so early, sir. Six months now. And it don't seem a day too long, as dear old Albert Chevalier used to say.'

Tommy Bloody Tucker looked pleasingly vacant; the history of the music hall was not one of his interests. 'Didn't he sing, "Thank heaven for little girls"? I hope you're not becoming a paedophile, Percy!' The head of CID was overcome by a sudden burst of hilarity at the wit of his suggestion.

Peach produced the sickliest of his vast range of smiles. 'That was *Maurice* Chevalier, sir. Different sort of cove altogether.'

'I see. Well, it's always a pleasure to exchange pleasantries with you, Percy, but we must get down to business. I want to run one or two things past you. One or two initiatives which I'm sure you'll welcome.'

He didn't look at all sure, and initiative was not a word Percy associated with Tommy Bloody Tucker. He said with heavy irony, 'Your overview of the wider crime scene and the society in which we operate gives you a perspective unavailable to the rest of us, sir.'

Irony was as usual wasted on T.B. Tucker. He said earnestly, 'It is part of my job to keep up standards in the CID section, you know. And I have to say that they seem to me to have been slipping lately.'

'In what respect, sir? We have kept the overtime budget strictly within the limits you defined for us before Christmas. Our clear-up rates are—'

'Dress, Peach, dress. Standards of dress are not what they were.'

'Ah!' At least the bee in the Tucker bonnet seemed relatively harmless this time.

'I have drafted a directive which I intend to circulate among the CID section. I wanted to run it past you before I issued it. If the Chief Constable approves, we could circulate it among the uniformed staff also. I have noticed a most reprehensible sloppiness among some of our younger officers.' The chief superintendent pushed a typewritten sheet across the desk to his junior.

Percy read the piece diligently and found himself struggling to prevent genuine mirth from bursting unbidden into his shining round face – a sensation he could never recall before in this room. 'It's – well, it's not quite what I was expecting, sir.'

Tucker took the sheet back and read aloud with some pride: '"It has come to my notice that the standards of dress which should be automatic and universally recognized among police personnel are not always being observed. Officers should remember that they represent the service and present a smart appearance at all times, except for those rare occasions when they are operating under cover. In particular, underwear should be of an appropriate colour, so as to be inconspicuous beneath whatever outer wear is adopted."'

He looked very satisfied with himself. Peach allowed the pause to develop towards the pregnant before he said with exquisite timing, 'Our girls been flashing their knickers on the main streets of Brunton, have they, sir?'

'What?' Tucker wore the bewildered goldfish expression which Percy always regarded as a mark of success. He said sternly, 'I wasn't thinking about women officers, Peach.'

Percy noted the welcome return of his surname. 'Fifty per cent of our younger officers are female, sir. They will take this as a direct reference to their breeks.'

'Breeks?'

'Panties, sir? Perhaps Mrs Tucker prefers that term? Unless of course she favours the thong.' An awesome picture-postcard version of the Wagnerian rear of Brunnhilde Barbara in a thong soared into Peach's vision and refused to be banished.

'You don't think it a good idea to circulate this?' Tucker's fifty-three-year-old features dissolved into the dismay of a child.

'I think our younger officers might treat it with derision, sir. The female ones might even react with defiance. They might choose to wear no underwear at all.' The vision of Brunnhilde Barbara disappeared at last with the advent of this vivid and wholly more delightful picture.

'I am the Head of Brunton CID, Peach, and not a man to be trifled with. They would disobey my directive at their peril.'

'Indeed, sir. But how would you ensure that it was obeyed? Would you hold regular inspections of underwear? I would of course offer you my personal support and assistance in the implementation of such a policy. But it might be tricky.'

'Tricky?'

'Yes, sir. The inspections would afford a considerable degree of personal satisfaction and even certain excitements, but they might be tricky to implement. Call me a Jonah if you will, but I foresee accusations of sexual harassment from some of our more feisty female staff. And what the papers might make of it, I shudder to—'

'Yes. Yes, I think I can see what you mean.' As always, the mention of media reaction and journalistic ridicule had Tucker's immediate attention. 'Well, perhaps I'll look at it again before I circulate it.'

'I think that would be advisable, sir.'

Tucker stared regretfully at the sheet in his hand. 'It seems a pity, though. I've spent most of my day on this.'

Percy Peach noted as he descended the stairs from Tucker's office that the sun had now set on the last day of January. He tried not to think of the cost to the public purse of the hours Tommy Bloody Tucker had spent devising the dress directive he had just aborted. At least it had prevented the real damage he could have caused by actually interfering in the business of arresting villains.

Things had been very quiet for the last two months. What

they needed was a serious crime of a really puzzling sort, so that the chief could worry about other things.

The man who had broken into Thorley Grange and stolen the jewellery was lucky. He was left unconscious by the side of the lane where he had fallen and been battered by his pursuer's boots. He wore a fleece, but his lower limbs and his wounded leg carried only jeans and trainers. On a freezing January night in this high and isolated place, hypothermia would have killed him before morning. But a little while after he had fallen, a motorist not only saw the prone figure but stopped to investigate it.

The hospital notified the police that a victim with gunshot wounds had been admitted, as was standard practice. The injuries were not life-threatening, but shock and the interval spent on the lane before he was discovered meant that the ward sister prevented the uniformed constable from speaking to him until three o'clock on the afternoon after he had been injured. He revealed that his name was Edward Barton, that he was twenty-two, and that he lived with his mother on a council estate in Brunton. Beyond that, he was resolutely silent, like a soldier taken prisoner who reveals only name, rank and number.

The constable reported to the station that it seemed unlikely that Barton's gunshot wounds were the outcome of a domestic incident. The matter was referred to CID with some satisfaction by the uniformed inspector. If this was going to occupy a lot of police time and produce nothing, let those clever buggers in plain clothes earn their money.

It was seven in the evening by the time Detective Sergeant Lucy Peach and Detective Constable Brendan Murphy arrived at the hospital. The nursing personnel had changed and the night sister was more amenable to police access to her patient. Possibly this was because there was a personable woman as the police presence this time; more likely it was because the patient had been surly, uncommunicative and ungrateful for what had been done for him. He had also threatened to discharge himself. The sister said, 'I can give you twenty minutes. I hope you get more out of him than we can.'

Edward Barton had a thin, alert face and a discontented expression. His deliberately blank pupils focussed for a moment on the blue-green eyes, vivid chestnut hair and dramatic upper contours of Lucy Peach, vividly presented beneath a dark green sweater. Then he saw the tall frame of Brendan Murphy behind her and realized that these were filth. Plain-clothes filth, and in one case filth in a very attractive guise. But filth nonetheless, and therefore worthy of his controlled hostility. He blanked them and said, 'I've nothing to say to you lot, I told that young sod that this afternoon.'

'Indeed you did, Eddie. It was because you were so unco-operative to our constable that DC Murphy and I have ruined our evening to come and see you now.' Lucy afforded him a dazzling smile. Be pleasant, until you knew for certain that wasn't going to work.

'You've ruined your evening for fuck all. That's all I've got to tell you.'

'Oh, you can tell us much more than that, if you wish to, Eddie. The question is whether you choose to do so or not.'

'I choose not to, bitch. I've already told you that. Are you thick or summat?'

Lucy smiled again, less friendly but still tolerant of his youthful defiance. She sat on the chair beside the bed and leaned towards the man within it, making him acutely conscious of her scent and her splendid bosom. Barton found both disconcerting, but he said determinedly, 'I've sod all to say to the likes of you.'

DC Murphy brought another chair and sat down close to his sergeant. 'You would be well advised to watch your tongue and be more helpful, lad.'

Barton transferred his attention reluctantly from the pneumatic DS Peach to the fresh face which was only a little older than his own. 'Or what, pig?'

'Or we might arrest you as you leave here and take you down to the station for further questioning.'

'And why would you do that, punk?'

'On the grounds of wasting police time, Mr Barton. On the grounds of refusing to assist the police in the investigation of a serious crime.'

Eddie wasn't certain whether they could do that, but he didn't want to risk it. He sank back on his pillow and gazed straight ahead of him across the ward. 'I don't know nothing.'

'Ah, so you know something. That's what we thought; that's why we're here.' Lucy Peach drew his attention back immediately. Eddie didn't understand double negatives, but he was obscurely aware that he'd made a mistake. He looked into those wide and lustrous female eyes and said, 'I can see why they call you Peach, darling! You're a ripe peach, aren't you? I wouldn't mind stroking your—'

'Who put those bullets into you, Eddie?'

'Get lost, bitch. I ain't no grass.'

Murphy leaned across and touched the slight mound in the blankets which showed where Barton's right thigh was bandaged, producing an immediate gasp and wince from the patient. 'Nurse! Nurse, I want you to see this.'

But apparently there was no nurse within earshot. Barton wished that he had been more appreciative and less surly about the medical care he had received earlier in the day. He tried to sound convincing as he said, 'I'll have you for police brutality for that, you bastard!'

Lucy smiled. 'For enquiring diligently after your health, Eddie? Perhaps you shouldn't twist around so much in your bed, if it's painful for you.' Then in a quite different, more businesslike voice, she said, 'Stop pissing us about, Mr Barton. How did you acquire the injuries for which you have been treated here?'

'I don't know. I don't remember. That happens, when you're in shock, doesn't it?'

'Sometimes it does – when people have been almost killed in road accidents, for instance. But not when they've received flesh wounds in the upper left arm and in the thigh.'

'Well, I don't remember.'

'You got a good kicking as well as bullets, didn't you? From a man who battered you unconscious and then left you to die. A broken rib as well as gunshot wounds. If I were you, I'd want some sort of revenge on a callous sod like that.'

Barton did, and for a moment he was tempted. But the episode had left him with a deep fear which was more powerful.

His face set into a sullen mask. 'I didn't see nothing. I hadn't done nothing. I don't know who he was or why he did it.'

DC Murphy let his arms float over the bed for a moment, as if he proposed further examination of the patient's injuries. Then he folded his arms and said, 'You were found outside Thorley Grange, Mr Barton. What were you doing there?'

'Thorley Grange. Where's that?' Eddie was rather proud of the furrowed brow of puzzlement he contrived for this.

'It's on high ground at the western edge of Brunton, Mr Barton. It's our belief that you know that perfectly well. So what were you doing there?'

'I don't know how I got there – I never go up there.' He managed to look genuinely puzzled. 'Perhaps that's why I don't remember anything. Perhaps I was shot in the town and then dumped up there after a good kicking. Lucky for me that someone found me and got the ambulance, I suppose.'

Murphy regarded him steadily for a moment, as if challenging him to further ridiculous speculation. He said tersely, 'You've been very lucky indeed, Mr Barton – so far. I've a feeling your luck is going to run out any second now.' He reached towards the heavily plastered bicep beside him. Barton winced away, but Murphy merely put it back under the bedclothes with exaggerated solicitude. 'Why were you in that lonely spot beside Thorley Grange?'

Barton stared straight ahead and spoke as if repeating a mantra he had memorized. 'I've no idea why I was found there. I don't even know where the place is. Someone must have dumped me up there.' Then he said with more animation, 'You lot should be trying to find who attacked me, not harassing a wounded man.'

Lucy Peach said quietly, 'That's exactly why we're here, Eddie. But unless you're prepared to help us, we don't stand much chance.'

'You don't stand much chance anyway. You're a waste of fucking time.'

DS Peach held her hand up as Brendan Murphy leaned over the bed again. 'We've wasted enough police time on you, Eddie Barton. There's been a uniformed copper outside the ward all the time you've been in here, to make sure no one could get at you. You'll be out of here soon and no one will protect you then. You've strayed out of your depth, but unless you're prepared to help us, there's nothing we can do to keep you safe. You should think about that, while there's still time.'

'Fuck off, pigs!' The reaction was automatic. Eddie Barton was no grass, was he? And the pigs didn't protect you, once they had what they wanted. He enjoyed his obscenities more because they were directed against a woman, and a pretty one at that – some vestige of ethics still told him it was more shocking to direct these things against a woman, even one who seemed to be as unshockable as this one.

She stood up now. The tall DC who was her sidekick stood too, between him and the window, blocking out some of the light, making the man in the bed feel suddenly more vulnerable. Lucy Peach said, 'If you want to help yourself, let the uniformed officer outside know and someone will be down here immediately to take your statement and initiate enquiries. I strongly advise you to do that. Please note that I made that quite clear to Mr Barton, DC Murphy.'

The two of them were gone then, without a backward look at him. They issued some instructions he could not distinguish to the invisible man in uniform who defended him against unwelcome visitors.

After they'd gone, Eddie lay for a long time looking at the high ceiling above the fluorescent lights. Out of his depth, they'd said. They were right about that, even if they were stupid. He was a small-time burglar, however expert he pretended to be in that. He'd strayed way out of his depth and he still felt a long way from the shore. Not waving but drowning, the poem he remembered from school said. He felt some of the panic that poor sod must have felt.

Eddie Barton felt more alone and more frightened than he had ever felt in his life.

THREE

A t Thorley Grange, the repercussions of Eddie Barton's attempted burglary were still being felt.

The man who had commissioned the new building on the site of the nineteenth-century cotton baron's site was a representative of the worst side of twenty-first century capitalism. A century and more ago, men who made fortunes from local industry had built their modern castles to display their wealth. Nowadays, fortunes came by other means. There were all sorts of rumours, but no one knew for certain exactly where the new occupant's money came from, or which was the most lucrative of his many enterprises.

Oliver Ketley was physically an impressive man. He was six feet two inches tall, with broad shoulders and hips and no noticeable embonpoint, even at the age of fifty-six. In his youth, he had been a fearsome centre half in amateur football; he had put on no more than half a stone in the last thirty years. No one knew whether he watched his diet or whether he was one of those fortunate people who could eat whatever they liked without adding inches to their waistlines. Certainly no one around him felt bold enough to enquire about it. He took little exercise save for the occasional game of golf at the North Lancs Golf Club, the best course in the area.

Ketley should have been a handsome man, but he was not. He had regular features in a large, square face, but they were for the most part expressionless, even when he seemed perfectly relaxed in convivial company. His inscrutability seemed always to carry a certain menace. He registered everything around him, but reacted to it as he pleased and when it suited him. His facial control gave him a sinister aura, which was enhanced by the fact that his eyes were a very pale blue, a shade which was inappropriate in such a face. No one enjoyed Oliver's stare. He had a good head of black hair, sharply parted and slicked straight back, in the style of an earlier era.

He was a physically powerful man, but none of those around him now had ever seen him use that strength in physical combat. When you made the amount of money that Oliver Ketley did, in the way he did, you made enemies also. He had killed, in the past – had murdered his way to the top, in the envious phrase of one of his contemporary villains. But he had long since acquired the hard men who were his carapace against opposition. He had muscle to defend him against any attack, muscle to enforce his will when that was necessary. In the twenty-first century, it was easy enough to hire hard and ruthless men as your enforcers, once you had the money to do that.

But loyal muscle was often unintelligent muscle, which could bring its own problems. Ketley was investigating one such problem now. James Hardwick was the head of his enforcers. This was a man who had also killed in his time, a man who carried the knife scars on chest and side which were the badges of loyalty and survival in the brutal world where he operated.

It was Hardwick who spoke now. If he was nervous about this investigation of his department, he gave no sign of it. 'It was Wayne Taylor who shot him. He saw him leaving the house.'

'Did he shoot to kill?'

'No. He was bringing him down.' Even in an increasingly lawless world, killing still excited irritating attention. Unless you could dispose of the remains swiftly and without any trace, it was better to avoid murder.

'Then why shoot at all?'

'Because the man would have got away with your wife's major jewellery. Taylor felt he had no alternative.'

Ketley nodded. You couldn't allow anyone to get away with a burglary here. Almost a hundred thousand pounds worth, retail. And it wasn't just the money. If the word got round that Oliver Ketley had been outwitted by a petty thief, it would provoke hilarity and loss of status for him, in an underworld where status was strangely important. 'So this sod nearly got away with it?'

'Yes. Almost got away scot-free. He was over the wall and

away, and he was faster than Wayne. Taylor brought him down with a couple of shots and gave him a good kicking. He took your stuff back and left him there.'

'Left him there unconscious. Almost against the wall of the property. He could have died there.'

It wasn't the possible death that was the concern, but the location and the possible consequences. If you killed a man, you dumped him elsewhere. You didn't leave the body on your own patch, where a body would invite in police snoopers. Best of all, you dumped the carcase beneath motorway concrete or in the ocean, and thus ensured it was never seen again. To leave a wounded man outside your walls invited investigation.

'Taylor miscalculated. He thought the man would get up and limp off home. He didn't think he'd be picked up and taken to hospital by a passing motorist.'

Both of them were silent for a moment. You didn't usually get brains and brawn together; the people who had both rose higher in the criminal world than being bruisers for others. Taylor should have either finished his man off or sent him on his way, too scared to utter a syllable about what had happened. Hardwick eventually said, 'Do you want me to fire Wayne Taylor?'

'No. Send him down to Birmingham. Let him operate there: the casino can always use a bouncer.' Oliver Ketley rarely sacked people. If they stepped seriously out of line, they would simply disappear from the world, eliminated by the machinery of which they had been a part. If they made minor errors, you gave them a warning and kept them on; it was better to keep employees who knew anything about you under the company umbrella, where they would certainly not reveal any of your business to others. Becoming a bouncer at the entrance to a Birmingham casino was certainly a demotion, and Taylor would recognize it as that. But he'd be grateful that the consequences of his mistake weren't worse. 'What happened to this bugger who broke into the place?'

'Eddie Barton, he's called. Small-time thief moving out of his league. This would have been his biggest-ever haul. He broke in before we switched the security system on for the night. Forced a window in the old library and went straight to your wife's jewellery in the dressing-table drawer.'

There was silence between them again, each knowing what the other was thinking. His wife was a careless fool to leave stuff like that among her smalls; it was inviting trouble, even in a house like theirs. Jewellery should be kept in a safe. These seconds of silence were the nearest Hardwick would come to voicing that opinion. His boss eventually said with ominous calm, 'Did he have inside information?'

'It's possible. He seemed to know where to get in and where to go. He didn't touch anything else except the jewellery and a couple of miniatures.'

'Cleaners?'

'It's possible. They'd be the ones who knew where your wife kept the stuff. I'm investigating discreetly.'

'Where's the thief now?'

'Barton? At present he's in the Brunton Royal Infirmary, with a uniformed copper on the door to prevent access by people like us. But his injuries aren't serious. He'll be discharged within a day or two.'

A small, mirthless smile flitted for an instant across Ketley's inexpressive face. 'Perhaps he ought to have a visit at home – just to make sure he keeps his miserable mouth shut.'

Detective Chief Inspector Percy Peach was finding married life splendid in all sorts of ways. One of these was the improvement in his diet. Not only was he eating better fare than that he had formerly procured from takeaways, but instead of returning to a cold and empty house he often found warmth and a meal almost ready for him when he returned to his ageing semi-detached home.

This night was different. His new wife would not be home until around eight as she had to interview a gunshot victim in hospital. But Percy was a modern man: he had declared it to his mother-in-law. So he set to and prepared sausage and mash and baked beans – the central principle in bachelor cooking, he had always argued, was not to be overambitious. The bangers were done to a turn when Lucy arrived: near-black all round, without being burnt. The boiled potatoes had just the right additions of milk and butter added to make them smooth and tasty after his energetic mashing. The beans were piping hot, with the superfluous tomato sauce in which they had been heated discreetly minimized on the plate. Perfection within simplicity: that was the secret.

Lucy found both the aroma of cooking and the warmth of the kitchen welcome. It was too often forgotten at the station that bachelor girls as well as single and divorced men went home to empty and unwelcoming houses and flats. She was too hungry to be anything other than highly appreciative of her spouse's efforts. When he then produced his pièce de résistance as dessert, she even offered heartfelt applause. Percy had only attempted rhubarb crumble twice before, so he must be a quick learner, he said, when Lucy announced loyally that it was just right. He beamed so affably that Lucy decided it was better not to remind him that this was an essentially simple dish. She was beginning to pick her way through the minefields of marital diplomacy.

It was not until they had the steaming mugs of tea, which Percy preferred to the elegance of cups and saucers, that they reviewed the events of the day. The CID section considered that DCI Peach was a man who feared nothing and was never shaken, but Lucy knew him well enough now to sense what made him nervous. Criminals rarely worried him. Appearances in the Crown Court and traps set by astute and unscrupulous defence barristers did. She sighed a final approval of her repast and said, 'How'd it go in court today?'

He did not shrug the query aside with a virulent obscenity, as he might have done at Brunton nick, where his iron-man reputation was unchallenged and carefully preserved. He said thoughtfully, 'All right, I think. As usual, I said as little as possible, until called upon for a professional opinion by the prosecution. We've given them a good case: verdict and sentence aren't until tomorrow, but I think the bugger will go down.' He spoke with considerable satisfaction. Brought up as a Catholic, he retained from that experience only what he called 'a starred A grade in A-level guilt'. The nearest thing he had to a creed was a personal crusade against the forces of the criminal army ranged against him.

As if he was embarrassed to reveal so much of himself, even to Lucy, Percy said quickly, 'I had a session with Tommy Bloody Tucker this afternoon. He wants to make sure all officers' panties are in order – I've offered to do the inspections on the female staff at Brunton, so long as he makes it an order in writing.'

'You're joking!' But it was never safe to assume anything in the case of Chief Superintendent Tucker, even though you knew Percy Peach would be putting the most damning interpretation possible on it.

'It's true! He wants to put a circular about dress around, with particular reference to correct underwear. It has to be neat and of an appropriate colour, he says. He got the idea from some equally deranged bugger in the Midlands, apparently.'

'Did you manage to talk him out of the idea?'

'No. I merely offered my assistance in inspecting the bras and pants of female personnel, as I said. I think I should confine that to the CID section; I might need danger money to tackle Diane the Dangerous Dyke in the uniformed division.'

Percy maintained that this lady had all the essential qualities for rapid elevation to chief constable in the modern police service: she had a degree, a black skin, lesbian preferences, and a total lack of imagination. Lucy was too tired to argue the lady's cause, the more so since she could hardly contain her amusement at the picture of Percy asking this particular woman to remove her uniform with a directive from on high in his hand.

Warm and replete, she almost dozed off before the latest episode of *Downton Abbey*, which they had recorded from Sunday night television. She had to get Percy to tell her what had happened. 'Great costumes, great setting, lousy dialogue,' he summarized sourly. 'And your mum's allowed to fall asleep in front of the telly, but a young flibbertigibbet like you isn't!'

'Must be married life with an older man.' She yawned and stretched her legs luxuriously. 'Speaking of marriage, shouldn't you have asked me why I was late home?'

'Not yet. If it happens three times in a week, I'll have you and your lover tracked by a private eye. Anyway, I know you were at the hospital. It was me who detailed Brendan Murphy to keep an eye on you. How'd you get on?'

She smiled. 'He's a good lad, Brendan. Very chivalrous – except that he felt he needed to defend my honour against a man with gunshot wounds and at least one broken rib. He behaved as if I'd never heard obscenities before.'

Percy grinned. 'It's the Catholic upbringing, you see. We believe every woman should be like the Virgin Mary. Until we learn better, of course.' He ran a hand appreciatively over her non-virginal thigh.

'We didn't get much out of the little sod in the hospital bed. I think he was scared, beneath his standard anti-police bluster.'

'Who shot him?'

'I doubt we'll ever know that. He was found unconscious outside Oliver Ketley's place. We think he'd tried a break-in and been spotted. But nothing from the house was found on him when he was taken to hospital.'

'Thorley Grange?' Peach was immediately interested. He had been disturbed when Oliver Ketley had moved on to his patch, but powerless to prevent it. The man was a known villain and a big one, but too slippery and too well defended for anything to stick. A major employer of dubious labour and a centre of criminal activity: just the sort of man you didn't want in your area. 'Who was employing this man?'

'Eddie Barton? My guess is no one. I think he's a petty burglar who got out of his depth and very nearly paid for it with his life. But we didn't get anything out of him to tell me whether I'm right or wrong. And I thought we agreed last week that we weren't going to talk shop at home.'

'You're transparent, Lucy Peach! You're a shameless hussy who only thinks about one thing. And I'm just putty in your hands – for the moment, at least. Lead me to your bed and remind me of my manhood!'

Three minutes later Percy Peach, who retained his magical capacity to disrobe at record speed, was between the sheets and conducting the first of his inspections of female underwear in CID, to the accompaniment of a low, appreciative growling. 'You've passed!' he said breathlessly as Lucy discarded the last of her clothes and joined him with a leap beneath the duvet he held up for her. He explored the now familiar but no less luscious curves which had excited even the wounded Eddie Barton. Several minutes later, his appreciative cry of 'Bloody 'ell, Norah!' signified both excitement and the imperious dismissal of all thoughts of work.

Indeed, it was not until the first light of a February dawn was seeping into the room that he reflected that sooner or later he might need to speak to this Eddie Barton himself.

DCI Peach would have been surprised to know that, forty miles to the south, a very different man was thinking about the owner of Thorley Grange, Oliver Ketley, at the same time as he was.

Jack Burgess was not a policeman, however. He was very much the same type of being as Ketley: an enormously rich man who acquired his wealth by dubious and occasionally shocking means. He operated a variety of industries, based largely in the great northern cities of Manchester and Liverpool. The legitimate ones, such as casinos, nightclubs and betting shops, made smaller profits but were very useful for laundering money from the illegal but highly profitable concerns. The latter were principally drug-running, prostitution, and an increasing amount of illegal immigration.

The scale of his wealth as well as the industries in which he collected it made Burgess a rival for Oliver Ketley. At forty-four, he was twelve years younger than Ketley and more newly on the scene, but he was now almost as big. He lived in Alderley Edge in Cheshire; his estate was much more modest than the rolling acres of Thorley Grange, but the house built for him here was outside the range of all, save for people like him and the Premiership footballers of Manchester United and Manchester City.

Two footballers had in fact been among the people entertained at Burgess's house on the last night of January. There had also been the leader of the latest boy band chart-toppers and two of the women who had got to the final stages of the last Big Brother series. Burgess was more prone than he realized to a little celebrity gloss. These people were happy to have hospitality thrown at them and they didn't ask embarrassing questions about where it came from. And Burgess maintained that it didn't do any harm with the public to show yourself alongside faces which featured in the innocent pages of magazines like *OK!*.

All of this was true enough. But Jack Burgess came from a working-class, single-parent background, where as a boy he had been left much on his own in the evenings. The most undemanding television had often blared out at him until nearly midnight. Perhaps he gathered people like this around him to prove to himself as well as to others that he had arrived. Well-known faces, however vacuous, demonstrated that he was now one of the richest and most powerful men in the country.

Whereas Oliver Ketley shut himself behind the high walls of Thorley Grange and eschewed publicity, Jack Burgess courted it. Whereas few of the people of Brunton even knew Ketley's name, Burgess's name was now known to many from the gossip columns and the photographs of *Hello*. Two very different men, most would have said. And yet increasingly bitter rivals.

One of the many useful qualities possessed by Jack Burgess was that he needed very little sleep. He had that in common with Margaret Thatcher, he told anyone who commented on it. Most of the people he associated with professed a great admiration for the Iron Lady. Hadn't she encouraged initiative in all sorts of unlikely places?

At one o'clock, Burgess's guests had left, most of them with serious admonitions from their host about driving carefully. The police reaped a rich harvest of speeders and drinkers on a particular stretch of road which most of them would be using. Most people in Jack's position would now have been happy to plod their way to bed, perhaps in a pleasant alcoholic somnolence. But Jack Burgess was neither drunk nor tired. He called in a man who had not been at the party. He wished to discuss business affairs, and in particular the way Oliver Ketley was beginning to trespass upon his territory and annoy him. In reality it was the other way round, of course: as the newer shark in this polluted sea, it was Burgess who was seeking to take away business from his older rival. But like most gangland bosses, Jack assumed a natural right to dominate the territory. He had long since passed the stage where his staff dared to point out anomalies in his assumptions.

'Ketley's been in touch with Van Heusen. What's he up to?'

Van Heusen was the international dealer who supplied drugs to the Burgess organization. In the mysterious and fabulously profitable world of illegal drugs, no one knew whether the man was Dutch or where his huge supplies came from. Van Heusen might indeed be an assumed name; even Burgess himself had never met him. Nor had he any desire to do so.

Geoffrey Day, the man he was speaking to, handled the dealings with Heusen's representatives, but even he knew little of the man himself and was content that it should be so. In this trade, knowledge was a dangerous asset; people who knew too much disappeared suddenly, with no one caring to follow up their deaths.

Day said uneasily, 'I don't know quite what he's up to. But we've no evidence that he's trying to muscle in on your territory.'

'Supplies aren't inexhaustible. Even Van Heusen's supplies. And the same goes for markets. Ketley isn't going to increase his sales without affecting ours.'

Geoff Day nodded slowly. 'There are more drugs being used every year. Everyone knows the government and the police are fighting a hopeless battle. But I agree: Ketley operates in the same geographical areas as we do. If he's planning large-scale expansion, it will affect us. I've got contacts with people who work for him. I'll make discreet enquiries.'

Jack Burgess had set things in motion. He felt for the first time in the day a little weary. He smiled acidly at Day and said, 'There's not one of them, but in his house I keep a servant fee'd. Eh, Geoff?'

Geoffrey Day looked suitably puzzled, as he had intended him to. Burgess said loftily, 'It's a quotation from *Macbeth*. Benefits of a public school education, you see.' Jack made the most of the scraps of knowledge he retained from his erratic schooling; he had once been a page in a production of the Scottish play. Nowadays he pretended to his followers that he was a Marlborough man; he liked them to think that he had an entirely different schooling from most gangland bosses.

At that moment, his patchy remembrance didn't extend to any consideration of what had happened to Macbeth at the end of that eventful play.

FOUR

Greta Ketley looked fondly at the emerald necklace, then picked it up and fastened it around her slim neck. 'I've always liked this. I'm so glad you didn't let that thief get away with it. I should have been very upset.'

Greta was Swedish, but she had lost all trace of her accent, save on the rare occasions when she was excited or angry. She was fourteen years younger than her husband. When she had married him twelve years ago, she had looked very much the trophy wife. She had had long, straight, blonde hair, green eyes, and the willowy but curvaceous figure which suggests both expertise on the ski slopes and enjoyment of the pleasures of the après-ski. Greta had never been stupid. She could play the dumb blonde when it suited her, but it was strictly an act, usually reserved for men whom she held in quiet contempt. If the act had been used less and less over the years of her marriage, that was simply because as time passed she saw less and less need for it.

At forty-two, she remained an attractive woman. She used that attraction when it suited her even more capably than when she had first come to Britain as a capable and dazzling au pair. She was sitting before her dressing table in a light-green silk slip when she donned the retrieved necklace. Oliver Ketley walked across the room and stood behind her as she looked into the mirror. He paused for a moment until her eyes rose to meet his in the mirror, then slipped his hands round her shoulders and on to the emeralds. 'They match your eyes,' he said softly. He stooped over her and slid his hands from the stones of the necklace to the smooth skin beneath it, then down to rest softly on to her breasts beneath the slip. 'You really should take more care of your jewellery, you know.'

He spoke like one addressing a favourite child, who repeats the conventional wisdom but knows he will not be obeyed.

'I know, Oliver. You've told me before. They should really

be locked away safely. But there aren't so many occasions in the year when you can wear stuff like this. I like to take my things out and look at them and handle them, even when I don't plan to wear them.'

'I know that. And I like to see you enjoying things. But valuable things aren't safe, in today's world.' He spoke as if he were one of the righteous bastions of that world, without any ring of irony.

'Even when my protector is Oliver Ketley?' She leaned her head back and looked up into those very pale blue eyes which she had come to know so well.

He smiled. 'Even then, my darling. The fact that that little toerag came so near to getting away with it proves that.'

'What will happen to him?'

He never knew how much she knew about his business and his actions, and Greta was careful to keep it that way. He had no idea whether she knew that the thief was in hospital and he didn't want to explore it with her. 'Oh, he's been taken care of. I don't think he'll be back here again.'

'Will you prosecute?'

The idea was outlandish and he fancied she knew that, but he affected to treat it as a serious enquiry. 'Oh, I don't think so. We've got our property back and the toerag has learned his lesson. No point advertising to the world at large that you possess stones like this and don't choose to keep them under lock and key.'

She put her hands on his and held them affectionately for a moment. Then she unfastened the clasp of the necklace and put it beside the rest of her restored finery, signifying that this moment of intimacy was at an end. 'I saw the chap who helped me with that puncture going out with a holdall this morning. He's not leaving, is he?'

'Wayne Taylor? He's going down to Birmingham for a few months. We need someone to help out at one of the clubs there.'

'He was very quick and helpful with that wheel when I was stuck near the gates. Promotion, is it?'

It would have been a foolish man who didn't rush to the aid of the boss's wife, Oliver thought. After all these years, he was still pleased to see small demonstrations of the power he held. 'It's a sort of promotion, yes. There'll be more opportunities for him there.'

'I see.' She nodded several times, as if she divined more than he knew. He was never sure exactly how much she knew about him. Did she ever think about where the money came from to support this huge place and the way she dressed and lived?

She put the necklace and the other jewellery away in exactly the place from which it had been stolen. Oliver Ketley knew as she shut the drawer that she would never put it in the safe and that he would never make her do so, but he could not explain to himself why that should be. The emotional world was a mysterious planet for him; he had laboured since his childhood to keep it so.

Greta thought as she completed her dressing and made up her face that he would be pleased to crush her emotions as he had his own. If she were not careful, she would become one of those cynical people who knew the price of everything and the value of nothing. She must make every effort to avoid that.

She waited until she was in her car before taking the mobile phone from her handbag and putting it on the passenger seat beside her. She drove though the big gates and alongside the wall until it fell away behind her and she was between open fields. Then she stopped the car, glanced into the rear-view mirror to make sure she was not observed, and dialled the familiar number. Her face lit up and the years dropped away as she heard the voice which answered.

Greta Ketley said, 'I'm on my way. I should be with you in half an hour.'

The man was impeccably dressed, impeccably mannered. He spoke excellent English in the preliminary exchanges. But he was patently not white Caucasian; that was the official term you had to use, Michael Knight thought.

He was the chef at Thorley Grange and he was interviewing for a new kitchen assistant. He was glad to have the chance to appoint his own staff, but he had little experience of interviewing. He glanced down at the letter of application in front of him. It had been typed on a computer and signed simply 'C. Lee.' He had assumed this would be an English applicant, probably a local man. He had thought choosing his staff would be a simple process; now it seemed to be a potential minefield. He wondered how he could investigate the man's background without being accused of prejudice by those damned race relations people. Mr Ketley wouldn't like that; he didn't like anything which brought any sort of publicity to the place. And that certainly wouldn't be good publicity.

Knight wasn't even sure of the man's age; you couldn't deduce anything from those smooth, regular, olive-skinned features. He looked down at the letter: it told him in the second line that the man was twenty-eight. He glanced through the rest of it again. There was nothing in it about a country of origin or work outside the UK. But then there was no reason why there should be. Applicants had been directed to summarize their previous work experience in relation to this post, and the details in front of him did just that, simply and expertly.

Knight tried to make it an informal, friendly enquiry as he said, 'Were you born in this country, Mr Lee?'

A small, very polite smile. 'No. I was born in Vietnam. But I have been here for years now; I feel quite British. I have a passport I could show you, but I did not think that it was necessary for this post.'

'No. No, of course it isn't. I was just doing my job, just finding out a little about you.' Michael Knight felt on the defensive, when it was surely the man seeking a job who should be nervous. An idea struck his spinning brain. 'We'll be working quite closely together, if you get the job. It's nice to know a little about each other.'

He couldn't be sure, but he thought the man leaned forward on his chair and gave him a tiny bow. 'My first name is Chung. I have a brother who plays football for Norwich City. Please feel free to ask me anything you wish.'

Chung threw in his footballer brother at all sorts of unlikely times; for some reason he had never fathomed, it seemed to reassure people, to persuade them of his reliability. Sure enough, the chef now nodded, as if he had been offered some convincing evidence of this candidate's kitchen competence. Knight glanced again at his letter and said, 'You seem to have the kind of experience which would be useful here, Mr Lee. You say you were doing "kitchen and other work" in the hotel at Preston. Why did you leave there?'

'I moved to a restaurant because I wanted to work in catering full-time, to get the experience I need. I hope that eventually I may become a chef myself.'

'Well, most of your work here would certainly be in the kitchen. If you do well, you may in time even stand in for me, when I have time off. But I would need to be convinced that you were up to the task, before anything like that was possible.'

'Of course. But I feel the work here would provide me with the experience I need to run a kitchen, whether here or elsewhere.'

He was a bit too sure of himself, this smooth-faced man with the clean hands and immaculate nails. Getting ahead of himself, voicing his ambitions about becoming a chef. Knight said sharply, 'Really? I'd better watch out for my own job, hadn't I?' He followed this with a laugh, but he didn't sound amused. There was a pause before he added, 'I should stress that this is quite a junior post. You'll get the sort of experience we've been talking about, but you'll be expected to help out wherever needed around the kitchen. You may also be serving food, when Mr Ketley has visitors.'

'I understand.' Another small smile, and this time Knight was sure that the man bowed.

'These will mostly be business visitors. Mr Ketley doesn't do a lot of private entertaining. You will need to be discreet about anything you hear.'

'Yes. I have always made it my practice to be so.' He had heard that phrase in a radio play and stored it away.

'It is very important that anything you hear at Thorley Grange should not pass beyond its walls.'

Michael Knight repeated the phrase which had been used to him on his own appointment, and again the man seemed to find nothing surprising in it. Chung Lee merely inclined his head again and said calmly, 'That has always been my practice.'

There was something irritating about this scrupulously presented individual, Knight thought. He said waspishly, 'It's quite a junior post, you know. Not particularly well paid.'

'The wages are adequate. It seems to offer the sort of experience I need.'

'Quite frankly, I have to wonder why you're applying here. We can't be offering much more than you're earning in your present post.'

'Money is not the first consideration, Mr Knight. The work is more important. And I understand from the details you sent me that the post is residential.'

'Indeed it is. The details also said that you would be expected to adjust your duty hours at short notice to accommodate the needs of the household.'

'That again is not a problem. I am, as we say, not afraid of work. And free residential accommodation makes the pay seem much more generous. I am a single man; at present I have to reserve a large fraction of my wages to pay for my accommodation.'

There were only two other applicants. This man was patently superior to either of them, in experience, attitude and the way he presented himself. It would constitute racial prejudice to ignore that. Michael Knight took a deep breath and said, 'In that case, I am happy to make you a formal offer of this post, Mr Lee. I'm sure we will be very happy working together.'

He stood up and held out his hand. Chung Lee took it and shook it up and down twice, as if concluding a formal ceremony. His hand was small but his grip was firm and confident. He gave his little smile again and said, 'Would it be possible for me to see the kitchen where I am to work and the room where I am to live before I leave today?'

Knight gave him a quick tour of both, then assured Lee that he was delighted he could move in so quickly. Chung had already given in his notice to the restaurant, which meant that he could take up his new post in two days' time. He was as polite and secure in his leave-taking as he had been in everything else.

Michael Knight rang the restaurant where Lee had been working after he had gone and was told that he had been a model employee in his short time there, that the owner had been disappointed when he had handed in his notice. He had even offered Lee a little more money, but the young man had said that he needed the more varied experience which the post at Thorley Grange would offer him.

Knight wondered why he should be worried about offering a junior post to a man who seemed both from his background and his bearing to be so eminently suitable. Perhaps the defi- · ciency was in himself rather than the candidate; perhaps he felt he would not be able to live up to the high expectations of this very contained man.

Perhaps Mr Chung Lee had seemed just a little too sure of himself.

Eddie Barton was discharged from hospital twenty-four hours after being interviewed there by DS Lucy Peach and DC Brendan Murphy.

He was proud that he had given the pigs nothing they could use, pleased to be rid of the succession of bored-looking constables in uniform who had sat outside the door of the ward to prevent any hostile access to him. Yet he found he felt almost naked without this attendance during his first few days of convalescence at home.

It was thirty-six hours before he limped out to the betting shop to place a bet, three days before a friend who visited him was able to persuade him to go to the pub in the evening. He relaxed a little on his second pint. 'I'm glad you dragged me out, Rob. Mum's a diamond, really, the way she looks after me, but I was getting stir-crazy in there.'

He refused to be drawn on the exact nature of his wounds. He also sat where he could keep an eye on the door of the pub, so that he could see whoever was coming into the place. It was early evening and there weren't many entries; the ones who came were mostly familiar. But after two pints Eddie had had enough. He said, 'These ribs are playing me up, Rob. The medics told me I'd have this pain. I'd better call it a day.'

'You seem nervous, Eddy.'

'Nervous? No. It's just that I realize I'm not quite as fit yet as I thought I was. They said I'd need to take it easy for a while. Do you think you could walk home with me? Just in case it gets worse, I mean.'

'No problem, mate. I go past your place, anyway.' Both his friend and his anxious mother were surprised to see Eddie back in the house before eight o'clock.

But as the days passed, nothing happened, Eddie felt stronger, and it seemed as if his vague fears were groundless. He realized now that he'd been too ambitious in trying to burgle Thorley Grange, that it was out of his league. A nagging voice beneath his fear protested that he'd almost got away with it, hadn't he? And those mysterious people up there surely couldn't want any further revenge on him. He'd escaped with nothing and they'd almost killed him for it. They'd probably forgotten all about him by now.

A fortnight after his failed attempt on the jewellery of Greta Ketley, Eddie Barton was feeling less threatened and more cheerful. It was the middle of February now and after a hard winter the snowdrops in the gardens he passed were making a brave show. In the sun beneath sheltering walls, the brilliant yellow and the deep blue of crocuses were proclaiming that spring was not too far away. He had called at the library and was carrying two of the romantic novels Mum liked and two thrillers for himself. He was secretly proud of the fact that he read, though he tended to conceal it from all but his closest friends.

There was no problem at the job centre. He was patently still unfit for the manual work which was all they could offer him and he had the medical notes to support him. When he threatened to display his wounds, the frosty-faced woman paid him his benefit without even the token reluctance she usually displayed. Money in his pocket always lifted his spirits. Even the pittance the social gave you made you feel comfortable, for a day or two. He'd be able to resume work in a week or ten days, so long as he didn't undertake any difficult entries. It would be a while before he could squirm through windows again.

He would be glad to get home. The bag with the four books wasn't heavy, but it was tugging a little against his damaged ribs, and he couldn't transfer it to the other hand because that was the arm with the healing bullet wound in his bicep. He'd take the short cut by the old gasworks, where the only houses left standing were a few squats. You didn't go that way at night, but it would be fine at eleven in the morning.

He could walk quite quickly again now; maybe he'd go to the pub on his own tonight. It hadn't seemed so at the time, but he was coming round to the view repeatedly expressed to him by the hospital nurses that he'd really got away very lightly, considering he'd had two gunshot wounds and a brutal kicking. He was supposed to see his own doctor this week, but he'd probably skip that, if the healing still looked good when he inspected it in the mirror.

He was so preoccupied with his own thoughts that he scarcely heard the big silver Audi as it glided up behind him. Posh car for these parts, Eddie thought automatically. He didn't realize that it was stopping until a man was beside him, holding his arm in a vice-like grip. 'Inside!' was the single word he said. He put his hand on Eddie's head and bent it beneath the roof as he shoved him into the car, like the police did with an arrest.

Eddie Barton was too frightened to make any protest. He felt, indeed, as if the breath for words might never come to him again. He could see the back of the driver's head, with the hair close-cut upon it; the man did not turn to look at him.

'We wanted a word,' said the man beside him. He had a Geordie accent, which for some reason made the words sound more sinister to Eddie. He fixed strong fingers and thumb on Eddie's bicep, finding exactly the place of the healing wound, drawing a sharp gasp of pain from the quivering face above it. 'You're lucky you're still 'ere, mate. You got away lightly.' He gave the arm another squeeze, as if contemplating what more serious damage he might now administer.

'First, you don't ever go near Thorley Grange again, toerag.'

'I won't! I won't!' Eddie wanted to convince them that nothing was further from his thoughts, but he couldn't find the breath for that.

'Second, you keep shtum. Absolutely shtum. If you breathe one word about what you did or what you saw up there, you're dead meat.' He accompanied each phrase with another squeeze on the arm, producing a series of terrified whimpers from Eddie. He seemed to enjoy these, for he accompanied his final word with a jab at the plaster which was all that now covered the broken rib in his side. 'Understood?'

A scream of agony. Then, lest the enquiry should be repeated, Eddie shouted. 'Understood!'

'Drive on,' said his torturer after a few seconds. He sounded disappointed that his work was over, and Eddie divined that this was a man who thoroughly enjoyed inflicting pain. He didn't protect his victim's head from the roof this time, or even leave the car with him. The Audi stopped after a hundred yards and Barton was flung from it into the doorway of a derelict house, his fall on his injured side eliciting a final yell of pain.

He lay still for a long time, as if he feared that any movement would be interpreted as a sign of defiance which would merit further punishment. Not until the sound of the Audi had died away into the generalized hum of distant traffic did he dare to lift his head and look around him. Then, slowly and painfully, he levered himself to his knees and looked at the squalid street around him. It was completely deserted. The rusting gasholder shut out the pale winter sun, making his isolation seem more complete.

Moving in slow motion, like a man who could not believe he had escaped more serious hurt, Eddie Barton gathered the scattered library books and returned them to the plastic bag. Then he limped homewards, feeling as wretched as he ever had in his young and eventful life.

FIVE

C hief Superintendent Thomas Bulstrode Tucker looked out of the window of his penthouse office in the massive new brick building which was Brunton police station. He could still remember the old market hall, with the big ball atop its square tower, which had fallen each day when the clock beneath it struck one. He had stood as a small boy with his hand in his father's to watch the demolition of that tower by the vandal civic developers in 1964. Now he could look out over the town to the countryside beyond, towards the splendours of the Ribble valley, which amazed those visitors from the south who had expected only the grimy terraces of an old cotton town.

Chief Superintendent Tucker was looking forward, anticipating that slowly approaching date when the cares of office would disappear and a fat pension would leave him free of worries. It was true that he had a formidable wife to confront at home, but he thrust aside that unwelcome prospect with the thoughts of carefree days on the golf course, when he would discover the elusive secret of that infuriating game and his handicap would come tumbling down. Like many another hopeless hacker, Thomas cherished the notion that leisure and more rounds would improve his golf. It would be some years before he faced the reality of Anno Domini. That would defeat all lessons and practice and eventually diminish even the very limited prowess Thomas possessed.

Tucker was at once a source of fun and a great frustration to his CID staff. He was a humourless figure, but not as stupid a man as most people thought. He was aware both of his own inefficiency and of his reputation among his staff. The iron rule of rank muffled most opposition. But he knew that there were constant mutterings about the chief whom that offensive man Peach had christened Tommy Bloody Tucker. He couldn't do without Percy Peach, whatever liberties the fellow took, because it was DCI Peach who produced the crime clear-up rates which had made T.B. Tucker a Chief Superintendent and head of CID.

He sometimes toyed with the notion of retiring 'on the sick', as he had seen some of his colleagues do. You claimed stress, which was very difficult to disprove, and spent the last years of your service either absent altogether or appearing only intermittently, with the real responsibility and the real work transferred to others. It was a tempting prospect, but it had one great drawback. Both his formidable wife and those acquaintances at the Lodge and the golf club who had no police contacts thought of him as efficient.

Self-esteem was important to Tucker. He believed that loss of reputation in the Lodge and the golf club were the worst disasters which could hit a man. You could survive many things, but loss of face was not one of them. Without a family, there were few other things left to Thomas but status.

That was a sad thought, and he was in many ways a sad, isolated man. He spent most of his days negatively. He did not try to be constructive, but fought to avoid mistakes, to keep his nose clean. His only consistent aim was to avoid the ultimate humiliation of a dressing-down by the chief constable and the suggestion that he should consider his position. His was neither a happy position nor a happy life. And now the hated Percy Peach, the man who was at once his saviour and his nemesis, was climbing the stairs to see him from the CID section where the real work was conducted.

Chief Superintendent Tucker determined once again to assert himself. One of his many faults was that he rarely learned from experience.

'I'm very busy, Peach. This is most inconvenient. What is it that you wanted?'

Percy took his time in running his eyes over the vast empty spaces of the executive desk. 'I see, sir. Still redrafting your memo to all CID staff, are you?'

Tucker sighed deeply, trying to demonstrate that he was as long-suffering as any saint under Satanic attack. 'You'd better sit down, I suppose. What on earth are you talking about?'

Percy's black eyebrows arched impossibly high beneath his

shining bald pate. 'Your directive about correct pants and bras for our staff, sir. I've been holding myself in readiness.'

Enlightenment dawned. Tucker said gruffly, 'The dress code, Peach? That is still under review.'

'Indeed it is, sir. Directly so in my case. I've been most careful in my selection of boxer shorts since we spoke last week. And I've kept a very close check on my wife's panties also, sir. I must say that in the case of DS Lucy Peach duty has combined with pleasure in a most agreeable fashion.' He stared reflectively at the ceiling and allowed a beam of ecstasy to steal over his features until his whole frame was suffused with bliss.

'I see. Well, as I say, I have decided for the moment to keep the matter under review.'

Percy's face fell. 'Your decision, as always, sir. But I must admit to a smidgeon of disappointment. Having volunteered my services when you broached the project, I was looking forward to a meticulous examination of the bras and pants of all the female officers under our jurisdiction.'

Tucker decided to try the man-to-man approach. 'Come, come, Percy! You know very well we'd never get away with such things without claims of sexual harassment.'

'The thought had crossed my mind, sir. But with the Head of CID prepared to assert himself and provide his usual strong and fearless leadership, I resolved as ever to carry out my orders. I would bring enthusiasm and thoroughness to the inspections, in the knowledge that you would be taking full responsibility for my actions.'

The mention of responsibility was as usual a red light for Tucker. 'The matter as I say is under review. But I will tell you privately that I have almost decided against issuing any directive on dress.'

'Ah! In that case I shall continue to conduct meticulous examinations of the front and rear elevations of DS Peach's underwear, so as to keep myself in practice for any future general order from you. But I shall not extend such tests to the rest of our female officers.'

'You asked to see me, Peach. What is it you wanted?' Tommy Bloody Tucker reverted to world-weary resignation.

Percy realized that it was time to wrestle with more serious police concerns.

'A very large criminal fish has swum into our waters, sir. A killer shark, in fact.'

Metaphor usually confused Tucker, but this time he surprised his junior. 'I presume you're referring to Oliver Ketley.'

Peach, who could not know that the chief constable had raised this matter with Tucker only that morning, was surprised by this unusual grasp of reality from his chief superintendent. 'Indeed I am, sir. From the amount of building he's already commissioned at Thorley Grange, I fear he intends to stay here indefinitely. Which from our view can only be distressing.'

For a few moments, the two were silent, a pair of senior policemen united by the threat of a major menace to life on their patch. Tucker's reaction was as usual negative. 'I have to remind you, however, that nothing major has so far been proved against Mr Ketley. As far as the law is concerned, he is an innocent citizen.'

'But you and I know better.'

'We may feel that we do, Percy, but there is nothing very much we can do about that.'

'A burglar attempted to rob Mr Ketley a fortnight ago, sir.'

'Then it's our duty to bring that burglar to court.'

'Indeed, sir. But we cannot provide the Crown Prosecution Service with a case, because the victim, Mr Ketley, refuses to provide us with the appropriate evidence. Refuses even to acknowledge that any such incident took place.'

'That is unfortunate, but there may be very little we can do about it. No doubt Ketley wishes to keep a low profile.'

'I'm sure he does, sir. But a member of his staff used a firearm against the intruder, who I am sure did not offer any violence himself.'

'Can you prove this?'

'Not yet, sir. But I have not yet taken a personal interest in the case myself. I feel that it is time I did so.'

'You must be very careful, Peach. Very careful indeed. This man may be a villain, but he has no convictions which declare that to the public. He has the resources to do us considerable harm.'

He was being warned off. But whatever Peach's shortcomings, he really cared about crime; he hated it with something approaching a missionary zeal. That was the thing which made him respected as well as feared by the entire CID section. He now pointed out to Tucker Ketley's known involvement in drugs, in prostitution, in gangland killings – known to the police, but so far unproved in court, because it had been impossible to persuade key witnesses to bear witness in court against him.

Peach spoke with a passion that reduced even the pusillanimous Tommy Bloody Tucker to silence. Then he mentioned the worst crime of all, in the minds of most policemen in Lancashire. Worse even than straightforward murder, for most of them. Worse than anything except the abuse of children, because the victims of this crime were numerous and almost as helpless as children. A crime committed as long ago as 2004, yet still in many respects unsolved.

Chief Superintendent Tucker listened aghast, and was quelled. All he said as he dismissed his DCI was a fearful, 'For God's sake mind how you go, Peach!'

It was still February. Everyone knew that there must be hard frosts still to come. There might even be more snow; indeed, from the higher parts of the course, you could still see whiteness upon the top of Ingleborough. But golfers, like most sportsmen, are optimists when it comes to weather, as in most parts of Britain you need to be.

The North Lancs Golf Club was the best one in the area. It was one of Chief Superintendent Tucker's permanent resentments that while DCI Peach's application for membership had been immediately accepted, his own had been turned down. The membership committee had politely pointed out that Tucker's handicap of twenty-four was not low enough for him to be considered, and his most intensive efforts over the years had not succeeded in reducing it.

On this crisp, bright Saturday, the present captain of the golf club, a local solicitor who had been a member since he was a boy, was playing one of his captain/pro challenges against two members. These were friendly encounters which led to a good deal of banter in the clubhouse; those pairs who beat captain and pro enjoyed congratulations in the clubhouse and entry to a small competition for all the winners at the end of the year. Those who lost made a modest contribution to the captain's chosen charity. These light-hearted, pleasurable occasions allowed the captain to play with people he might otherwise not have encountered on the course.

The professional played off scratch and the other three received the appropriate stroke allowance, according to handicap. The challengers this time were a new member, Oliver Ketley, and the man who had introduced him, a local bookmaker. This man had realized that he could no longer compete with the big boys and sold his three betting shops to Ketley's organization. The captain was glad that the bookmaker, whom he had known for years, was part of the four-ball, for he had found conversation with the new member difficult.

Oliver Ketley was not a natural communicator: he had found little need for it over the years. As his power and his reputation had grown, the men around him – save on the few social occasions he allowed himself, it was always men – had adopted the habit of speaking only in response to some enquiry of Ketley's. Unless Oliver initiated conversation, there was very little of it around him. The pro was a taciturn individual who when on the course concentrated upon producing his best golf. For eighteen holes, the conversational exchanges were largely between the captain and the bookmaker. If Ketley noticed that things were socially rather strained, he did nothing to alleviate that.

The captain found him a difficult, intimidating figure. New members were traditionally nervous in the presence of their captain; he had grown used to easing their tensions and lightening the atmosphere. Oliver Ketley had no need for his assurances that this was only a game and not to be taken too seriously. He seemed indeed to be a serious man. With his commanding physical presence, the shorter clubs looked like toys in his hands. He generally hit the ball straight, if not with quite the distance you would have expected. He accepted congratulations on his better shots with the merest nod and the smallest of smiles. His pale blue eyes registered no satisfaction, but they did give the impression of taking in everything around him. He did not seem to approve of much that he saw, though his mouth when it spoke uttered conventional phrases. He won the match with a solid par on the eighteenth, then shook hands with the briefest of smiles.

In the clubhouse, Ketley bought the first round and unbent a little over the drinks. The captain had many other people to talk to here, lots of cheery greetings and golfing chatter, so it was easier for him in the club lounge. Oliver was drinking brandies, but they seemed to have no effect upon him. When someone mentioned drink and driving, he said that his driver was picking him up and offered a lift to anyone who thought they might be unsafe to drive. No one took him up on his offer.

Oliver said nothing out of place, as befitted a new member. He offered no opinions on politics or religion, even when the talk turned to the challenge of Militant Muslimism, a hot topic in a town where a quarter of the population was now Asian. He smiled when any of his companions said anything humorous, but the small movement of the lips on the square, expressionless face scarcely constituted mirth. There was certainly no sign of amusement in the very pale blue of eyes, which seemed too small for that large face.

Just before he left the club, he asked the captain about his chosen charity. 'It's the Brunton Hospice,' the captain said. 'They do wonderful work and they're always short of funds. But you don't owe anything: you won our match.'

Ketley's thin lips tightened again into his small, humourless grin. He produced his cheque book. He said nothing as he wrote, then stared at the cheque for a moment before he signed with a flourish. 'I agree that it's a wonderful cause. Please add this to your gift fund. I'd rather the source remained anonymous.' He handed over a cheque for two thousand pounds, waved aside the effusive reaction, and prepared to leave the club. News of his generosity would get out, despite his request. In his experience, people could never keep completely quiet about gifts, if they were large enough.

From a much noisier table on the other side of the busy golf-club lounge, Oliver Ketley's every movement and reaction were carefully noted. Beneath the bald head with its fringe of black hair, the darkly glittering eyes of Percy Peach were studying his man.

Oliver Ketley's greatest rival did not play golf. In the office behind his Manchester casino, Jack Burgess sat with Geoffrey Day and awaited the arrival of a third man. Whilst Ketley was taking his exercise, the workaholic Burgess was furthering his interests. Jack liked that idea. He liked the thought that it was his industry which had taken him ahead of his rivals, which would presently enable him to overtake Ketley.

Saturday was a busy day in the new casino, which stretched across the extensive floor of a converted mill. In a few hours' time, garish neon lighting outside would be beckoning the punters inside and roulette wheels would be spinning to make money for the owner, as cotton looms had once done in this city they had called Cottonopolis. But at the moment all was quiet. There was the faint sound of vacuum cleaners at work on the carpets of the big room where the public squandered its money, but no other activity.

Burgess looked at his watch. 'Better get down to the back door, Geoff. Bring the man straight up here.'

Day nodded. They had offered to meet him at his own place, but he hadn't wanted them there, hadn't wanted any visitors which might give watching eyes a clue about the work he did. He would come to the back door of the casino at the time he had arranged. Crowded cities were a much better cover for him. He felt happier with crowds around. If you wanted to survive in his trade, you took every possible precaution.

He was beside Geoff Day before Day saw him, even though he was watching for him at the back door of the casino. The man was fit and wiry, without a surplus ounce of fat on him. His eyes were set deep in his gaunt face, making him seem at first glance ill, almost as if he might be suffering from some terminal disease. He would have attended to that if he'd known it, as he would have anything which made him other than ordinary. Anonymity was his cloak and he had become almost paranoid in his search for it. He looked up and down the narrow street behind the casino, then followed Day into the building.

'Mr French to see you, sir,' said Day. He shut the door carefully behind the visitor and moved away from the room. You accorded a contract killer the respect of a 'Mr' and a private audience. You moved away whilst the boss negotiated the hire of his services. George French wasn't alone in thinking that the fewer people who knew about his business the better. If things went wrong, which of course they wouldn't, it was much better that you knew nothing about whatever sinister bargain had been concluded.

In the small, very warm room Day had left, hirer and the putative hired sat down opposite each other. French slid his anorak off his shoulders and on to the back of his chair and Burgess nodded and smiled. It was almost two years since he had last seen French, but he didn't shake his hand. He ignored the man's sallow cheeks and the dark patches beneath his eyes. 'You're looking well, George. And prosperous, I trust.'

'Well enough.' The speed with which his answering smile appeared and disappeared showed how awkward he felt with such pleasantries. 'You want a job done, or I wouldn't be here.'

'You're right. I do.'

'Twenty thou in advance. Twenty thou on completion.'

Some people shied away when they heard the price. The fair-haired man on the other side of the desk wouldn't do that, but it was as well to agree the terms from the outset. Jack Burgess smiled, eased himself back in his chair for a moment; even with a job like this, he liked to pretend that as the employer he was in charge. He thought of producing the bottle of malt whisky from the cupboard behind him, then decided against it. French would certainly refuse and those who turned down expensive spirits always seemed to him to be asserting some subtle moral superiority. But moral wasn't a word you should apply to this man's trade.

'This will be a big one, George.'

French was immediately wary. 'Not a politician is it? I don't do politicians or policemen. Backlash is too big.'

Burgess nodded. He approved of that. The attention the authorities would accord to such killings, with huge teams assembled and the search continuing for years if necessary, made murder the wrong solution. There were other methods of dealing with political enemies; you found their weaknesses, which were usually sexual, and then set them up for lurid exposure in the tabloids. Burgess appreciated the realism and the diligent preparation which made French the best in his trade. 'This man isn't a politician or a policeman, George.'

'Then who is it?' French didn't like the use of his first name, which always made him feel patronized. But he wasn't going to object to it, with a lucrative commission in the offing. He forced a wan smile. 'You'd better tell me who you want to disappear.' He always put it like that. Even the blackened souls who employed him sometimes shied away from words like murder.

'Oliver Ketley.'

The bombshell was dropped quietly. French did not flinch, still less whistle, as the name sounded in his ears. Nevertheless, both men knew that it was a bombshell. A few seconds passed before French said. 'Ketley's different. I'm not saying impossible, I'm saying difficult. An extra ten k difficult.'

'And why would that be?'

'More danger for me. More preparation. Ketley has his own muscle – men who aren't just enforcers but personal body-guards. It wouldn't be easy to get near you with Geoff Day and his buddies around you.'

Jack Burgess smiled again, ran a hand quickly through his rather untidy blond hair. What French said was true enough, but it was never mentioned. The comment from this cold, impersonal man he was about to employ was a reminder to him that even he was vulnerable, if someone should have the will and the resources to attack him. He said, 'All right. I see the difficulty. Fifty k altogether, then; half in advance and half on delivery. When?'

'You must leave that to me. This will need a lot of planning. I'll need full detail of his movements, but I can get that. Have you got a deadline for this?'

'No, but I don't want it to drag on indefinitely.'

Or until Ketley decides you're too dangerous, and hires me or someone like me to dispose of you, thought French. The thought amused him, but he allowed no trace of that to appear on his cadaverous features. 'It won't do that, but I'll need the right opportunity. You don't want a failure.'

'And you want one even less.' Burgess did allow himself a grim smile at that. Failure would mean death for the man sitting opposite him.

'Exactly. That's why I can't give you a deadline. There are no near-misses allowed in this game; the only two results are complete failure or complete success. I'll need the opportunity and you can't make that. But I'll deliver, sooner rather than later. Hopefully within a month, but no promises.'

'Fair enough. You'll have twenty-five k within the next few days.'

'In used notes.'

'That's no problem. This place takes in as much as that, on a good night.'

'No further contact beyond that. The job will be done as soon as possible. Maybe days, more likely weeks.'

Now, at the last possible moment, they rose and shook hands, sealing their grim bargain. Geoffrey Day could not have been far away, for he appeared immediately when Burgess summoned him. George French left as swiftly and unobtrusively as he had arrived.

Jack Burgess sat very still in his office for a long time after he had gone. It was a big decision to take out Ketley. But once you had made the decision, it was good to have the money to employ the very best in the trade.

SIX

Luke Gannon was a year older than Eddie Barton. Eddie realized in retrospect that that was why he seized on Luke's offer. Gannon had been a year ahead of him at the comp. He'd seemed big and strong then, the leader of his gang. Eddie had held him in awe at school, and it was some hangover from those days which made him go along with the scheme.

Luke wasn't a close mate of Eddie's, but he came over to him in the pub and asked how he was getting on with his recovery. They didn't discuss how he'd got his injuries; from the effective local grapevine of the small-crime world, Gannon would know all about how he'd been damaged. Indeed, Eddie found that his wholly unsuccessful attempt to burgle Thorley Grange had marginally increased his standing. After all, it had been an audacious effort, and gunshot wounds always carried more kudos than a routine beating.

Luke Gannon discussed the patient's state of recovery as if he were an anxious aunt. Then he said, 'You won't be climbing any drainpipes or clambering over any high walls for a while then, Eddie.'

The way he delivered this made it clear that it was something he had prepared in advance, so Eddie just grinned ruefully and waited for what would follow. Sure enough, Gannon, after a glance round the pub, said quietly, 'I might be able to put an easy thing your way, if you're interested. For old times' sake, like.'

In all truth, there hadn't been many old times, thought Eddie. He'd been too young to be in Luke's gang at school and they hadn't done any jobs together since then. He should have rejected the offer at the outset, because Luke wasn't a good bet. He didn't operate in the areas where Eddie had built up his expertise, and he'd already got a couple of convictions. To put it at its bluntest, Luke was thick. He wasn't bright enough

to foresee the difficulties in a job which Eddie would have
seen immediately. That meant in turn that he didn't do the
careful preparations which had kept Eddie clear of the courts.
But the hangover from school was stronger than Eddie realized
at the time.

It was a simple enough proposition. They borrowed a van
from Luke's cousin. Then they drove it to the local golf
club. They dressed in sweaters and respectable trousers –
definitely not jeans, Luke said twice. This was because jeans
were banned in golf clubs and they were going to pass
themselves off as members. 'But aren't we too young for
that?' asked Eddie, who had never in his life set foot in
such a place.

'No. They have young 'uns like us. They even have lots of
kids, nowadays. And they have so many members that no one
knows 'em all.'

'But they'll have locks on the doors. We can't just walk
into the place.'

Luke smiled his most patronizing smile. 'That's where
you're wrong, mate! That's just what we're going to do. They
have a security code system on the doors and you have to
know the number to get in. The members have cards. But all
we do is hang about by the door until someone comes out,
then thank him and take the door from him. They just assume
you're another member – especially if they're rushing out to
get on the course.'

'It can't be as easy as that.'

'It is, mate. Believe me. I've done three jobs like this before.
Piece of piss, mate.'

This was where Eddie didn't ask the right question. He
should have suggested that people would be more ready for
them, more aware of the danger, if Luke had pulled the stunt
three times before. But Eddie had never attempted this sort of
brazen, broad-daylight crime before. So all he did was ask
lamely, 'What happens when we get inside the place?'

'We're in the dressing rooms then. If there are people there,
we nip into the bogs, come out when we can hear that everything's quiet. You whip through their trousers then. You'll be
surprised how many of the daft buggers leave twenty or thirty

pounds in there – even more, if you're lucky. And there's wallets and credit cards and the odd decent watch.'

'Sounds a bit hit and miss.'

'Nailed on piece of piss, mate.' Luke Gannon wasn't sensitive to mixed metaphors. 'I agree that what you get from the trousers can vary, but what we're really after is the sets of golf clubs. Thousand pounds new, some sets are.'

'But we don't get that for them.'

'No mate, we don't. But that's where we're well placed, see.' Gannon looked round the pub again, leaned towards Eddie, then tapped the side of his nose with immense relish. He didn't often get the chance to enlarge on the subtlety of his plans. 'I've got this contact. We pass on all the golf gear fast as shit sliding off a shovel. You don't get a big price, but you move the hot gear on fast.'

'And how do we get these sets of clubs?'

Again the crafty, confidential grin. At this moment, Luke himself could hardly believe how clever he was. There's wooden lockers all along the walls. Each with a set of clubs in. They're locked, but I've got keys that will open most of them. If they don't, you'll find a ten-year-old could force them.'

He was so enthusiastic that Eddie had to force himself to ask the obvious question. 'And what are the members doing while we're pinching their gear?'

'Out on the course enjoying their daft game, most of 'em, if we choose our time right. Course, the ones whose gear we pinch from the lockers aren't there at all.' He watched whilst Barton nodded dubiously. 'You in, then?'

Eddie's mind was screaming a no, telling him that it couldn't be as easy as this and that Luke Gannon was far too confident for his own good. But he was grateful for the offer, even a little flattered to be considered.

So his lips said, 'Go on then. I need the cash, don't I?'

Greta Ketley conducted the affair with the utmost caution from the start. That was made easier by the fact that no one seemed to consider it possible that anyone would attempt to stray from the bed of Oliver Ketley. She rather enjoyed that thought, just as she enjoyed the enormity of her treachery. Greta was a woman who had discovered many years ago that she enjoyed danger. That was what had induced her to marry the strangely menacing Oliver Ketley, when both her friends and her saner instincts had told her that marriage to a man like him would be at best a foolish and perilous adventure.

It had proved in time to be just that. Greta had been thirty when she married Ketley twelve years ago. She had thought of herself as experienced and worldly-wise; in most senses she had been both of those. But she had retained one naivety which is common in most of her sex: she thought she could change the character of a man through love. Oliver might be a harsh and, from what she had heard, brutal man. But he would surely respond to her devotion and her loving kindness. Every man had a feminine side, they said; she believed that every man had at least a softer side, which would find free expression when a loving woman committed herself to him for the long term.

It had not proved so. Oliver kept her resolutely out of his affairs. She had learned after one or two fierce humiliations that she should not try to interfere with the way he made his money or the way he treated people. The last thing you wanted to be was an enemy of Oliver Ketley's. She knew now that even a wife could become an enemy, if she tried to be more than bed-mate, ornament and hostess.

She could have jewellery and expensive holidays and all the clothes she wanted, so long as she expected not love but lust from him and chose not to see his frequent bedding of other women. She could furnish the big new house and what was left of the old one exactly as she wished, with expense no problem. Oliver would afford her a good life, with all the luxuries she fancied. But it would be strictly on his terms.

All of this Greta now understood. You learned more about yourself as well as others through experience, even when that experience was unpleasant. She knew that it would be highly dangerous to take a lover when you were married to Oliver Ketley. But she now knew also that she loved that very danger. What she missed in her comfortable, affluent life was the element of risk. She had failed to make a decent human being out of Oliver. The sex had been good, in the early days, until she realized that any supple female body would do for him and that she could not love an automaton, even a dangerous one. She would look for love and for danger somewhere else.

There were a number of glamorous young men who swam in and out of her orbit, because Ketley's various business ventures involved a wide range of men. But most of them were far too careful of Ketley to risk a pass at his wife, or even to react to encouragements from her. Men were a foolish sex, but they were more realistic than women. When they measured the possible delights of secret meetings with Oliver's indisputably bed-worthy wife against the retribution from Ketley, they decided against both. And Greta had her pride: she didn't want a coward in her bed. What she really needed was a man who would appreciate danger as she did, a man for whom danger would add a unique element to lovemaking, as it did for her.

She found such a man in Martin Price. For both of them, the possibility of discovery brought with it a spine-chilling excitement they could have taken from nothing else.

Price had served for eight years in the SAS. He had risen to the rank of Captain in that impressively daring and impressively vicious organization. He had been forced to leave the army because he had broken a rule in even the elastic code which was peculiar to the SAS. It was an organization which needed to countenance much more than the regular army if it was to achieve its perilous goals, but Price had done something which even the SAS could not ignore. Greta had still not found out exactly what he had done. Nor had she pressed Martin for details; his vague and undefined offences brought a touch of mystique to the man which added to her excitement.

Martin Price had first met Greta at this stage of his life. Immediately after he had left the SAS, he had been doing some covert work for Oliver. Mystery had combined with dashing good looks to imbue him with glamour, but he had then disappeared for six years to operate as a mercenary soldier in different parts of Africa and Asia.

His experience in the SAS gave him the ideal background for such work. He had a capacity to weigh the chances of success and failure in any battle exercise more accurately than any of the native troops he commanded. He was not only experienced but cool and dispassionate. People zealous for a particular cause usually entertained delusions of military glory which undermined calculation. Price estimated the realities of combat and his chances of success with cool efficiency.

When he resurfaced in northern England, Martin was older, harder and even more captivating for Greta Ketley. His reappearance coincided with her final realization that she was never going to change Oliver Ketley, that she was never going to be more than an exotic appendage in her husband's life. When Price appeared from nowhere beside her on one of her shopping expeditions to Manchester and asked her to join him for coffee, she agreed immediately. Months later, both of them agreed first that she had not hesitated for a moment before doing so and secondly that each of them had known that this was a commitment to something much more serious.

Martin Price did not live in a city. In the small town of Chorley, between Preston and Manchester, a Georgian mansion had been converted into four luxury flats. Martin lived in the larger of the two ground-floor flats. It was much easier to see who was coming and going in Chorley than in the city, much easier to note the presence of any stranger who might be checking on the movements of people in the new flats. You took such precautions, when you had lived as Martin Price had lived.

He kept his blond hair short, not to disguise the advent of baldness, as some forty-year-old men did, but because it was a habit he had acquired in the SAS and maintained in the rainforests of Africa. Long hair brought lice, when water was scarce; it also made you vulnerable in close combat. Greta stroked his hair now, delighting in its familiar springiness beneath her fingers, gazing from no more than a foot into those blue eyes which were so much darker and more alive than Oliver's. Martin had a good mouth, too, so much more active than—but comparisons were odious, when you could and should enjoy a man for his own sake.

He levered himself up on his elbows on the silk sheets and smiled down at her. She wondered how he had managed to preserve such perfect teeth through the danger and the violence he had encountered. 'Fag?'

'Yes, please.'

It was quite the strangest of the little rituals they had adopted to confirm the uniqueness of their relationship. Neither of them smoked; when they compared notes, they both appeared to have given up at the same time, when they were in their twenties. But Martin was an admirer of the films noirs and the Hitchcocks of the fifties and sixties and he had converted Greta to them. Bogart and Cary Grant and seemingly everyone else smoked then. Partly in memory of them, but much more to seal their own bonding, they had taken to smoking a single black Turkish cigarette as a post-coital rite. Neither of them inhaled any more, but they blew out long wreaths of aromatic smoke, which seemed as they mingled to symbolize their own happy pairing.

Greta had left her clothes well away from the bed and she would shower thoroughly before she dressed, lest a husband who suspected nothing should pick up the traces of smoke on her clothes. She might be daring, but she was not stupid. One of her frustrations was that Ketley was never far from her thoughts. That was probably why she now said without any forethought, 'I wish I could stay here for ever.'

Martin blew a long funnel of smoke, then watched it slowly disintegrate like incense as it rose towards the high ceiling. 'And I wish you could, too.' It was a more measured response than her original thought had been, but it surprised him even more because of that. Commitment had been an alien word for him throughout his life. He was sure that Greta also had intended nothing permanent when they had started this. She snuggled a little closer and he slid his arms beneath the shoulder blades which had recently writhed so passionately within his grasp.

'I'll have to go soon.' But she made no effort to move. Instead she moved her body softly against the arm beneath her and raised both of her hands to stroke his.

There was a long pause before he said slowly, 'If you'd really like to make us more permanent, we shall have to think what we should do about that.'

Now she did move, turning on to her side so that she could

look directly into his face again. 'There's nothing we can do. Oliver's not a man to cross. I worry enough already about the danger I've put you in.'

'The danger I put myself in. I went into this with my eyes open.'

'But you didn't think then that we'd be talking like this.'

He smiled at her, that slightly lopsided grin that could make her tremble, even now. 'No, I didn't. I don't think I thought too clearly about it then. I knew that you were the most attractive woman I'd ever met and I lusted after you. I didn't think much beyond that.'

She was suddenly afraid for both of them. 'Perhaps it would have been better if it had stayed like that.'

'It would have been simpler, certainly. But not better. You can't regret the way we feel, just because it makes life more complicated.'

She looked at him for a moment full of wonder. Then she took his face between her hands and kissed him long and tenderly, feeling the renewed stirrings of desire as he stroked the small of her back. 'So what do we do about it?'

'Nothing in a hurry. Nothing without serious thought.' He was a soldier again; a soldier-lover, planning a daring sally to secure his woman.

Pleasure lasted in Greta for scarcely a moment. Fear was abruptly stronger, surging up and over her gratitude to him. 'You shouldn't even think about it! Oliver wouldn't consider divorce, unless he'd initiated it. He'd punish me. And the first step in that would be to eliminate my lover.'

'I can look after myself.' The lover's eternal, blinkered assertion.

'Not against Oliver Ketley, you can't. That's no reflection on you, my darling. It's just that he has resources you can't match.'

'But we have certain advantages. He doesn't know about us, does he?'

'No.'

'You're sure of that?'

'I'm sure. I'd know about it, if he had even an inkling. And you'd probably be dead. Don't underestimate him, Martin.'

'I shan't do that. But whilst he doesn't suspect us, we have the advantage.'

Greta nodded, still fearful, but feeling the tense excitement which danger always brought to her. 'What are you going to do?'

'I don't know yet. But as long as he doesn't know about us, we needn't hurry. We can lay careful plans.' He took her impulsively into his arms again, pressing his lips hard against hers, feeling her tongue move urgently against his teeth, exulting in the stirring within the length of her body as he held her tight against him.

He held her for a long time like that, then reluctantly thrust her away from him to look into her face. 'Once we have made our plans, we'll make our move. It will need to be swift and decisive.'

Eddie Barton should have heeded his instincts. The golf club job had felt wrong from the start. Nothing in its execution changed that view.

Yet it began easily enough. They managed to park the battered white Ford van quite near to the entrance to the men's changing rooms at the golf club. A portly man who was shouting to his friends that he was on the way round to the first tee held the door open for them obligingly and scarcely glanced at them as he left.

But they were too nervous to make the most of the pickings from the trouser pockets in the big room and they were interrupted repeatedly by members coming through to use the toilets. Eventually they grabbed two bags of clubs from the lockers and left, forcing their legs to move casually rather than to run to the van.

In his anxiety, Luke Gannon gunned the accelerator too hard as he started the van. Eddie thought they must surely excite attention. But no one came running from the clubhouse. They were away between the high posts and out of the golf club car park within seconds. Eddie glanced behind him at the booty on the floor in the back of the van. They wouldn't get much for what they'd pinched and the risk hadn't been worth it. But at least they'd got away with it. They'd need to get rid of the hot stuff fast, though.

The police car was waiting at the end of the cul de sac. It eased sideways across the road as they approached, making it totally clear that the main road and the wide world outside was not for them.

Luke Gannon sprang from his seat and made a token effort to evade the strong arms of the law. They encircled him before he had gone five yards. The constable was still quite young; there was real jubilation in his tone as he voiced the words of arrest. His first 'collar': a story to retail to his girlfriend that night. Gannon and Barton would no doubt emerge then as bigger, stronger and more fearsome than the defeated pair who now meekly surrendered their golf club pickings.

Eddie Barton journeyed towards Brunton nick and formal charges with his heart in the shoes he had polished for the occasion. He clasped his aching ribs and wondered whether a life of petty crime was quite the easy option he had thought it a month ago.

SEVEN

DCI Peach and DS Northcott observed things carefully whenever they went into a room. It was a CID habit. They had seen hundreds of rooms like this one. They had seen hundreds of people like the defeated figure who was centre stage. The woman's blonde hair needed urgent attention at the roots. Beneath the badly buttoned cardigan, her drooping breasts cried out for a better bra. There was a faint smell of stale food. The plastic containers of the supermarket curry were still on the sink beside the unwashed pots. Yet the rest of the room was tidy and clean; it strove against the odds for shabby respectability.

The woman was weighed down with care, but not stupid. The tired grey eyes quickened with apprehension as they showed their warrants. 'A detective chief inspector and a detective sergeant? My Eddie isn't in that league; he don't do that sort of job. He don't do anything, hasn't for weeks now. He's been injured. What you got against him?'

Peach found himself sorry as he often did for the mothers of young petty crooks. Probably she'd struggled to bring the lad up on her own after the departure of a feckless partner, warning him frequently against the dangers of bad company and the need to get a steady job. Now there was only the prospect of increasing disappointment and increasing hurt from yet another son who thought he could buck the trend and flout the law. 'He tried to pull that daft trick at the golf club last week, as you know perfectly well, Mrs Barton. But we're not here to arrest him. We need to speak to Eddy, for his own good.'

She didn't believe that. It was always for their good, not yours, with the cops. She hesitated, looking at Peach and the tall black detective sergeant behind him. She'd had the odd copper in here before, but never plain clothes men and never these exalted ranks. She said, 'Eddie's in his room. You'd better go up.'

He'd heard them, of course. He'd turned his television down and listened hard to the conversation in the living room, just as his mother would no doubt hear most of what was going to happen now from the bottom of the stairs. Peach left the bedroom door a fraction open; when you were talking sense, let the older generation hear it too. Mum might even reinforce your arguments, after you'd gone.

'I've nothing to tell you,' Eddie Barton said defensively. He sat on the edge of his bed and kept his eye on the very black face of DS Northcott; the big man looked as if he might be inclined to beat the shit out of him if he stepped out of line. The fact that the DS was six feet three and said very little only made him seem more menacing in the small, hot room. When neither of them responded to his opening statement, Eddie blurted out nervously, 'I'll be pleading guilty to that golf club thing. Never should have got involved in it. All we got was a couple of lousy sets of clubs.'

'You're right there, sunshine!' Percy Peach nodded agreement, switched off the television, and sat down in Eddie's favourite chair, his round, enquiring face no more than six feet from his subject's. 'Only Luke Gannon would go back to the place where he'd pulled the same stunt only seven weeks ago. Almost like giving himself up, that was. All our lads had to do was follow you down there and block your exit. You're nicely recorded on the CCTV at the golf club. And a right pair of twats you look!'

He allowed himself a smile at such stupidity. Eddie couldn't help noticing that DS Northcott did not smile at all; he looked unpleasantly like a Rottweiler awaiting a command. Barton licked his lips and said as boldly as he could, 'You're wasting your time here, then. I've told you we'll be pleading guilty.'

'Of course you will. That's not that we wanted a word about, though, is it DS Northcott?'

'No sir.' Clyde Northcott seemed to take the question as an invitation to become more involved. He stepped forward and stood beside his chief for a moment, then moved smoothly to sit beside the man on the single bed. Eddie cringed away from him, but all the DS did was to turn his head sideways, as if to observe an interesting specimen from a different and more intimate angle. He said in a deep voice which Eddie thought full of menace, 'We need Mr Barton's cooperation on a much more important matter.'

'Oliver Ketley,' Peach announced briskly.

Fear flashed on to the thin face and stayed there. Then, belatedly and pathetically, he said, 'Who's Oliver Ketley?'

Peach laughed outright at that. 'Don't ever go in for the stage, Eddie. You're supposed to conceal what you're thinking if you do that. Let's try to cut a long story short, shall we, because it's bloody hot in here and I can see my colleague's getting impatient. You were guilty of breaking and entering at Thorley Grange and you were shot while escaping by one of the gorillas who guard Mr Ketley and all he surveys. How am I doing so far?'

'Don't know what you're talking about,' said Eddie, sullenly and hopelessly.

Peach proceeded as if he hadn't spoken. 'You were taken to Brunton Royal Infirmary with gunshot and other wounds. We put you under expensive police guard there. When you were fit to speak, we sent a detective sergeant and a detective constable to interview you about your injuries, but you refused to cooperate. As a direct result of your criminal offence and the retaliation of your victim, you have been a burden on the NHS and wasted a considerable amount of valuable police time and resources.'

Eddie felt a need to arrest this torrent of words and accusations before it engulfed him. 'She were a right cracker, that sergeant you sent in. Lovely bum and tits on 'er. Wouldn't kick 'er out of bed, mate.'

'I see. Well, I'll tell my wife what you said, Eddie, but I wouldn't hold out any great hopes, if I were you.'

Barton's face registered first incomprehension, then consternation, then abject fear. He turned his eyes from Peach's faintly amused round face to the ebony features beside him, and found that for the first time DS Northcott was smiling. His mouth looked very wide and his teeth looked very white. His amusement was an even more frightening sight than his previous impassivity.

Peach said, 'You're a lucky lad, Eddie. We're not going to

prosecute you for the Thorley Grange business. If you offer us full cooperation, we might even put in a good word for you with the JPs on the bench when that golf club nonsense comes to court. Might even suggest you were led astray by an older man.'

Eddie said automatically, 'I ain't a grass. I don't cooperate with no pigs.'

Peach shook his head sadly. 'I was hoping you'd have more sense – your mum seemed to think you were quite an intelligent lad. But then mums do, don't they?'

'I'm not stupid. If I grass that lot up, they'll—' He stopped abruptly.

Peach made the most of Barton's mistake by allowing a smile to creep very slowly across his expressive features. 'And who would "that lot" be, Eddie?'

Barton shook his head glumly, not trusting the tongue which had already got him into trouble. Peach said earnestly, 'We protected you whilst you were in hospital, Eddie – used expensive manpower to do it, as I pointed out to you a moment ago. But we can't protect you for ever, now that you're back in the community. You must have realized by now that you bit off more than you could chew up at Thorley Grange. There are some very nasty people up there. Your best policy would be to have us pigs on your side.'

'Fat lot of use you lot were, when—'

For the second time he had reacted without thinking; for the second time Peach welcomed it with a broad beam of comprehension. 'They've already visited you, haven't they, Eddie?'

Barton's hands felt automatically for the still painful ribs on his left side. He did not deny Peach; words only led you deeper into the mire with this persistent man, who seemed to know most things and to understand everything.

The DCI moved his own hands slowly and unthreateningly to the young man's slim waist, then lifted the shirt as tenderly as a nurse. The blue, green and yellow hues of various bruises covered most of the lean torso. 'You could sue them for this, you know, even though you committed the first offence. Use of excessive violence, the lawyers call it.'

'But I'm not going to, am I?'

This time Peach's smile was small and rueful. Barton was right; Ketley and his minions would never allow a hostile witness to make it into court against them. The very suggestion might bring serious injury or worse to this pathetic creature who had strayed so far out of his depth. 'No, I don't believe you are, Eddie. Off the record, I can't even recommend that you should. But I think you should tell us everything you know about the set-up at Thorley Grange right now.'

Barton glanced at the tall figure beside him. DS Northcott nodded vigorously; even his encouragement seemed to carry menace. 'There's not much I can tell you. I was trying to pinch Mrs Ketley's jewels. I knew just where they were, see?'

He paused automatically, expecting them to ask about the source of his information. But all Peach said was a soft, 'How'd you get in, Eddie?'

'Through the old building; through the room they call the old library. I forced a window and slipped in. Piece of piss, it was.' For a moment, his pride in the speed and efficiency of his entry shone through. Then he recalled to whom he was speaking and said hastily. 'Then I was up the stairs and into the bedroom. I took the jewels and a couple of miniatures from the dressing table. Ignored everything else.'

'Very professional,' Peach murmured drily. 'I expect you're going to tell us you almost got away with it.'

'I did. I was back through my window and away before anyone saw me.'

'But someone did see you, didn't he?'

'Not until I was out of the place and away on my toes he didn't. I was away the way I came and back over the wall before he was. I'd have outrun him, too. I was leaving him well behind when he gunned me.'

'Who was he, Eddie?'

'I don't know. I don't know anything about the place, except where the jewels were.'

'And how to get in.' Again Peach didn't ask about the source of his knowledge. That would only put someone else in danger.

They asked him more questions, but his answers only confirmed that Barton had already told them all he knew. Eddie

Barton rose automatically from the edge of his bed when he
felt the easing of the springs as the big man beside him stood.
He saw Peach go through the door, prepared to shut it behind
his sidekick and collapse in relief on to his bed. But DS
Northcott turned at the door to face him. Eddie thought for a
moment that he was going to take a handful of his shirt, but
he did not touch him.

Instead, Clyde Northcott stood tall above him, pinning his
man against the wall by his very presence. 'You're probably
not going to heed this. Daft buggers like you never do listen
to good advice. But get yourself a job, son. You may think
you've not got a lot going for you, but you're not on drugs
and you've got a mum who still loves you. Get yourself a job,
turn up on time, and do what you're told to do. That's what
the Poles are doing and it's working for them. It might not
pay much but you won't end up inside and you won't have a
chest and a belly like that.'

Eddie cringed instinctively, but the man did not touch the
bruises as he had expected. He held Eddie's eyes against his
own deep brown ones for a second, then turned and went down
the stairs without a backward glance.

Both officers were quiet as Clyde Northcott drove the police
Mondeo back towards the station. The frowning Peach was
thinking how a huge problem had appeared from nowhere
with the arrival of Oliver Ketley and his crew at Thorley
Grange.

Clyde Northcott reflected that they hadn't got very much
out of Barton because he hadn't had much to give. Clive hadn't
been Percy Peach's bagman for very long. But he had already
learned that his DCI was an expert at making sizeable bricks
from very little straw.

The work you do for a man gives you a different perspective. The people who served Oliver Ketley in any of his business
ventures estimated him in almost the same way as the police
who sought to trap him. He paid well, as you had to for work
which was physically dangerous or outside the law. But they
knew he was a villain, just as clearly as they knew that
they must keep that knowledge strictly to themselves. Ketley

didn't favour discussion of the work they did, even among his own staff.

But you saw things differently if you were merely the kind of domestic staff whom any person with Ketley's resources could afford to employ. Thorley Grange was a big house. When you added the old original wing to the vast modern complex which had been built so quickly, there were in all fourteen bedrooms in the place, as well as suites of entertaining rooms and a large indoor swimming pool in the basement. There were two gardeners, a housekeeper and a large domestic staff.

Yet for most of the year these facilities were not extensively used. This meant that the people who maintained the Grange enjoyed what was most commonly called 'a cushy number'. Except for a few occasions in the year when the rooms were full and the meals in the dining room elaborate, the work was easy and the pay was good. If you kept your mouth shut and did your limited work conscientiously, it was an easier life than that experienced by most people who did domestic work.

Janey Johnson certainly found it so. She had worked at the Grange from the outset, being taken on two years ago, when the new building work was completed. She had worked here for a few weeks before even Oliver Ketley and his wife had moved in. She was thirty-five, small, dark, quietly pretty and self-effacing. The experienced housekeeper who had taken her on had recognized at interview a woman who was by no means stupid but had few qualifications, having left school to support an ailing mother without taking GCSEs. Just as important, she was a widow who needed the work. She was likely therefore to be uncomplaining and reliable.

Mrs Johnson proved just that. Like most of the staff, she lived in Brunton and came in daily to work at the Grange. She was never late; she could be relied upon to work steadily without being supervised; she never 'threw a sickie' to take time off when it suited her. On the rare occasions when there was room for it in a house that ran so smoothly, Janey Johnson showed initiative, as well as the eminent common sense which characterized most of her behaviour.

It was no surprise that the housekeeper developed a liking for the unobtrusive and uncomplaining Mrs Johnson. She was originally employed purely as a cleaner, moving as she proved her efficiency and trustworthiness from the kitchens and the more public rooms to the living quarters and bedrooms of the senior household staff and occasionally even into the quarters occupied by Oliver and Greta Ketley. Janey was willing and able to turn her hand to most things. She waited at table when a full house required it. She showed a talent for flower arrangement, so that eventually most of the floral displays in the house, including the one in the hall which everyone saw, were put together by her.

In her three years at Thorley Grange, Janey Johnson had scarcely spoken to the owner. Oliver Ketley was a man you only addressed when you were spoken to, and he had little occasion to speak to the unobtrusive Mrs Johnson. But a week after Eddie Barton had attempted his burglary at the house, she was called into the presence of the owner. She stood before him as demure and quiet as ever, but she felt her heart beating like a trip hammer in her breast at the interview.

With his very pale blue eyes, slicked back hair and square, automaton's face Ketley was a sinister figure, especially to one who had never been alone in his presence before. His size made him even more intimidating to the diminutive Janey. She was glad when he sat down, then fearful again as he looked her up and down for several seconds without speaking. The fact that he obviously intended to make her apprehensive only added to the effect. He left her standing in front of him for what seemed a long time before he said abruptly, 'Sit down, Mrs Johnson.'

Janey sat down as demurely as she could on the dining chair in front of him, crossing her trouser-clad legs at the ankles, feeling very exposed. She wished that he had taken her into the business office where she had never been, so that at least there would have been a desk between them.

Ketley assessed her legs for a moment, running his gaze slowly up her thighs and stopping without shame at her crotch. Then he said heavily, 'I wanted a word with you about the burglary we had here a couple of weeks ago.'

'Yes, sir. I don't know anything about it. I wasn't even here at the time. It happened on my day off.' She poured out every fact she could think of to establish her innocence, in a flow that only made her sound more defensive and more guilty.

'I know that. You wouldn't be still working here if I thought you'd any connection with what happened.' He tried to smile, to put her a little more at ease; he quite fancied this trim woman he had never noticed in his house. But smiling didn't come naturally to him. The only effect of his words was to leave her in no doubt that whoever crossed this man could expect big trouble.

'I'll tell you whatever I can, sir.'

'That's all I need. As nothing was eventually taken, it didn't seem necessary to involve the police. Mr Hardwick and I have already conducted an investigation into the affair and we now have a clear idea of what happened. Do you know Mr Hardwick?'

'Yes, sir. Not well, sir. We don't see each other very often.' Nor did she wish to. James Hardwick, bodyguard and enforcer for the boss, kitchen gossip said. There were dark tales of some of the brutality that unsmiling man had arranged in the course of his work, but Janey knew that rumour always exaggerated.

'No. Mr Hardwick is largely concerned with my business affairs. But as he lives in, he has a detailed knowledge of the workings of the household.'

It sounded like another warning that she should hold nothing back. She wanted to assure him that she had no intention of doing that, but she merely nodded, her attention all on the big, expressionless face which made her feel as if she was sitting naked on her chair. Because he said nothing and she felt an overwhelming need to fill the silence, she blurted out, 'I heard the man didn't get away with anything.'

'He didn't. And he's been dealt with.' A trace of satisfaction coloured the inscrutable voice for an instant. 'But we are naturally concerned that there should be no repetition.'

'No, sir. Of course not.'

'It appears that the man who broke in was given certain information. What do you know about that?'

This was why she was here, then. To help in the hunt. Janey didn't want to incriminate anyone, but she knew in the same thought that she wasn't going to risk denying anything she knew to this man. She heard her voice shake as she said, 'I don't know anything, sir.'

Another of those terrifying pauses followed. The pale blue eyes regarded her like those of a wild animal which has its prey cornered and helpless. 'You probably know more than you think you do, Mrs Johnson. I stress that no suspicion attaches to you, but you would be most unwise to try to withhold information.'

'I shan't do that, sir.' She managed to hold her voice steady this time, to imbue the simple statement with some of the conviction she felt.

'It seems likely that someone informed the intruder about certain things. He seemed to know the most vulnerable window to force. He knew the way to our bedroom. Most significantly of all, he knew exactly where Mrs Ketley's jewellery was kept. He could only have been fed that information by someone who works here.'

'Yes, sir. I follow that.' She managed with difficulty not to protest her own innocence again.

'Not many of the staff have access to my wife's bedroom. Not many of our domestic staff live-in.'

'No, sir.'

'What can you tell me about Amy Collinson?'

She had known that would be the name. 'Not much, sir. She's younger than me.'

'But she lives near you in the town.'

Janey felt a new thrill of fear. They'd been checking on her. But of course she'd filled in her address on an application form when she came here; Amy must have done that too. 'Two streets away, sir. But I hardly know her.'

'You went to the same school.'

'But not at the same time, sir. We were never at the comp together. She's much younger than me.'

'Yes. Almost exactly the same age as the man who broke in. Do you think they knew each other?'

'I don't know, sir.' She bit her lip. 'It seems likely.'

'It does. Especially as they were in the same year at the school. Can you think of anyone else who might have fed our burglar with the information he needed?'

She made herself pause, hoping that he would think she was giving the matter some thought. 'No sir, I can't really. But I don't know anything.'

He looked hard into her brown eyes for a moment, as if he wished to probe the darkest secrets of her soul. She was an attractive woman, slim but curvy. Janey: he filed away the name for future use. Then he said, 'Thank you. That will be all.'

She stood, paused for a moment to try to check the nervous trembling in her knees, then walked as steadily as she could to the door. It was a relief to find that there was no one in the staff loo. She pressed her forehead hard against the cold smoothness of the mirror.

Amy Collinson disappeared quietly from the house and her employment there. A week later, Janey was relieved to see her four aisles away in the supermarket. Her treachery hadn't brought any more retribution than dismissal from her cosy job without a reference. Ketley didn't want to excite attention by eliminating low life.

On the next morning, the housekeeper, Mrs Frobisher, a seemingly unflappable woman of around fifty, called Janey in at the end of her morning stint. She smiled at her. 'You've given complete satisfaction in your work here thus far, Mrs Johnson.'

'Thank you. I'm glad to have the work. I like to feel I can turn my hand to most things.'

'You're a widow, aren't you?'

'Yes. For five years, now.'

'And you've no children?'

A flicker of pain. 'No. We were planning a family at the time of Sam's death.'

'How would you feel about a residential post here?'

'All right, I think.'

'It would represent promotion and a higher wage. You'd be expected to turn your hand to all kinds of things, but you've already shown you're capable of that. And the accommodation would be free. In real terms, this would give you a substantial rise in income.'

'Yes. Thank you.'

'I'll give you a job description and details of the wages and the pension scheme this afternoon. You may wish to have twenty-four hours to think about it.'

'I shan't need that, Mrs Frobisher. I'll take the post.'

The housekeeper relaxed a little. 'That's good. I don't think you'll regret it, Janey. I'm a widow myself, you know, and it wasn't easy in the early years.'

'No, it hasn't been for me. But I'm coping better now. And this will be a big help. Thank you for thinking of me, Mrs Frobisher.'

Five days later, Janey Johnson moved into a surprisingly comfortable room in the new part of Thorley Grange. It was more spacious than she had expected and it had its own built-in bathroom. Service had moved on a lot since the chambermaids and skivvies of the nineteenth century skipped up and down the narrow servants' staircases in the old wing. Amy Collinson had been a fool to blab out secrets and lose herself a job like this.

Janey hung her three dresses and her coat in the wardrobe. She needed only half of the spacious drawers to accommodate her tops and sweaters and underwear. She set out the delicate silver bonbon dish and the slender glass vase which were all she had brought with her from the wedding gifts she and Sam had received fourteen years earlier. The rest of her treasures she had taken to be stored at her mother's and father's house in Leeds.

She placed the wedding photograph of her parents on top of the slim chest of drawers in the corner of the room, pausing for a moment to smile at them fondly in their innocence. She hadn't thought when she left school before her exams that her mother would still be alive now. Then she unwrapped the picture of her husband.

She set Sam for a moment beside her parents, then reluctantly rewrapped the picture and slid it beneath the clothes in one of the drawers.

EIGHT

Janey Johnson settled in quickly at Thorley Grange, as she had known she would. She had worked there since the new building was completed two years earlier. The transition was only to residential accommodation and a more trusted role. The housekeeper, Mrs Frobisher, kept an eye on her protégé and was well pleased with what she saw.

It took Chung Lee, the new employee in the kitchen, rather longer to find his feet. His work was good. The chef, Michael Knight, watched him closely in the kitchen and found him competent and speedy – speed is always a virtue for a chef, who has to work under pressure when his work is most on show. Lee's English was fine, though his slight accent was a steady reminder to the people working with him that he had not begun his life in Britain.

Because he wanted to convince the chef that he was as English as possible, Lee had told Knight at interview that he had been in the country for a long time. He had in fact arrived only three years ago. Though he was bright and intelligent enough to pick up the language and customs quickly, he still felt himself in an alien culture when it came to socializing. As a result of one or two rebuffs in the past, Chung was cautious in forming new friendships. This meant that being part of the residential staff at Thorley Grange proved at first a lonely life for him. He was surprised how comfortable the room provided for him was, but there weren't many possibilities of new friendships when so few of the staff lived on the premises.

Janey Johnson, whose room was only three doors down the corridor from Chung Lee's, felt sorry for him: the man with the smooth olive skin and the pleasant, unassuming smile must surely be very lonely, when he was not working in the kitchen. But they didn't see each other much in the course of their work, since she seldom ventured into the kitchen and he rarely worked outside it. And Janey was cautious herself about new friendships; she had long ago learned that a pretty young widow was a honeypot to questing bees, that friendly exchanges could too often be accepted as invitations by hormonal males. She kept a careful distance between herself and her new employer; now that she was living-in, Mrs Frobisher had dropped discreet hints about Ketley's occasional assertion of something like *droit de seigneur* with junior female staff.

Ten days after she had moved in at the Grange, there occurred one of those days when important business associates and senior staff of Oliver Ketley met for a day at the Grange. As Mrs Frobisher had warned her, it was a day when all hands were called to the pumps; Mrs Johnson was needed to act as a waitress at the tables for the major meal in the early evening. The kitchen, as is usual on such occasions, was not a place for the sensitive. Michael Knight, very anxious that all should go well, bellowed orders at all and sundry, with choice epithets added whenever the pace seemed to slacken or attention to wander.

In the event, the meal was excellent and the serving of it went off smoothly. Whatever crimes Ketley oversaw to make his wealth, he enjoyed playing the role of lord of the manor. As his guests retired to what had once been the old library for port and cigars, he came into the kitchen to compliment the chef on the meal and the rest of the resident domestic staff on the service. He offered gracious words of thanks, even though his pale eyes conveyed no pleasure and his sphinx-like features scarcely altered as he spoke. There would be a little bonus in the pay packets at the end of the week.

Whatever they thought of his bearing, the staff were pleased that he had acknowledged their work and the hard fact of extra money was well received. There were bottles of excellent wine to finish up with their own meals and at last they could relax. Most of them agreed that the boss was a fair employer, not a bad chap at all, once you got used to him.

There was one exception to the general approval. Janey Johnson was surprised to see the usually bland and unreadable Chung Lee give Oliver Ketley a look of pure hatred as he left the kitchen.

* * *

DCI Peach's preference would have been to arrive without warning, but he had to make an appointment to see Oliver Ketley. The police might know the man was a villain, but as far as the law went he was still pure as the driven snow. Or as Peach put it to Tommy Bloody Tucker, as pure as the driven slush. Ketley, like all major criminals, had his own well-paid, efficient and conscienceless lawyer at his beck and call. Oliver was simply a member of the public who must be asked to act as a good citizen and give the police whatever help he could.

Ketley saw them alone. Help was available at the end of a phone line if he should need it, but his habit of secrecy dictated that even those he employed were told as little as possible of his interests and activities. He sat this curiously dapper little man and the black sergeant who was such a contrast to him in comfortable armchairs. That way, they were a little lower than him as he steepled his fingers behind his big desk. 'Always happy to give the law whatever help I can, of course, but perhaps I should tell you that I've cleared a half-hour window in a busy day to accommodate you. This will need to be brisk, gentlemen.'

'It will be as brisk as you choose to make it, Mr Ketley,' said Peach aggressively.

Oliver transferred his pale gaze from sergeant to inspector. 'I may choose to make it very brief indeed, if you continue that attitude. I may choose to have you shown out without even declaring your business. I would be within my rights to do so.'

'But as a model citizen, you will obviously be anxious to give us whatever help you can,' returned Peach drily.

Ketley was not used to verbal combats. It was years since anyone had cared to challenge his opinions or statements. 'What is it you want, pig?'

'Ah! More the language I would expect from the gutter.' Peach nodded his satisfaction. 'We're here to arrest whichever of your staff shot a man and put him in hospital. No doubt you will be able to identify the culprit for us.'

'I've no idea what you're talking about.'

Peach sighed elaborately. 'On the thirtieth of January, a twenty-two-year-old man named Edward Barton committed the offence of breaking and entering here. He stole valuable jewellery. He was fleeing from the scene of his crime when he was twice wounded by rifle shots fired by a member of your staff. Our officers questioned your staff immediately after this incident and received nil cooperation. The law says that you are allowed to employ reasonable force against a burglar. You are not permitted to employ a weapon which might well fatally injure a man, especially when he has already taken flight.'

'The Americans are much more sensible about that.'

'Possibly. But I am not here to debate the shortcomings of English law but to make an arrest. Am I to have your cooperation?'

'I cannot give you that, because no such crime took place.'

'You deny the shooting?'

'There was no such retribution by a member of my staff, because there was no burglary here on the thirtieth of January.'

'And if I produce a witness to say there was?'

'You will be able to produce no such witness.'

'Because you nearly killed that witness in the first place, then beat him up to make sure he kept his mouth shut when he was still convalescent, you mean? Well, I dare say you're right about that. I'd be reluctant to appear in court myself, if I had murderous thugs like the ones you employ to fear. Don't trouble to deny it – we both know you won't let it come to court. We'd like to speak to one of those thugs, though. A man with various aliases, most recently calling himself Wayne Taylor.'

If Ketley was surprised by the extent of CID knowledge, he gave no sign of it. His expressionless face was silent for a couple of seconds. Then he said, 'Wayne Taylor is indeed a very junior member of my organization. He is presently employed in our Birmingham casino. He has been working there since the twenty-fourth of January.'

It was Peach's turn to disguise any trace of surprise or disappointment. 'Strange that you should be so certain of that date, with such a junior employee. Well, as you say, this may never come to court. But we shall keep a note of Mr Taylor's offence, against the day when he is arrested for some other

violent crime. It is surprising how much men like him will
tell us, when they're facing a long stint in the big house.'

'I've had enough of this. I've business to conduct.'

'I believe you, Mr Ketley. It's almost the first thing I've
believed since I set foot in this room.'

'In our modern world, even detective inspectors who get
too big for their shoes can disappear mysteriously.'

'Threat duly noted, Mr Ketley. But you know as well as I
do what happens when you kill a policeman. The whole might
of the law is released upon you. There'd be so many boys in
blue and plain-clothes men turning over this place that even
your organization wouldn't survive it.'

'Forgive me if I don't feel threatened. And now your time
is almost up.'

'You're safe enough, for the present, Ketley. But not for
very long, now. Things happen fast, once those at the top begin
to topple. All sorts of people in your organization may be
anxious to sing all sorts of songs, once the Special Branch
gets you for your crime on the fifth of February 2004.'

This time Ketley was shaken. DS Northcott, who had
watched him keenly throughout, caught a tiny wince in his
body, even though his face remained as unyielding as ever.
Ketley blinked those sinister light-blue eyes and said, '2004
is a long time ago. And I've no idea what you're talking about.'

'Oh, but you have, Ketley. The cockle-pickers in Morecambe
Bay. Twenty-three deaths in one appalling night, all down to
you.'

'Perhaps you need to be reminded that a man has already
been convicted of the manslaughter of those people. A man I
have never even met.'

'Lin Liang Ren. Now serving fourteen years. But no one
thinks he was the only person involved in what happened that
night.'

'But the case has been closed. Things move on, Detective
Inspector Peach.'

'The case remains open. Money's no object to the Special
Branch, lucky buggers. They'll get you, sooner rather than
later. And then lots of other things will come out, once the
rats begin to leave your sinking ship. I look forward to that.

In the meantime, keep your filthy fingers off our Brunton patch, please. And don't ring me about a round of golf: I play with almost anyone, but even pigs find some company beneath them.'

He was gone before Oliver Ketley could produce any appropriate words of dismissal. They were almost back at the station before Clyde Northcott said from behind the wheel, 'Do you really not feel in any danger from him?'

Percy Peach allowed himself a grim smile. 'I'm relying on the fact that he doesn't know Tommy Bloody Tucker's in charge of CID.'

As Oliver Ketley reviewed once again his connections with that awful February night of 2004, his rival racketeer Jack Burgess was covering his traces in a more contemporary crisis.

The police had that morning revealed they had arrested a group of Asian men in Rochdale who had been systematically 'grooming' white girls of thirteen and fourteen for prostitution. It would cut off a substantial source of income for Burgess, who had financed the organization and made substantial profits from it. But at the moment he was more concerned that the police could not connect it with him.

'Is there any way they can show a link between us and the Rochdale group?' he asked Geoffrey Day.

'No. I paid those men myself, in cash. It was local; we didn't need any other link.'

'Will they talk? Those Pakis I mean, now they're under arrest?'

'No way. Most of them didn't know where the money was coming from and had the good sense not to ask. We ran an incentive scheme: the more girls they delivered, the more they were paid. In effect they were paid on commission. And paid bloody well. It was a lucrative enterprise for them as well as for us.'

Burgess relaxed a little. 'Sex always is, Geoff. Always will be. You just identify the demand and supply it. People will always pay.'

'There's just one man who knows the money came from

us. He was the intermediary; he was our contact with the men
who found the girls and did the grooming.'

'And boys. There's plenty of demand for them, in our
enlightened society.'

Geoff Day shook his head. 'Plenty of demand, but a fair
supply. The rent boys don't charge enough. There isn't the
same profit margin.' He spoke as dispassionately as a marketing
man in a retail store. 'Ketley's organization runs a few boys'
groups in Liverpool, but the vast majority of his grooming
empire is based on young girls; they're easier to come by than
they used to be. And they pay better.'

'Speaking of Ketley, hasn't he burned his fingers with his
grooming rings? There have been three cases in the Brunton
area since he moved his headquarters there.'

Day smiled. Burgess kept his eye on everything his rival
did, especially when he came unstuck. 'They haven't even
come near Ketley. He runs as tight a ship as you do. The child
protection people spot lots of Asian men approaching and
grooming under-age girls, but that's as far as they get. Plenty
of convictions for sexual activity with children and supplying
drugs to them. The men involved get pretty heavy sentences
at Preston Crown Court. But the police never get to the big
boys who are doing the systematic organization and supplying
men with young, mainly white girls.'

Jack Burgess became thoughtful, as he usually did when
they reached the subject of Oliver Ketley. It worried Geoffrey
Day, because it was the one area where you couldn't rely on
the boss to be totally objective. Usually he assessed risk and
reward with cold calculation, his aim always being
maximum reward with minimum risk to himself and his organization. But his contest with Ketley was more personal, and in
Day's experience when things became personal objectivity
suffered. He would be glad when the governor's scheme to
eliminate Ketley and take over his empire was safely achieved.

As if he read the thought, Burgess now said, 'Any news on
George French? Do we know how near he is to success?'

'No word.' Neither of them mentioned the killing of Ketley,
almost as if they were superstitious that putting it into words
would endanger the mission. 'French is a loner, like all

contract killers. He'll proceed in his own way, but in the end he'll give us what we want. He'll plan to ensure the least risk for him, but that suits us as well. He knows Ketley's weaknesses, like his liking for shoving his hand up the newest skirt in the vicinity, and he'll use them if it gives him an opportunity. We don't want this traced back to you. That means it must be efficient and anonymous. But Ketley's well guarded. French will need to wait for his opportunity rather than try to force it.'

Burgess nodded ruefully. He recognized that George French was the best in his specialized business, but he was used to being able to prod those he hired. 'We'll need to replace our Rochdale business by taking over some of Ketley's. Let's hope French delivers soon.'

NINE

Percy Peach was a man who constantly startled those around him. The Brunton criminal fraternity found he turned up in unexpected places and knew all sorts of unexpected things. His colleagues in Brunton CID had ceased to be surprised about that. But they had speculated for several years about who would secure the permanent affections of DS Lucy Blake, the bright young woman with the chestnut hair, ultramarine eyes and disturbing curves, who figured in the sexual fantasies of all ranks. There was amazement when this most delicious of prizes was secured by the bald, round-faced, divorced Percy Peach, a man ten years her senior.

For the Brunton public at large, bred on Northern comics and traditional humour, the most surprising thing of all about Peach would have been something quite different and altogether more mundane. DCI Peach loved his mother-in-law and she returned his feelings in spades.

Long before Percy had roared like a comet into her life, the then Lucy Blake had known that her mother was a remarkable woman. What she had not expected was that the man who had seemed initially to be the embodiment of all the traditional male prejudices should also find Agnes Blake remarkable. Still less had she expected her mother to trumpet the virtues of this unpromising-looking candidate as the ideal husband for her only and much-cherished daughter.

It had helped that Percy Peach was a prominent local cricketer, a fleet-footed batsman who regularly made half-centuries in the Lancashire League, where each team employed an eminent professional and the standard of cricket was very high. Agnes had been delighted to find that the man universally known in the police force as 'Percy' had the initials D.C.S. He had been christened Denis Charles Scott by a cricket-mad father, who had been a youngster alongside the young Denis Compton in Hitler's war.

A very young Agnes had been taken to Old Trafford by her father in 1948 to see Compton take on the Australians. He had been hit on the head and carried bleeding from the field, but had insisted on returning with a mere sticking plaster on the stitched wound – no helmets and no health and safety rules in the days of Denis. He had then scored 145 and etched himself for ever in the memory of the child Agnes. To have a man named after her hero as first the boyfriend and now the husband of Lucy was a dream fulfilled for a lively widow now entering her seventies.

For the first time in several months, Percy and Lucy were visiting her mother in her cosy cottage at the base of the broad flank of Longridge Fell, to assist in the splendid ritual of high tea. Agnes loved baking and Percy loved whatever she baked. After years of coping with a daughter who protested that she must watch her weight, Mrs Blake found it bliss indeed to have a man who smacked his lips and never mentioned calories.

And Percy knew his part in this cosy domestic drama. He stepped into the tiny dining room which was almost filled by the fully extended table, groaning under the goodies assembled upon it by their shyly smiling hostess. There were home-roasted ham and thinly sliced brown and white bread, buttered scones and strawberry jam, queen cakes, sponge cake, rich fruit cake. Percy stopped spellbound before the feast. 'You've surpassed yourself, Mrs B. We wouldn't have any crime in the world, if people could all eat here!'

'Go on with yer, Percy.' Agnes beamed her approval of her son-in-law and stood for a moment with her weight on one foot, as she had done as a blushing seventeen-year-old when a boy complimented her.

'We certainly wouldn't have the energy to chase them, if all the police ate here,' said her daughter more soberly. It was one of the great delights of her life to see the two people she loved most in the world getting on so well together, but they were a formidable alliance, when they ganged up on her. She would try to control their wilder sallies during the meal and its aftermath.

There was no immediate problem. Percy had lived alone

for ten years after the break-up of his short-lived first marriage and existed largely upon takeaways. His admiration for Agnes's baking was genuine and profound. He was a bouncy little figure, certainly not skinny, but without the paunch he should have been developing at thirty-nine. Whatever he ate, he never put a pound on, Lucy had learned resentfully. He now proceeded to do ample justice to the efforts Agnes had made for him. 'That Nigella Lawson's not bad, in her own way,' he said, carefully damning the delectable kitchen goddess with faint praise. 'But she could learn a thing or two from you, Mrs B, when it comes to baking.'

Agnes's giggle was positively adolescent, her daughter thought uncharitably. 'I'll brew the tea, Mum. That's if it's safe to leave you two lovebirds alone for two minutes.'

'Just you watch your tongue, our Lucy,' said Agnes, finding the simulated shock on her son-in-law's face the occasion for a renewed outburst of hilarity.

'Two minutes wouldn't be long enough for us, love,' said Percy magisterially. 'Your mum's an artist and artists can't be bound within the squalid restraints of time.'

When Lucy returned with the tea, Percy had been persuaded to accept a second slice of fruit cake and the pair were dissecting England's Ashes triumph in Australia. She proposed an adjournment to the sitting room with their teacups, in the vague and totally mistaken belief that the pair might be easier to control from there.

The technicalities of batsmanship in the five-day game and the one-day game occupied them for some time and excluded her from the conversation. Lucy gazed fondly at the silver-framed photographs in pride of place upon the mantelpiece. The left-hand one showed her dead father in black and white, leaving the field after a notable bowling performance in the Northern League. The right-hand one was in colour and more recent. It showed Percy looking dapper, his red cap a little on one side and a smile of pure pleasure upon his face as he mounted the pavilion steps. Her mother's careful black print below announced that this was 'D.C.S. Peach, leaving the field after another attractive Lancashire League half-century for East Lancs.'

Perhaps her mother caught the direction of her glance, for she reiterated a familiar theme. 'You gave up cricket far too early, Percy. I blame our Lucy for that.'

'He'd retired before I ever met him!' Lucy protested with renewed indignation.

'Only just! You could have talked him out of it, at that stage.'

'That's true, I suppose,' Percy pronounced magisterially. 'I was just putty in your hands, Lucy. A slave of your every whim.' He widened his eyes into a schoolboy's helpless erotic stare and trained them upon the ceiling.

'You've never been helpless in your life, Percy Peach. You gave up because you bloody well wanted to!'

'Language, our Lucy! Not in front of the mother who bore you and bred you and baked for you, please! I'm sorry, Mrs B. It must be some of the people she mixes with at work. And the criminals aren't much better, these days.'

Agnes giggled and rocked herself to and fro on the sofa in front of the open fire, delighted by the idea that a one-time mill girl and a woman who still did a part-time stint in the supermarket could be shocked by a simple 'bloody'.

Lucy tried desperately to shake the pair's mutual delight in her discomfort. 'Anyway, golf's his game now, Mum. He's doing very well at it, I'm told. I'm thinking of taking it up myself.'

'GOLF!' Agnes forced many years of derision into that single upper-case syllable. 'Wash your mouth out, girl. Not a sport at all, that. Don't you dare compare it with cricket!'

'It's not like the old days, Mum. The top golfers have to be athletes now, like other sportsmen. Tiger Woods is an athlete.'

As soon as the words were out, she knew she had chosen the wrong example. But there was no chance to arrest the derision flooding into every well-loved wrinkle of her mother's face. 'Don't give me Tiger Woods, young lady. That's golf for you. He's so bored with the game that he has to jump into bed with every young floozie that offers. Goes round *paying* for it! I ask you.'

'Makes it worse, does it, paying for it?'

'You can't play cricket for ever,' Peach said hastily. His traditional values told him that a discussion of the precise moral differences between a sportsman paying for sex and leaping gratefully into the many beds which were freely offered would be interesting, but scarcely seemly between mother and daughter. 'There's nothing worse than seeing your scores decline and hearing people mutter when you go that it should have been two years earlier. Golf isn't the game that cricket is, never will be, because it's much more selfish.' He noted with relief a certain softening in the grim visage of Agnes Blake. 'But it's a new challenge to take up.'

'Is that what I was? A new challenge?' said Lucy, who was still tuned for aggression.

'Well, golf leads you to explore some interesting places,' said Percy thoughtfully. 'It's like you in that respect. And it calls for constant physical ingenuity and invention.'

'HUH!' Another upper-case monosyllable of supreme contempt from Agnes. She plainly had a talent for this verbal compression, and the outburst banished the subject of golf as comprehensively as her greeting had blackened it.

Lucy looked fiercely at Percy, but found no help there. After a few seconds of heavy silence, she said desperately, 'How's the vicar getting along, Mum?'

The young clergyman who had married them in the old village church was a nice man, she thought. He was underpaid, like most of his calling, and suffering from a religion riven with conflict over women bishops. He had also taken on a picturesque fifteenth-century church which was a perpetual drain on finances. He was in favour of women priests and could see no logical reason why they should not in due course become bishops, but suffered from the fact that most of his parishioners were ageing, conservative and much inclined to the old ways. If they saw their vicar as dangerously advanced in his ideas, they would be less inclined to fund the new roof which was urgently needed.

'He's doing all right, is Reverend Davies. He's managed to get one or two of the young families in, to replace us old folks.'

Agnes looked hopefully at Lucy, who said hastily, 'That's

good. And I heard in the village that one of your benefactors is a member of Percy's golf club. So it can't be all bad, can it?'

It was a nice bit of golf propaganda, so welcome to her that the words were out before she could suppress the thought. Agnes said, 'The man who's paying for the bell to be recast? He's never a golfer, is he?'

'Oliver Ketley? He is, you know. Percy said he was there when he was in the club last Saturday. So golf can't be all bad, can it?'

'Four thousand, he's paying. And him not even a believer! But a church is part of the community, he says, and he wants to pay for the cracked bell to be recast to support our village.'

'You might not be so happy if you knew where that money came from, Mrs B.' Percy Peach, who had been settling down for a doze in the warm, low-ceilinged room, was suddenly deadly serious.

'Is he a wrong'un then, Percy?' Agnes, who had been looking forward to hearing the peal of bells restored to the old church, was abruptly cast down.

'He's a bad 'un, Mrs B. You can take my word for that. As bad as they come, in my view. But don't you go around saying that, because he's a clever bad 'un. We can't pin him down, so that as far as the law's concerned he's a blameless man as well as a very rich one. And he who sups with the devil needs a long spoon, as your vicar well knows. But you take his money, same as the captain of the golf club took a couple of thousand quid for his chosen charity last week. Better it's used for things like that than some of the things Ketley spends it on. Just don't have anything to do with him personally, that's all.'

'I don't think we'll need to do that. He just sat down and wrote out a cheque, the vicar said. Isn't he the man who's done all that new building at Thorley Grange?'

'Yes. He's installed himself there now. He's busy playing the lord of the manor and trying to win a reputation as a major local philanthropist.'

Agnes Blake, who had lost ten years when she was so

delighted by Percy's earlier banter, seemed suddenly a frail old lady. Her face was lined and troubled as she said, 'Perhaps we shouldn't be taking his money after all.'

Lucy glanced at Percy. 'You take it, Mum. Percy's right, it's better spent on a cracked bell in an old village church than on other things he might choose. But don't say anything about Ketley. In due course, it will probably come out that he's a villain. They usually get too bold and go too far in the end. In the meantime, don't venture an opinion.'

Agnes looked very disappointed. 'That might be difficult, when some of the daft creatures in the village are singing his praises.' Then she was suddenly fearful. 'He won't come round here, will he?'

The old lady looked very small and frail in her favourite armchair. Lucy reached across and took her hand. 'No, he won't come round here, Mum. He's not that sort of villain.'

They talked about other things then, and she watched the colour and animation come gradually back into her mother's face. Percy cheered her, as he always could, with talk of cricket and then anecdotes of the more trivial and comic episodes in the task of policing the nation.

Percy thought of Agnes when they were driving back to Brunton. Would doubts about her safety surface again when she was left alone in her cottage, with the night closing dark and cold around her? He watched a hungry winter fox scurry across the road in his headlights, then said, 'I'm sorry I told your mum about Ketley. Much better if she just thought of him as a local benefactor, but I spoke before I thought.'

She was silent for so long that he thought he was not going to be forgiven. But then she moved a little closer to him in her seat and said softly, 'It was me who introduced the name, not you. You're a good man, Percy Peach. It was out before you could stop it because your habit is to speak the truth to your friends. I'm glad Mum is one of those.'

He squeezed her arm in thanks and they drove the last two miles of the short journey in companionable silence. When they reached the house, he walked automatically to the kettle, filling it for the last hot drink of the day, feeling a pleasant lassitude in his limbs after his indulgence at Agnes's table.

Lucy went to the phone to check if there were any messages, as was her usual habit.

She listened twice to the terse message, then handed the phone to Percy in the kitchen without a word. There were no details in the official police voice and scarcely a hint of excitement. But the facts were clear and unembroidered. A suspicious death. A man believed to be Oliver Ketley had been found shot dead in his car.

TEN

C hief Superintendent Tucker was present in the CID
section on Sunday morning. Even in death, Oliver
Ketley was powerful.

Tucker marched from one section to another of CID, ill at
ease at this level because he spent so much more time in his
penthouse office on the top floor of the new brick building. 'This
is going to be a big one!' he told DCI Peach unnecessarily.

'Very big!' echoed Peach. But where there had been apprehension in Tucker's tone, there was satisfaction in his. Whoever
had removed Ketley from the world had done that world a
service, in Peach's view. Delivered it from evil.

'Is there any chance it could be suicide?' asked Tucker
hopefully.

'Every chance, at the moment. Ketley was found with the
death weapon in his hand, apparently.' There was a lot of stress
on 'at the moment'. Peach didn't believe the man he had
confronted a few days ago would have chosen this way out.

'You don't think he might have been filled with remorse
for his crimes and chosen to end it all?'

'Do you, sir? Considering the things he's done, it would
have been a pretty belated remorse. If he didn't choose to end
his life the day after all those cockle-pickers were killed in
Morecambe Bay, I doubt whether he'd have done it all these
years later.'

'Not even if he felt the police net closing on him and arrest
inevitable?'

Peach looked at him keenly. 'Unless you know more than
I do about the police net, that wasn't the case. My impression
is that now they've pinned one man down and put him away
for life for that 2004 crime, the others who were involved can
breathe a little more freely. I think Ketley felt that. I tried to
give him a bit of a scare about it last week – told him the
Special Branch had infinite resources and they wouldn't rest

until they had him. He didn't seem very worried about the threat they represented.'

'We'll need to be careful, Peach. As far as the media are concerned, Ketley was a blameless citizen and a prominent local benefactor. We can't go around blackening his reputation without chapter and verse to back us up.'

'No, sir. My feeling is that chapter and verse might be forthcoming, in due course, but only after we've sorted out exactly how he died. Death always brings its own halo, in the short term. For the present, we can expect the press to treat Ketley as a dead hero.'

The two very different men were silent for a moment, contemplating the vices of the fourth estate. In due course, the tabloids would switch shamelessly from glorification to vilification. Hadn't Robert Maxwell gone from war hero to vicious tyrant overnight, once it was safe to reveal the unethical habits of his press-baron autocracy? The next best thing to a saint cruelly removed from the world was the unmasking of a shameless villain who had posed as a saint. But that usually waited for a while.

In due course, the shabby ethics and shocking crimes of Oliver Ketley would be exposed in every salacious detail. But for the moment he would be a great man cut down in his prime, with an inefficient police service struggling to provide answers to the tragic mystery of his death.

'You'll know more when you've been to the scene of the crime,' said Tucker pointedly.

'Indeed I will, sir. DS Northcott and I are off there this minute, sir.'

Tucker looked doubtfully at the tall black figure who had appeared behind Peach. 'Well, take it carefully. I'm the man who will have to answer to the media for any insensitivity you show.'

'Yes, sir, we'll remember that. DS Northcott and I are noted for our sensitivity. Perhaps you could set up the house-to-house enquiries in the area, whilst we are out at the crime-face.'

Tucker glanced at his watch. 'I'll do that. If you have anything significant to report later in the day, please contact me by phone.'

'I shall do that, sir. What time will you be home from golf?'

Tucker had made the mistake of sitting down. He now followed Peach's glance down to his feet and hastily stood again. His posture had revealed his ankles and with them the lurid yellow long socks that he wore with plus twos for his Sunday golf. He said with all the dignity he could muster, 'Report anything you have as soon as you get it. And for God's sake, tread carefully!'

A Bentley, no more than a few months old. Oliver Ketley had enjoyed driving a classy motor. It showed others where you stood and where they stood. With his death, it had become no more than a tawdry bauble.

The Bentley was a very dark blue. The crimson staining its windscreen didn't clash with its colour, but the irregular shape and the splashes around it would have offended the car's designer, who had striven to make everything in his design regular and harmonious.

'Bit above our station, lad, this motor,' said Peach to Clyde Northcott.

'Running costs a bit high for me. I think I'll stick to the bike.' Black humour, the defence of Peach and Northcott, as with most police in the face of death. There was nothing irreverent or disrespectful about that. It was simply an attempt to keep the starker facts of their working lives at a decent distance. You needed something, if images like this and much worse ones weren't to disturb the long, dark hours when you tried to sleep.

They stood beside the police car, forty yards from the Bentley and the activity in and around it. They had an easy relationship, deriving from the way Northcott had arrived here. He had been a hard and violent teenager, slipping down darker paths as he moved into his twenties. His black skin and his inclination to solve disputes with his fists had made him much feared but little liked in the electronics factory where he had then worked. He had begun to deal in cocaine, successfully enough to buy the powerful Yamaha R1 motorcycle he craved. He had then extended his dealing.

The event which had changed his life had been his

looked at the spotless rear floor wells and asked Chadwick, 'Anyone in there with him when he died?'

'We've gathered a few fibres. Whether they were left there yesterday or on some previous occasion we don't yet know and may never know. Anything else will wait until forensics get busy. I expect those boys and girls will enjoy taking a Bentley apart far more than they would a Nissan Micra.'

Peach exchanged grim smiles with Chadwick. 'I don't expect this to be easy, Jack.'

'Don't be such a bloody pessimist. You've already got the murder weapon.'

'Murder weapon, Jack? That's very unprofessional, when we don't know yet that anyone killed the sod.'

'Perhaps my official report will have to say that. But I know a bit about Ketley, Percy, though no doubt nothing like as much as you do. I wouldn't have thought he was likely to top himself. And I know how disappointed you'd be if this was suicide, my old mate.'

Peach grinned, taken back ten years to when they had been keen young CID sergeants together, before the serious gunshot injuries which had ruined Chadwick's promising career. Then his face darkened. 'If this is a killing by one of his business rivals, it's going to be a contract man.'

Chadwick looked again at the man and woman systematically covering the ground around the car, at the photographer waiting patiently to take his final pictures after the body had been removed. For the first time, his reaction was that of the civilian rather than the CID stalker he had once been. 'At least Ketley's gone for good. The world is rid of a man it will be much better without.'

At one o'clock, Greta Ketley stared at her mobile phone and hesitated. She looked anxiously down the long stretch of the bedroom and dressing room, though she had already checked twice that there was no one within earshot.

Then she took the decision she had always known she was going to take and punched in the number. Two rings later, the familiar voice responded. She said simply, 'You've heard?'

'Yes. It was in the radio news summary at twelve. The

television news is reporting from the scene now, but the car's screened off. Have they contacted you?'

'Yes. Two women PCs came this morning. Gave me the barest facts they could. He was found last night. Dead at the wheel of his Bentley, they said.'

'Did they say it was a suspicious death? That's the phrase they use.'

'I don't think they did. I don't remember those words. But I was upset. I asked them if there'd been an accident. They said no, they didn't think so. That's when the older one said there were gunshot wounds.'

'Did they say it was suicide? Or that it looked like suicide?' His voice was calm, even matter-of-fact. But she knew he was nervous, because he was running his questions together in his anxiety to know the facts.

'No. I don't think they ever used the word suicide. I tried to get more out of them, but they said that was all they could say at this stage. All they knew themselves, I think they said. Then they said that the man in charge of the case would want to see me later, that he might be able to tell me more.'

'That's just routine. Nothing you should be worried about.'

'No. I'll be glad when it's over, though.'

'Of course you will. That's perfectly natural. But it's better that we don't meet for a few days. They might have someone in the frame by then.' He paused, then said more grimly, 'They won't be short of suspects. Did they mention identification of the body?'

'No.'

'They'll probably want you to do it. If you find that too distressing, they'll find someone else. But if you can face it, it might be a good thing to do. It would be the first step in what they usually call closure.'

'I'll do it, then.' Her voice was heavy with the emotional weariness which often assails the next of kin. 'I don't feel up to much questioning, though.'

'They'll treat you as gently as they can. They always see the spouse of the deceased first. It's because that's normally the person who can tell them most about the habits and the movements of the victim.'

It was the first time either of them had used that word. And despite what he said about her knowledge of Oliver, both of them knew that the spouse was always the first suspect, the person police had to investigate before they could move out into a wider circle of possible killers. 'I'll be glad when it's over. I'm surprised how upset I feel about Oliver.'

'That's normal enough. Happier times are bound to come back to you. It might be an idea to ring a doctor and get him to prescribe something. That's a form of protection in itself – you can always rely on him to say you're too disturbed to be persecuted with questions.'

'Or her.'

'Or her, indeed. Get the sorority on the job. Is there anyone around who could be a friend and a help to you? Someone who could come in if you were getting upset and say you'd had enough?'

'There's the housekeeper, Mrs Frobisher. She's friendly enough, but a bit distant. There's a young widow who's only become resident a week or two ago. I quite like her. I'm sure she'd help, if I needed her.'

'Bear it in mind, then. But the police questioning is likely to be straightforward and sympathetic, as far as you're concerned. I know you won't tell them about us, and I can't see any reason why they should ever get on to that. Anything else should be straightforward. And don't be nervous.'

She forced herself to grin at the invisible presence at other end of the conversation. 'Of course I won't be nervous. I've nothing to be nervous about, have I?'

'Of course you haven't. And I look forward to seeing you, as soon as the heat's off. It's best that you don't phone me. I'll be in touch, when I think it's safe. If I ring, it will be at four o'clock exactly, the time we've always used. Usual arrangement: if there's no reply after two rings, I won't persist. Goodbye, my darling.'

Martin Price stared at his mobile for a moment after they had finished speaking. He wondered why he had used that old-fashioned phrase about the heat being off. And he wondered just how long that process would take.

ELEVEN

I t was three thirty when the police came to Thorley Grange. A short, cheerful-looking man in a neat grey suit, who said his name was Detective Chief Inspector Peach, and a very tall, smooth-featured, black man, whom he introduced as Detective Sergeant Northcott. Greta Ketley watched them climb out of the police car by the stone pillars of the old house and wondered why they seemed familiar to her. Then she remembered: she'd seen the same pair in almost exactly the same place ten days or so ago, when they'd called to see Oliver in his office.

There was no time to speculate about the reason for that visit. Within thirty seconds, they were offering their apologies for having to disturb her at such a sad time. She touched her white face, feeling for the puffiness around her eyes, and said what she'd decided she would say before they came, 'You mustn't worry about disturbing me. Of course I'm upset and shocked, but I want you to find out who did this, for all our sakes.'

Peach wondered quite who was included in that last phrase, when she had no family around her, but perhaps the little shrug of her shoulders indicated that it comprehended the household in general. He felt a sharp sympathy for this pale, dignified figure who had suddenly been thrown from the background into the very centre of things in this huge house, responsible now for staff whom she might never have wanted. She had a slight, attractive, Scandinavian accent which seemed to make her an even more isolated figure, a lonely Lady of Shalott in a world she did not understand.

All of which was probably romantic nonsense, Peach told himself firmly. This pale figure with the long fair hair and the high-cheeked, attractive face might be a hard-headed gold-digger; she might have known and approved of the methods by which her husband had become so rich. She was certainly now allowing herself to be treated as the lady of the manor. One of the servants had led them into a large drawing room where Mrs Ketley was already sitting in a large armchair, wearing a long, dark blue dress and shoes in matching leather.

It was an appropriately sombre hue for the situation, but he noticed how admirably it complemented her Nordic complexion and hair. Surely a natural sense of style didn't make a woman more calculating? Greta Ketley smiled wanly, as if she read that thought, and said, 'I see the reasons for this meeting, but I hope it won't take very long.'

'It shouldn't do. It's largely a matter of routine, but I assure you it's very necessary.'

'Mrs Johnson also knew my husband. She lives in the house. Will it be all right if she stays with us? I'm sure I shall be all right, but I'm feeling a little weak.'

Peach had been concentrating on his first estimation of his hostess as the victim's wife. He glanced for the first time at the woman who had led them here and saw a figure who might have been chosen as a physical contrast to her mistress. Mrs Johnson was slight and dark, and demurely pretty. She seemed a little embarrassed by her mistress's request for her presence. Early to mid thirties, Peach's experienced eye said. Divorced, he supposed, though you could never be sure of circumstances without checking. Probably that was why she was able and willing to take a residential post; you must live very cheaply as a resident here and be able to save most of your wage.

He said, 'Of course we have no objection. It will ensure you're not outnumbered by policemen – I know DS Northcott doesn't like that.' The face beside him, hitherto as inscrutable as that of an African god, cracked into a smile at this gentle witticism. Clyde directed the smile towards Mrs Johnson, as though it made them companions here, as minor players in the scene.

Peach's bonhomie briefly took in the whole company. Then he darted his first question at the widow, 'How long were you married to Oliver Ketley?'

'Twelve years.' She watched Northcott's large hand scribble a note, then caught the calculation in the police eyes and responded to it. 'I was thirty when I married him. Quite old enough and quite experienced enough to know what I was doing.'

There was an air of challenge in the statement, which Peach welcomed. He found it much easier to deal with women of spirit than drooping flowers, even if they occasionally antagonized each other. The whole point of this first meeting was to get as much information as possible. That was a fact they sometimes offered as an apology, but the widow really was the person who could usually tell them most about a victim. He was already sure in his own mind that Ketley was a victim, not a suicide.

'You're telling me that you married him with your eyes wide open. That you were well aware of how he made his money.'

'No. I'm merely trying to be as honest with you as I can. I'm trying to tell you I knew a little about the man he was and why he attracted me – that I wasn't an impressionable teenager who knew nothing about life. I had very little idea then how he made his money and I have probably even less idea now.'

Percy doubted whether that was true, but it wasn't the right time to press the thought; he was interviewing a widow less than twenty-four hours after her husband had been brutally murdered. Instead, he took up the other issue she had raised and offered her a different challenge. 'I shouldn't think teenagers, impressionable or otherwise, would have been much drawn to Oliver Ketley.'

She did not smile at the thought. She was not relaxed enough for that. She chose her words carefully, as if she were the alien she had once been, picking her way through the minefield of the English language. 'It is true that young people shied away from Oliver. His face was not easy to read and he was not a man it was easy to know. He liked it that way. But some women prefer a certain mystery in a man. It sets him apart from the others, makes him more of a challenge, I think.'

'And did you solve the mystery, after you were married?'

Greta looked at him steadily for a moment, aware that each of them, in sizing the other up, was anxious not to give ground. 'That is a private matter, Mr Peach. I do not think you should be asking about it.' She glanced sideways for support, but Janey Johnson was apparently very interested in the carpet at her feet.

'I apologize for the intrusion – apologize that it should be necessary. But I have already indicated that I do not think this was suicide. In that event, the nature of your relationship with your husband has to be important. You have said that at least one of the man's attractions was a certain mystery. I am asking how much more you learned about the man and the way he lived his life after you married him.'

Greta glanced again at Janey Johnson, caught the tiniest of nods from the younger woman. She spoke slowly, wanting to be aware of the implications of every word she used. 'I grew to know the man rather better. I knew his likes and dislikes. I knew what pleased him and what made him angry.' She stared hard at the Detective Chief Inspector, daring him to ask if this was a sexual reference, but Peach said nothing. 'I knew nothing of the ways he made his money or the ways he conducted his business.'

For the first time, Peach arched those expressive black eyebrows, implying disbelief, without the direct insult of words. 'Nothing?'

'Nothing, Mr Peach. I learned very quickly that Oliver liked it that way. It took me a little longer to realize that I also preferred to preserve my ignorance.'

This time he allowed her to see his smile. 'That is what many women would have done, in the same circumstances. I know that this will seem crass and perhaps even cruel, coming so soon after your husband's death. But I feel I should tell you that he was under police investigation on several fronts. He was suspected of some very serious crimes.'

She wavered a little, as was surely appropriate. But she knew the line she had to take and it gave her confidence that she had agreed it with Martin Price. 'I am sorry to hear that. To be perfectly honest, it does not surprise me. I did not like some of the people he associated with. I did not like some of the people who came here. But I knew nothing of his business affairs or the way he went about them.'

She saw no movement between the men, but it was Clyde

Northcott who now said in a soft, deep voice, 'Wasn't that a little ostrich-like, Mrs Ketley? Even a little cowardly, when you were married to the man?'

She flashed Northcott a look of sudden, naked hostility which told them she would make a formidable opponent. But it was banished from those classically beautiful features as swiftly as it had arrived. When she spoke she was perfectly controlled, choosing her words as fastidiously as previously. 'Not cowardly. My word would be realistic, Detective Sergeant. I don't know if you are married: I suspect not. But if one wishes a marriage or a long-term relationship to endure, one learns to accept certain – certain limitations. I learned quickly that one of these limitations for me involved keeping my nose out of my husband's working life. We struck a bargain, if you like. Oliver never grudged me money. He accepted that I would spend what I thought necessary on this place and on my own pleasures.' She looked round appreciatively for a moment at the huge, luxuriously fitted room. 'In return, I accepted that I wouldn't question either his businesses or his methods. You may call that cowardice, if you like. I call it realism.'

Northcott looked at her steadily for a moment, then made a note on his page without further comment. It irritated Greta that she could not see the notes he was making, could not see how far he was accepting what she said and how far noting it as an area for further exploration. It was Peach who said, 'Let us accept that you knew little or nothing of the way the money arrived. But you've told us that you learned much more about the man during your marriage, as one would expect. How close would you say you were?'

She allowed herself a wan smile. 'Shouldn't you say, "on a scale of one to ten", as the medical people do? Of course I got to know him better, to know his likes and dislikes, just as he learned more about me. I knew what clothes he liked me to wear. I knew the jewellery he preferred. I learned what pleased him in bed and what—'

She was suddenly in tears, dabbing her face with a tissue she must have clutched in her hand throughout, shaking her head violently from side to side, trying but failing to produce words of apology.

Janey Johnson sprang to her side, grasping the hand without the tissue between both of hers. She glared at them resentfully. 'That is surely enough for today, DCI Peach. More than enough!'

'I agree. I am sorry again that we had to intrude today, Mrs Ketley.' He stood and moved a step towards the door, as did Clyde Northcott. Then he turned. 'One final question, on a simple matter of fact. When did you last see Mr Ketley?'

Greta held up a hand as Janey moved to protect her. She wanted this fact established as much as they did. 'At around seven o'clock last night. We ate early because he said he had to go out.'

The food was good in the Thai restaurant. It was in one of the older streets of central Brunton. Thirty years ago, it had been a restaurant serving British food, with the menu fashionably printed in French, as it tried to go upmarket. Thirty years before that, it had been the town's finest cake-shop, with a small café upstairs, where middle-class ladies in fashionable hats discussed the ways of the post-war world and this new-fangled welfare state.

Chung Lee knew none of this. He chose the darkest corner he could and ordered just a starter and a coffee. He picked at his food, for he had already eaten all he wanted in the small staff dining room beside the kitchen at Thorley Grange. Chung felt conspicuous sitting on his own at the small square table with its white linen and shiny cutlery. He relaxed visibly when a man no taller than him and with a similar Asian skin came into the restaurant, looked around, and responded to his urgent signalling.

Fam Chinh was perfectly at home here. He knew the proprietor and had suggested it as a meeting place. He now ordered a full meal and proceeded to enjoy it unhurriedly. Chung Lee made desultory conversation as he watched his companion eat, wanting all the time to snatch a look at his watch. He didn't know Chinh well. But then he didn't know anyone in Brunton well. That was the difficulty about being a natural loner in a strange country.

He'd worked alongside Chinh whilst he was broadening his

experience of restaurant work, immediately before he had been appointed at the Grange. He'd found him an affable, easy-going man and a good partner to work with. They'd both started by stacking crockery and working the big old washing-up machine, both graduated to more demanding kitchen tasks as they had proved themselves reliable to the Indian proprietor. They'd looked out for each other, covering up each other's small mistakes and occasional late arrivals for work.

That was as far as it went. They'd been friends and they'd liked each other, but they had seen very little of each other outside work. Chung had taken Fam's telephone number and the friendship might have developed if they'd had longer together. But then Chung Lee had gone for the job at Thorley Grange. They had not seen each other since then. Fam Chinh had been surprised that morning when Chung Lee had rung him at home and asked if they could meet.

Now Chung watched his friend with mounting impatience as he worked his way towards the end of his meal. Lee's confidence was ebbing as he realized how little he really knew of this man. He remembered that Fam was married, that he cherished his wife enough to go straight home to her after work, as not all of the English men seemed to do. But he could not remember if he had any children, could not make the connections which would establish that they were real friends and that friendship carried obligations.

Just when it was no longer needed, as Fam Chinh finished his meal and wiped his lips appreciatively upon his paper napkin, Lee found a topic of conversation which engaged them both. He talked about the old times in Vietnam, about the tensions with Laos and Cambodia in which they had both been involved, as children growing up near the borders. Usually he spoke little about his early days, finding it best to pretend that he had been in Britain longer than he had. Now the conversation became animated, as Chinh lapsed into a series of comic anecdotes about his boyhood and sought to find if they had joint acquaintances.

Eventually, Chung Lee looked openly at his watch and sounded not Vietnamese but very British as he said, 'Is that the time? I shall have to go soon.'

'It's been good to see you. We must arrange to do this again,' said Fam Chinh. He was still rather puzzled by this meeting, pleasant as it now seemed, because he had never really expected to see Chung again.

'There was something I wanted you to do for me,' said Chung. He had blurted it out suddenly in the end, not led up to it craftily, as the English would have done. But he wasn't English, was he?

Fam, though his English was not as good as Chung's, was a little more Anglicized in his ways. He smiled and said, 'I'll do whatever I can for you. But I don't see much I can do. You have moved up in the world and I'm still where I was.'

Chung wondered if that was meant to be cutting, if the man really felt he had moved up in the world. Had he been disloyal, in leaving him behind working for the Indian? Perhaps he should not have pitched the attractions of work at Thorley Grange so strongly when he was struggling for something to talk about whilst the man ate his meal. It was too late to worry about that now. He wanted to introduce what he wanted casually, so as to make it seem less of a favour. But he hadn't the skills to do that.

He looked again at his watch and said, 'I really must go. Things at the Grange are in turmoil today, as you can probably imagine.'

'Turmoil?' Chinh spoke as if dealing with a strange new word, as perhaps he was. 'Why is that?'

Chung realized with a sinking heart that like many foreigners far from home, Fam paid little attention to local news. 'Did you not hear about the death?'

Fam Chinh looked blank for a moment. Then, to Chung's relief, understanding flooded into the olive features. 'Someone from the Grange was killed, yes? In suspect way?'

'Suspicious circumstances, yes; that is what the police say. And it was the man who owns the place – owned the place, I suppose I should now say. So there is much confusion and we wonder what will happen to all of us. That is why I have to get back.'

'Yes. Yes, I understand. I must not delay you.'

'But there is something I have to ask you.'

'What is that?'

Chung thought he saw shutters closing on his friend's face. He said desperately. 'It is not much, really. I need you to say that I was with you last night.' Then as doubt flooded into the face across the table, he said desperately, 'We could say we were here, if you like.'

Chinh spoke English adequately for his needs, though he was not as fluent as Chung Lee. Under pressure, his control of the language always deteriorated. 'Why you need this? Why you need me to say you with me?' His eyes widened in horror. 'You kill this man? You kill your new boss?'

Chung managed to laugh, to show the man by relaxing his body how ridiculous that notion was. In the crisis, he was much better than he had been in the preceding hour. 'No, of course not! I scarcely got near enough to Mr Ketley even to speak to him.' He chuckled again at the absurdity of the notion of himself as killer, then said, 'But the staff talk to each other up there, and it does sound to me from what I've heard around the kitchen and the rest of the house as if someone killed the boss. I'm foreign, like you, and we know what it's like, don't we? We always seem to be the first suspects, when anything goes wrong.'

To his immense relief, Fam Chinh nodded. There'd been an incident last week when money went missing and he'd been sure everyone was looking at him suspiciously. He'd been very relieved when the money was found. He said, 'You not really involved in this?'

'No, of course I'm not. But I haven't been up there very long and everyone else there seems to be British. I just want to be able to say I was with someone when this happened, that's all. A sort of safety blanket for me.'

'A safety blanket.' Chinh weighed this strange phrase he had never heard before and took a decision. 'All right. We were here, weren't we? We had a full meal and were here for the whole evening.'

'That's right! We were!' Lee wrung the man's hand warmly in his relief, almost as though they were both British. 'I'll do the same for you some day, Fam! Though it's only a precaution, you understand? I'm entirely innocent. I had nothing to do with this.'

'Of course you are! Of course you didn't!'

Chung Lee carried his elation out with him into the street. It survived the cold there and lasted until he was back in his room at Thorley Grange. It was only after two hours there that he wondered how resolute Fam Chinh would prove if put under police pressure.

TWELVE

As Senior Investigating Officer, DCI Peach gathered his team on Monday morning to bring people up to date before releasing them to their allotted tasks for the day.

Winter darkness is a great aid to those who wish to conceal their actions, but Bentleys are more often noticed than run-of-the-mill cars. Two people had seen the vehicle driving out of Brunton to the suburb where it had been located on Saturday night. A resident of the area had actually noticed the big car after it had parked, but had assumed that it was empty, whilst the owner was merely visiting one of the nearby houses. It had been a late-night dog-walker who had actually examined the car and discovered the body.

'We shall have the PM report and the first findings from forensics later today, but you can assume this is murder. An efficient murder, as far as the SOCO officer and I could determine at the scene of the crime, so don't expect anything startling or helpful is going to be handed to you on a plate by forensics. This one will stand or fall by our efforts.'

Peach paused whilst the tasks of the day were allotted and there were a few muffled groans. 'Most of you will know the reputation of Oliver Ketley. I probably know more than any of you. I consider it one of the blackest days in the many years I have spent in Brunton when Ketley decided to move on to our patch. He was a villain: a blacker villain than most of you will ever have encountered. I believe the full extent of his vicious career will only be revealed over the next few years.

'But the man's character must not influence you and the way you go about your work. As far as all of us are concerned, Ketley is now a victim. If we start picking and choosing among our victims, we might as well all give up this job. We need an arrest and a prosecution, to show that no one can murder on our patch and get away with it. Our mission is to uphold the law and murder is the worst affront of all to the law. We want a result here, as fervently as we would want a result in any other murder investigation.'

It was a long speech for Percy Peach. The team filed away in sober mood, with many fewer words than usual. They accepted what he said, but they understood also what he hadn't needed to say. If this was a gangland killing, the removal of one big villain by a rival, this was going to be time-consuming, difficult and possibly dangerous. And the nearer they got to an arrest, the more dangerous it would become.

Peach's own arrangement of his day was disrupted by the phone call he received two minutes after he had briefed the team. It came from a superintendent in Manchester whom he had never met.

'DCI Peach? I was referred to you by Chief Superintendent Tucker.'

'Yes, you would be.'

'He said that you were the man in touch with the detail of the case.'

'Yes, he would do.'

There was a tiny pause whilst the man at the other end of the call translated this police-speak and divined that Tucker was a wanker. 'It's about Oliver Ketley. A suspicious death?'

'A murder. That will become official by lunch time.'

'Yes. I may have a candidate for you. Nothing I can prove. Information from a snout.'

'A reliable snout?'

'A very reliable snout. Otherwise I wouldn't be ringing you.' The first touch of acerbity in the tone. Every CID officer has his snouts – usually small-time crooks or ex-crooks who move about in the underworld and keep their ears open. They are almost always men and they deal with men; it is much more difficult for the growing number of female officers reaching the higher CID ranks to build up a network of informers.

'I'm sorry. Thanks for the information. What next?'

The Manchester superintendent passed on the one significant piece of information his snout had brought to him, then said,

'It's your case. We don't want crossed wires, do we? I think you should do the interview. I'll give you what we know. It's significant, but it isn't a lot.'

Not enough for you to clear up a murder and take the credit, then. But fair play to the super: the fact and the name he passed over were significant. Peach said. 'I'm grateful for the information. Can you give me an address?'

'Twenty-four Egerton Gardens, Oldham. I know it's thirty miles or so from Brunton, but if I were you, I wouldn't try to make an appointment in advance. He wouldn't be there, probably wouldn't be within a hundred miles. He's inclined to shirk publicity, George French.'

Greta Ketley wanted desperately to speak to Martin Price. Speaking to your lover seemed so much the natural thing to do, after the ordeal of the police interview. She wanted to tell her man about the strangeness of the CID pairing – that your initial reaction was to be scared of the powerful black man who looked so formidable and never smiled, whereas it was the bouncy little chief inspector with the bald head and the black moustache who was the real threat. He asked most of the questions, then seemed to weigh every answer as if you might be lying. She wanted to warn Martin about that; but then if all went well Martin might not even need to speak to the police, lucky man!

He had told her that it made sense not to contact each other for a few days. She could see the logic in that, though at this moment she resented it. She needed to talk to someone, because she felt very isolated. There were staff all around her, but she had no idea what they were saying among themselves, what was the gossip below stairs about Oliver's death. She saw Mrs Johnson arranging flowers in the hall and called her into the drawing room where she sat, trying ridiculously to read a book.

'I'm sorry, I don't remember your first name.'

A small, embarrassed smile crept into the pretty, serious face beneath the dark hair. 'It's Jane, ma'am. Most people call me Janey.'

'Then I shall do that also. And you should call me Greta.'

'Please do call me Janey if you wish to. But I do not think that I should call you Greta. I don't think Mrs Frobisher would approve of it. And it would make life difficult for me with the other staff.'

The English system for employers and employees was a strange one: she doubted if she would ever work out all its subtleties. You paid these people, but you still couldn't arrange things as you wished. 'I see. Well, I shall call you Janey. And I shall ask Mrs Frobisher that you shall be my personal maid – my dresser when I need one, and things like that.' She threw in the last phrase rather desperately. What she really needed was a friend, but a confidante such as she had seen in old-fashioned plays might be the nearest she could have to a friend.

'Thank you.' Janey was not sure she welcomed this new intimacy, but she could hardly reject it and it might well be a good thing. It wouldn't make her popular with the other staff, but it might in due course mean more money.

'How did you think it went yesterday?'

Janey looked a little blank for a moment before she under-stood the question. 'When the CID people came here, you mean?'

'Yes. Do you think they were satisfied?'

'Yes, I think so.' She looked at Greta for a moment with her head a little on one side. 'They said it was just routine, didn't they? They said they always saw the spouses of dead persons first, because they knew most about the person who had died.'

'Yes, that's what they said.' Greta smiled with relief. She was glad she'd asked this sensible woman to be her friend. Janey seemed so innocent, to have things so much in perspec-tive. She herself had lived for so long in the shadow of Oliver Ketley that she had forgotten how ordinary people looked at the world. The police interview was probably as straight-forward a matter as Janey thought it was. Greta said almost apologetically, 'The police always regard the wife or husband of a murder victim as the first suspect, you see.'

'Do they? Well, I'm sure they don't in this case. I'm sure they're satisfied you're completely innocent, after speaking to you yesterday.'

'Well, that's good to hear, from someone who was present at that meeting.' Greta looked more relaxed as she smiled again. 'I'm glad we've become friends, Janey. I was feeling very lonely.'

'That's natural enough, when you've lost your husband. I felt very lonely indeed, when my Sam died.'

'Yes. It helps to talk to someone who's been through the same experience.' Greta wanted to ask how Sam had died and how long ago it had been, but she sensed that for the present she had pushed far enough into the life of this slightly reluctant new friend.

Janey Johnson took her silence as an indication that she could get back to her household duties. As she vigorously polished the silver punchbowl in the dining room, she wondered if Greta Ketley's anxiety meant that she had rather more to hide than Janey had hitherto assumed.

Twenty-four Egerton Gardens Oldham was not at all the sort of residence DCI Peach had expected.

It was a small detached bungalow, no more than five years old, with a neat garden at the front and a small new greenhouse between the garage and the weedless lawn at the rear. It was one of many such properties on a large modern estate; Egerton Gardens was a cul-de-sac off a wider road which was lined with much larger houses. This was obviously the section of the estate designed for retired couples; had it not been a bitter, overcast February day, they would no doubt have seen elderly men working in the gardens and passing the time of day with their neighbours.

Percy looked hard at the front door with its neat brass numbers. There was no sign of life within. 'Let's hope the bugger's at home. You introduce us, Clyde: it might be an occasion when we want the hard bastard to the fore.'

His companion glanced at him without emotion. Northcott could do other things as well as frighten people, but Peach knew that bloody well; when life was quiet, Percy liked to rub friend as well as foe up the wrong way. Clyde dutifully rang the bell, then listened to the noise echoing in what sounded like an empty residence. There was no other sound, but within five seconds the door was opened wide before them and a slight figure in jeans, sweater and open-necked shirt stood interrogatively in the aperture.

'Mr George French? I am Detective Sergeant Northcott and this is Detective Chief Inspector Peach. We'd like a word with you.'

The man eyed them up and down with curiosity but without apparent fear. 'You'd better come inside.' He looked for a moment at the police Mondeo at his gates before he turned away from them, for all the world like a suburban householder who was worried that a police vehicle left there for any length of time would excite speculation amongst his neighbours. He led the way into a small, immaculate sitting room and gestured towards the sofa, whilst he took one of the armchairs in the comfortable, slightly old-fashioned three-piece suite.

Peach looked round unhurriedly, sizing up the lean man with the blue-grey eyes deep-sunk in his sallow cheeks. It was those deep-set eyes which made him look a little older than the highly fit man he actually was. His shoulders were narrow, but his frame was wiry and carried no surplus weight. His hair was cut quite short, but not cropped; it took a keen eye to detect the few strands of grey in it. Around thirty-six, Peach decided. And in this setting, expertly camouflaged.

Percy gave a few seconds to each of the two original art works on the wall before he said, 'Business good, is it?'

George French looked at him steadily. An ordinary citizen in his own home would have asked them what they were about by now, but he was content to let them make the running; it was his habit to reveal nothing of himself until he chose to. 'Business comes and goes, for a consultant engineer. But it's good enough, yes. I have been divorced for seven years now and I have only myself to think of. I collect enough commissions to avoid working for a monthly wage. I like to be my own master.'

Peach gave him a broad smile, then rocked to and fro very thoughtfully upon the sofa, seemingly moved by some private mirth. 'Consultant engineer, eh? Well, it's as good a cover as any. I expect you've even got an engineering qualification, if we go back far enough. I expect you could even provide us with details of some of the work you've undertaken in the last year, if push came to shove. So I won't waste my time and yours: you probably have plenty, but we've got villains to lock away, haven't we, DS Northcott?' Peach glanced not at his sergeant but through the wide double-glazed window at the row of neat dwellings. 'You're posing here as a model citizen, Mr French. Shouldn't the pose include morning coffee and biscuits for your unexpected but welcome visitors?'

'I don't offer hospitality to strangers who insult me in my own home. I think you should state your business and then be on your way.'

But Peach, despite his assurance that their time was valuable, was playing this slowly. He had only one telling fact at his disposal and he would reserve it for a little while longer. Even men as cool and apparently unshakeable as this one could become nervous, if you delayed your strike. 'You must feel honoured to have such high-ranking CID men in what you would no doubt call your humble abode. Your name and address were given to us by someone of even higher rank in the Greater Manchester police. You've excited their interest, you see, and they're keeping an eye on you.'

French had known why they were here since he had seen them climbing out of the car, but he would play out his part in this preliminary charade as long as he could. Whilst you revealed nothing of yourself, it was still possible that they knew less than you suspected they did. 'If what you are telling me is true, I can't think why they should do that. A case of mistaken identity, perhaps. People tell me the police system is nothing like as effective as it should be.'

Peach glanced again at the paintings. 'You collect enough commissions to live comfortably, as you say, George. But not as a consultant engineer. Work is much more rewarding for a contract killer.'

French looked from one expectant face to the other. 'I suppose I should laugh at such a bizarre idea. Instead, I find myself both bewildered and annoyed.'

Clyde Northcott had to exercise all his powers of concentration to prevent him stealing a glance at Peach. This man seemed so genuine and unthreatening that he wondered whether they had indeed been given a bum steer, whether this was an innocent member of the public going about his business and they were about to be acutely embarrassed.

Peach was beset by no such apprehension. He was about to play his single trump card, but he would play it as if he had four others to follow. 'A contract killer. A man who has to kill regularly to maintain his income, to pay for things like this.' He glanced again at the paintings on the wall.

French smiled like one being patient with a recalcitrant child. 'Engineering pays well enough, if you're efficient. I'm quite good at costing major new projects, although I say it myself. If you ever need a new bridge or want to know the cost of clearing a site for a new supermarket, you should come to me, Mr Peach. I'll give you my card before you go.'

'What weapons do you use, George? Pistol and an Armalite?'

'As it happens, you touch on a hobby of mine. I'm a member of the Rochdale Shooting Club, though I can't attend as regularly as I should like to do. I even have the odd trophy in the spare bedroom. The weapons I use are licensed and documented.'

'I'm sure they are, though I wouldn't rule out totally different and undeclared armaments as well. Where were you on Saturday night?'

French took care to look surprised by this abrupt arrival of the question he had been expecting since he saw the police car at his gates. 'Saturday? Let's see now. Saturday was cold and clear – quite a good day for February. I dug over my little vegetable patch. Meant to do it in the autumn, really, but it was pretty wet in November. Then we had that early snow in December, which meant there was no gardening at all for nearly a month.' He was enjoying stringing this out, talking like one of the neighbours he exchanged gardening tips with – that man was sixty-seven and retired, and George thought he was doing a pretty good imitation of him.

'I haven't much room for vegetables. They give you pocket-handkerchief-sized gardens with these modern properties, so it's not a big patch. But my muscles must be out of practice. They were protesting a bit after the digging, so I allowed myself the luxury of a hot bath. Almost fell asleep in there, as a matter of fact. Then I had Thai fishcakes I'd bought from Marks and Spencers and watched an episode of *Midsomer Murders* I'd recorded on my Sky Plus. Followed it up with *Match of the Day*, where I found Arsenal particularly impressive.'

'No witnesses. Make a note of that please, DS Northcott.' Clyde was already doing so, with his smooth features displaying all the scepticism he could muster.

French for his part showed every sign of enjoying this strange little game. He put his hands on the arms of his chair and sat back a little. 'I seem to remember that detective on *Midsomer Murders* saying that the innocent often had no alibi, because the innocent had no idea they would need one.'

'I think you were fulfilling a contract on Saturday night, George.'

'And I think if you are going to persist in your ridiculous fantasies I would prefer you to address me as Mr French.'

'They aren't fantasies, George. We have hard evidence.'

'And I know that is a lie, because no such evidence exists. I think you should leave now.'

'We know you received an advance payment of twenty-five thousand pounds, George. Have you had the second twenty-five k yet?'

The delay in playing the trump card was justified. French was clearly shaken. Although his face showed it for only the most fleeting of moments, both men on the sofa saw it. That was what made his words unconvincing when he said, 'It may surprise you to know that I haven't the faintest idea what you're talking about.'

'Fifty thousand for a single killing. Good money, that, George. You don't need many of those in a year to live in comfortable suburban obscurity.' Peach looked out with amusement at the immaculate garden in the foreground and the bland modern housing beyond it. 'But you probably don't get as much as that for every killing. I can see that Oliver Ketley would justify a higher fee than your normal one. Still, mission achieved, with a minimum of fuss. I could admire your professionalism, if murder wasn't involved.'

'And I could admire the tales you spin, if they didn't involve malicious slander.'

Peach pursed his lips. 'We don't do plea bargaining here – not officially. But we'd be willing to tell the judge you'd offered full cooperation, if it was true. I'd say your best policy now would be to come clean and give us all the details you can about the people who paid you to do this. Jack Burgess, was it?'

Again the pallid face with the sunken eyes was disturbed for a split second by what might have been panic. But when French spoke it was as calmly as ever. 'I've no idea who this Burgess is and I haven't the faintest notion what you're talking about. I've heard of Mr Oliver Ketley because I've read about his death in this morning's *Telegraph*. He seems to have been a prominent local benefactor and I hope you eventually arrest his killer. If your performance here this morning is anything to go by, I hold out no great hopes of that.'

'And I hold out no great hopes of your being here to plant your spring vegetables, George. The career you've chosen pays well, but it doesn't pay forever. We'll be back for you, sooner rather than later.'

George French turned on his heel as the three stood up. He disappeared into the adjoining room and came back with the card he had promised. He said urbanely, 'If you know anyone who is contemplating a major engineering project, you might like to ask them to—'

'Keep it, French. Take my card, instead. And consider how you might set about reducing your sentence. The world is well rid of Ketley, but this is still murder.'

THIRTEEN

Chief Superintendent Thomas Bulstrode Tucker prided himself upon his PR talents. His skilfully coiffured hair had just enough silver at the temples to suggest maturity and calm judgement. His grey eyes gazed out confidently through the rimless spectacles he had lately adopted. His regular, firm features and immaculately cut uniform – he always preferred uniform to plain clothes for his television appearances – conveyed a man with vast experience who was still vigorous enough and adaptable enough to be a bastion against crime.

Appearances, as Percy Peach said, could be very deceptive; that was a very good thing for Tommy Bloody Tucker.

The Head of CID was giving an interview to BBC North-West television, which would be shown on that evening's news bulletins. He sat expectantly in the background whilst his young interviewer introduced the item. 'This is Janet Dickinson reporting from north-east Lancashire. The normally quiet and well-ordered town of Brunton has been rocked by the news of the brutal murder of one of its most prominent citizens. Oliver Ketley lived at the former stately home, Thorley Grange, which he had restored and considerably extended over the last few years.'

This was an important enough death to warrant a helicopter budget, and impressive views of the older part of the mansion, the entrance to the new building and the acres of the walled estate were fed into the item at this point. Then the young female voice resumed, 'Mr Ketley, a relatively recent arrival upon the Brunton scene, had established himself as a prominent local benefactor, and his death has already been lamented by the Brunton hospice and several other local organizations who were recipients of his financial support. He was found shot dead in his car in a Brunton suburb on Saturday evening and the police immediately confirmed that this was a suspicious death. We are now certain that foul play was involved. In other words, this was murder. Detective Chief Superintendent Tucker is in charge of the Brunton CID department. What can you tell us about the progress of enquiries, Superintendent?'

Tucker stared frankly into the camera, as the media course had told him to do. 'Well, Janet, you will appreciate that this shows every sign of being a complex case.'

Young faces are excellent at displaying surprise, and Janet Dickinson too had had her training, much more extensive than T.B. Tucker's. Her eyebrows rose high beneath a puzzled frown. 'Why would that be, Mr Tucker? A man as well-liked as Mr Ketley can surely have had very few enemies?'

'He was a highly successful businessman, Janet. Such people usually have enemies. That is an unfortunate fact of life.'

More puzzlement. 'You're saying that envy was the motive? That Mr Ketley was despatched by a jealous rival?'

Tucker gave her a patronizing, elder-statesman smile. 'It's far too early to say anything like that. You mustn't put words into my mouth, Janet.'

'I wasn't aware that I was doing that, Mr Tucker. I was merely trying to establish the present state of your enquiries.'

'Ah! Well, it's very early to say anything definite.'

'No one is at present helping you with your enquiries?'

Tucker allowed himself a silent chuckle at such naivety. 'What a strange phrase that is! A whole range of people have been helping us with our enquiries. We have a large team allocated to this crime, as you would expect, and my officers have been diligently questioning the public, the family and the staff at Thorley Grange about this.'

'I see. With what results?'

Tucker tried not to look ruffled. 'It is too early to say yet. I'm sure you will appreciate that much of the material we are assembling must remain confidential until we can—'

'This seems to me like official jargon to disguise the fact that you have made little progress so far. Have you any significant leads?'

'A whole series of items which may or may not prove significant are at present receiving our attention.'

'Does this mean that you are scrambling desperately for clues, Superintendent Tucker?'

Those men Paxman and Humphreys had a lot to answer for. Interviews hadn't been like this a few years ago. You'd said your piece and smiled confidently at the camera. Your interviewer had listened, nodded soberly and passed on to the next item without challenging you. Tucker wanted to slip a finger inside his collar and loosen it a little, but the media course had said that was the last thing you should do. He leaned forward and looked earnest. 'We have various leads, as I've already indicated. They are being vigorously explored, but it would be quite unfair to reveal our thinking at this point. I have every confidence in my team. I am confident there will be progress over the next few days.' Tucker jutted his chin rather desperately at the camera.

'We all hope so, Superintendent. Indeed we do. Meantime, the public, who are naturally very concerned to know who shot dead a well-loved local resident, must wait and see. It seems a rather invidious situation.'

The last shot was of Tucker, who was not quite sure of the meaning of invidious, fingering the inside of his collar.

Chung Lee had known it would come. It would have been strange if it hadn't. All the staff at Thorley Grange were being interviewed after the murder of its owner. Even those who only came in by day, even the cleaning lady who came for only two mornings a week, were being questioned by the police. They used the office by the front door where he had been interviewed when he was appointed assistant chef at the Grange. There were two people in uniform and most people were in and out in ten or at most twenty minutes. Many of them seemed quite excited to be involved in a murder investigation.

Chung asked the chef why they hadn't got round to him yet.

'They're saving you until last because they want to give you a real grilling!' said Michael Knight. Then, seeing dismay turning to panic on the young man's face, he took pity on him. 'It's not that, you daft ha'p'orth. I reckon they don't want to be accused of prejudice by doing the foreigners first. PCs have to be more PC than most, these days!'

Chung grinned weakly. He didn't understand the joke and he didn't know what a 'daft ha'p'orth' was. But he was relieved to hear that the chef didn't think he was a special case for the police.

The reason he came towards the end of the interviews was in fact quite simple. The residential staff were being interviewed by CID. Those who had been most recently appointed were naturally of most interest to them. So much so that they were reserved for the attention of the top brass. When Chung Lee was eventually ushered into the square room by the front entrance, he was confronted by a short, alert man who announced that he was DCI Peach and a tall, unsmiling black man who was apparently DS Northcott. The inspector wore a light-grey suit and very shiny black shoes, which seemed to mirror the small black moustache and the black fringe around the bald head at the other end of his frame. The sergeant had navy trousers and a tight-fitting black sweater which followed the lines of his muscular torso, as if he wished to convey the message that a physical beating would be the consequence of any attempt to deceive them.

They took his details, comparing them with the letter of application which Michael Knight had held in this very room on the day he was appointed here. Then, as if trying to put him at his ease, the smaller man said, 'You speak very good English, Mr Lee.'

'Yes. I have been here a long time, now. I pick things up quite quickly – people say I have a good ear. My written English is not so good.'

'And yet you completed your application for work here very well. I've seen a few police constables who wouldn't have done as well as you did. Did you write it yourself?'

'Yes.' Then his brow furrowed in his anxiety to say nothing which could be questioned later. 'I wrote down my answers on a different piece of paper first. I might have shown it to someone to take his advice.'

'You were careful. That is commendable. Not many younger people take such care nowadays. Tell us about your previous work, please.'

This was all right, so far. Perhaps it was just routine, as all the other employees had said; perhaps it wasn't going to be anything like as bad as he'd feared. He still had the piece of paper he'd referred to in his room; he was glad he'd read through the rough draft of his application again just before he'd come down to see them. He took them through the last three years, emphasizing the catering work he'd done in the snack bar at the seaside and even more the work in the Brunton restaurant immediately before he came here. It was almost as though he was being interviewed for the assistant chef's post again.

And then Peach posed almost the same question Michael Knight had asked him, 'Why did you want to come here, Mr Lee? Why did Thorley Grange attract you?'

'I'm interested in restaurant work. I want to become a chef eventually, with responsibility for my own kitchen. I felt there would be more opportunity for me at Thorley Grange.'

'I see. But you must have been serving many more meals in a busy restaurant than you do here. Wouldn't you have learned more there?'

'No. I was more junior there. I'd learned all that I could do. Mr Knight gives me more responsibility in the kitchen here. I enjoy the work more here. And when we have important visitors and big meetings here, we do elaborate menus. We prepare dishes I would never have learned to cook if I had stayed in my post in Brunton. I am happy here, because I am learning much more.'

It all sounded rather like a prepared answer to Peach. But probably it was and quite innocently so. Lee must have said something much like this when he was interviewed for the work here and was merely adding to it a little now for this situation. They'd already asked the head chef about him as a new arrival, and Knight had said that Lee was conscientious and a quick learner; he'd emphasized that he was pleased with him.

Clyde Northcott, perhaps wishing to prick the bubble of merit around this smiling, olive-faced man, said with a hint of sarcasm, 'And no doubt the money is better here as well.'

Chung Lee did not think, as an Englishman might have done, that it was churlish to raise as sordid a motive as money. He nodded earnestly and said, 'The pay is not much more than I was receiving in Brunton. But the conditions are good and the work is much more interesting to me. Also I have been given a pleasant room here, and the accommodation and my food are free. That means I spend very little and can save most of my wages.'

Peach nodded, then shot another question at him with crossbow fierceness. 'Who killed Mr Ketley, Lee?'

This time the shock showed on the features which had previously been so difficult to read. 'I don't know that. Why do you think I would know that?'

Peach gave him an innocent smile. 'Well, you live-in here; you're at the heart of things. You no doubt saw Mr Ketley's comings and goings. And you seem to me an intelligent chap, from what I've seen and from what other people say about you. I thought perhaps you would have formed an opinion, even if you've nothing definite to support it. Whatever you tell us will be in strict confidence.'

'I don't mix very much with the other staff, except in our breaks when we're working. There is much talk of course. Much special – no, that is not the word I want . . .'

'Much speculation? You mean people are wondering who did this and coming up with their own ideas?'

'Much speculation, yes.' Lee articulated each of the four syllables carefully, as if committing a new word to his vocabulary. 'But mostly we are all worried about what will happen to us. We have been told that for the moment there will be no changes, but we are all trying to look further into the future, to see if we shall have to search for new jobs.'

'That is understandable. But I've no doubt people will also be wondering who killed Mr Ketley. Or do they think they already know who did it?'

Chung's eyes opened a little wider with surprise, or possibly apprehension. 'No. No one knows who did this.'

'But people are only human. There must be speculation about who did it.'

That word again. Chung mouthed it silently, as if he were determined it would not escape him. Then he repeated, 'No one knows who killed Mr Ketley. I have not heard anyone suggesting who it might be.'

'I see. Well, try to listen to what people say in the kitchen and in the rest of the house. You may hear some opinions which might be useful to us, by the time we speak to you again. By that time, we shall also know much more about how Mr Ketley died.'

'You will wish to speak to me again?' Lee couldn't resist the question. His apprehension showed on the smooth features which had revealed so little for most of the interview.

'Oh, yes, I should think so. When we know more, we shall no doubt have some more precise questions to ask you.'

Chung nodded, trying to digest the implications of this. Peach offered that thought to most of the people they saw; he found it useful to see what their reactions were. You had to be careful not to suspect too much when you saw dismay – often innocent people found the prospect of further questioning quite daunting. If you knew you were innocent and yet found yourself being drawn into the centre of the case, you were no doubt fearful that innocence might not be enough.

And now, just when it seemed to Chung that the interview might be over, the forbidding-looking DS Northcott said in a deep, even voice, 'Where were you on Saturday night, Mr Lee?'

'Why do you wish to know this? Are you asking everyone this question?'

Clyde exchanged a meaningful glance with Peach, building up the tension as he had seen that Torquemada of interviewers do. 'We're asking most people this, yes. Is it difficult for you to answer?'

'No. It is not difficult. But I am glad you ask everyone. I have been told that British police want every time to pin crimes on foreigners.'

He wasn't exactly playing the racism card. The two men in the room with him had met that all too often when black or Asian suspects were under pressure. This man seemed to be voicing a genuine fear. Peach said calmly, 'You will be treated in exactly the same way as anyone else involved in this case, Chung. The people who may find themselves in trouble are those who try to deceive us. We shall have little sympathy for them, whatever part of the world they come from. Would you answer DS Northcott's question, please? Where were you on Saturday night?'

'I met a friend of mine. A man I used to work with before I came here.'

'Name?' the ballpoint pen and notebook looked tiny in Northcott's huge hands.

'Fam Chinh.' Chung spelt the name out carefully for the big man.

'Address?'

'I do not have his address.' Chung realized this was a mistake; he should have got it from Fam last night.

Northcott looked up at him, savouring the moment, not hurrying his question. 'A friend of yours, you said. But not a very close one, if you do not know where he lives.'

'I have never needed his address. I can give you his phone number.'

Chung duly did so, but he had to pull his diary from the pocket of his trousers to find it; he would have liked to rap it out immediately from memory.

Just when he had focussed on his contest with the big detective sergeant, it was Peach who took up the interrogation again. 'I think you had better tell us the nature of this friendship before we speak to Mr Chinh.'

He made it sound like a threat. Chung felt near to panic. They were questioning him in detail about this, the weakest part of his story. He had been prepared for all kinds of other questions about his residence and his work at Thorley Grange, but he had thought his whereabouts on Saturday night would be merely a brief statement of fact and a nod from the detectives. 'Fam was a man I worked with in the restaurant in Brunton before I came here. The Indian who owned it was a hard man and he didn't give us much credit for the good things we did there. Fam and I are from the same part of the world and we looked out for each other.'

'I see. And now Mr Chinh is looking out for you again.'

Lee looked very puzzled. 'I am sorry. I do not understand this.'

Peach studied him unhurriedly. 'I rather think you do, Chung. We are not accusing anyone of killing Mr Ketley. But

we shall want to know where everyone in the household was
at the time of his death. That is standard procedure. We like
to eliminate as many people as possible from suspicion.'

'Eliminate, yes.' Lee sounded each syllable carefully again,
as if he were committing to memory another new and useful
word. 'So this will eliminate me from suspicion.'

'It seems so, yes. Provided Mr Chinh confirms that he was
with you for the hours which matter on Saturday evening.'

'What time did Mr Ketley die?'

Peach smiled at him as if he were an intelligent but naïve
child. 'We're not yet certain of the exact time. When we are,
we shall probably keep the information to ourselves. You'd
better tell DS Northcott exactly when you were with Mr Chinh.'

'For the whole of the evening.'

Northcott nodded, licking his lips like a predatory tiger. 'We
shall need exact times, Mr Lee.'

'I cannot give you exact times, but I will do my best. We had
a meal together in the Thai restaurant in Market Street. We
met there at about seven o'clock. I was back in my room at
Thorley Grange at ten twenty. So I was probably with him
until about ten.'

Peach said without apparent irony, 'That's commendably
precise, for one who thought he would be unable to give us
exact times. Do you have your own transport?'

'Yes. I have a Nissan Micra. I used it on Saturday night.'

They took the colour and the number. Then, when he thought
it was over, Clyde Northcott said, 'What did you eat in the
restaurant, Mr Lee?'

Chung looked appealingly at Peach. 'Does this really
matter?'

'It may do, Chung. What you ordered may enable us to
establish you were really in that restaurant on Saturday, if we
cannot find other diners who remember that you were there.'

He hadn't thought of other diners. He realized for the first
time how meticulous they could be, when they were investigating murder. 'I'm not sure I can remember what I ate. The
main purpose was to spend some time with an old friend. To
exchange notes.'

Northcott gave him that smile which made his stomach

Chung grinned weakly. He didn't understand the joke and he didn't know what a 'daft ha'p'orth' was. But he was relieved to hear that the chef didn't think he was a special case for the police.

The reason he came towards the end of the interviews was in fact quite simple. The residential staff were being interviewed by CID. Those who had been most recently appointed were naturally of most interest to them. So much so that they were reserved for the attention of the top brass. When Chung Lee was eventually ushered into the square room by the front entrance, he was confronted by a short, alert man who announced that he was DCI Peach and a tall, unsmiling black man who was apparently DS Northcott. The inspector wore a light-grey suit and very shiny black shoes, which seemed to mirror the small black moustache and the black fringe around the bald head at the other end of his frame. The sergeant had navy trousers and a tight-fitting black sweater which followed the lines of his muscular torso, as if he wished to convey the message that a physical beating would be the consequence of any attempt to deceive them.

They took his details, comparing them with the letter of application which Michael Knight had held in this very room on the day he was appointed here. Then, as if trying to put him at his ease, the smaller man said, 'You speak very good English, Mr Lee.'

'Yes. I have been here a long time, now. I pick things up quite quickly – people say I have a good ear. My written English is not so good.'

'And yet you completed your application for work here very well. I've seen a few police constables who wouldn't have done as well as you did. Did you write it yourself?'

'Yes.' Then his brow furrowed in his anxiety to say nothing which could be questioned later. 'I wrote down my answers on a different piece of paper first. I might have shown it to someone to take his advice.'

'You were careful. That is commendable. Not many younger people take such care nowadays. Tell us about your previous work, please.'

This was all right, so far. Perhaps it was just routine, as all the other employees had said; perhaps it wasn't going to be anything like as bad as he'd feared. He still had the piece of paper he'd referred to in his room; he was glad he'd read through the rough draft of his application again just before he'd come down to see them. He took them through the last three years, emphasizing the catering work he'd done in the snack bar at the seaside and even more the work in the Brunton restaurant immediately before he came here. It was almost as though he was being interviewed for the assistant chef's post again.

And then Peach posed almost the same question Michael Knight had asked him, 'Why did you want to come here, Mr Lee? Why did Thorley Grange attract you?'

'I'm interested in restaurant work. I want to become a chef eventually, with responsibility for my own kitchen. I felt there would be more opportunity for me at Thorley Grange.'

'I see. But you must have been serving many more meals in a busy restaurant than you do here. Wouldn't you have learned more there?'

'No. I was more junior there. I'd learned all that I could do. Mr Knight gives me more responsibility in the kitchen here. I enjoy the work more here. And when we have important visitors and big meetings here, we do elaborate menus. We prepare dishes I would never have learned to cook if I had stayed in my post in Brunton. I am happy here, because I am learning much more.'

It all sounded rather like a prepared answer to Peach. But probably it was and quite innocently so. Lee must have said something much like this when he was interviewed for the work here and was merely adding to it a little now for this situation. They'd already asked the head chef about him as a new arrival, and Knight had said that Lee was conscientious and a quick learner; he'd emphasized that he was pleased with him.

Clyde Northcott, perhaps wishing to prick the bubble of merit around this smiling, olive-faced man, said with a hint of sarcasm, 'And no doubt the money is better here as well.'

Chung Lee did not think, as an Englishman might have done, that it was churlish to raise as sordid a motive as money. He nodded earnestly and said, 'The pay is not much more churn. 'I'm sure it will come back to you, if we give you a moment to think about it.'

Chung couldn't face that moment of silence. He blurted immediately, 'Thai green curry. And I had ice cream afterwards. I was too full for anything except ice cream.'

Northcott took what seemed a very long time to write this down. 'Good. I'm sure Mr Chinh will be able to confirm this, in due course.'

Everything sounded like a threat, when you knew you were telling lies. He'd need to get hold of Chinh on the phone and agree what food both of them had eaten, and whether they'd had coffee. Chung was beginning to wish he'd told them that he'd stayed in his own room and watched his small television set there. For a moment, he wondered whether he should do just that. But even as he wondered, he knew he wouldn't do it. He couldn't face this contrasting pair following up why he had chosen to lie, as they surely would. He'd never be able to convince them of how lonely and threatened you felt, when you were on your own in an alien country, with a major crime committed and all the forces of the law lined up against you.

Peach said earnestly, 'Chung, have you any idea who killed Mr Ketley?'

'No. I've already told you I don't.'

'If you have heard anything around the place which sounds like the motive for action against your employer, you must tell us now.'

He tried not to show his relief that they had moved away from his whereabouts on Saturday night. 'No. I have heard nothing.'

Peach stood up, apparently satisfied. He gave him a card and said, 'Well, keep your ears open, please. Pass on to us anything which sounds even faintly suspicious. We shall make sure you do not suffer any penalty for doing that.'

Chung nodded vigorously, overwhelmingly anxious now for this to be over. 'I hope you will soon arrest the man who did this.'

Chung Lee would have been surprised to hear the first subject raised in the police car as it drove between the high stone gateposts and out of Thorley Grange. The English, as he had always thought, had strangely indirect minds.

DS Northcott said, 'I bet that Nissan Micra isn't taxed and insured.'

DCI Peach came back in less than a second. 'You're on. A fiver says it is.'

Clyde grinned; he hadn't expected to be taken up on the bet. 'Why do you say that?'

'Because I think Mr Chung Lee is a meticulous young man. He wouldn't risk breaking our laws in a small thing like that. I also think he's an intelligent man and a quick learner. I think he might make a very good chef, in a year or two. If that's what he really wants to do.'

FOURTEEN

The post-mortem and forensic reports didn't give the team much that was new. The pathologist for the most part confirmed what the SOCO examination had already suggested.

The most useful additional information supplied concerned the time of death. Oliver Ketley had died instantly as a result of a shot fired from the weapon found in his right hand. The shot had entered at his right temple and emerged at the left-hand side of his forehead. In other words, the path of the shot had been slightly forward as he sat in the driving seat of the Bentley. This would have been very unusual for a suicide. People finishing their own lives often shoot themselves in the mouth, but the temple wound is almost as common. However, the bullet normally goes straight through the head or slightly backwards, rather than on the path this one had taken.

In the case of suicide, the weapon would almost certainly have fallen from Ketley's hand after the fatal shot. There were no prints on it other than Ketley's, but that was almost certainly because the pistol had been wiped clean before being placed in his hand. All the signs were that some person unknown had killed Ketley with a single shot and placed the weapon in his hand afterwards, in an attempt to convey the impression that he had taken his own life. This could have been done from outside the car, but the window or the door would have had to be open at the time for that. It was much more likely that the killer had been in the back of the car when the fatal wound was administered.

The analysis of stomach contents showed that a meal had been consumed two to three hours before death. Enquiries at Thorley Grange had established that Ketley had eaten an evening meal there between six thirty and seven, so this gave a probable time of death between nine and ten on Saturday night. The body had been discovered by a sixty-six-year-old man walking his golden retriever at eleven fifteen.

The most interesting facts from forensics related to the fatal weapon. The pistol which had been found in the dead man's hand was a Ruger 9mm pistol. The number showed that it had been bought in the USA and illegally imported into Britain; almost certainly it was one of sixty-six weapons smuggled through Manchester's Ringway airport by Stephen Greenoe, who was now facing trial in North Carolina for his crimes. The case had raised major security issues in Britain. Many argued that the handguns, which had been taken apart to stow within luggage and then reassembled for sale at around £5000 each in Britain, could just as easily have been bombs.

Most of these powerful pistols and revolvers, purchased openly in the USA, were undoubtedly now in the hands of criminal gangs in north-west England. There was a ready demand, since the ban imposed on handguns in Britain after the Dunblane shootings in 1996 had been largely effective, making it very difficult for criminals to obtain them. The Ruger had been purchased during the previous June and smuggled through the airport a month later. It was very new: it was possible it had never been fired before the shot which ended Ketley's life.

Clyde Northcott looked at Peach as they digested this. 'George French?'

'Very possibly. Contract killers have their own chosen weapons, but a Ruger would have been an excellent addition to anyone's armoury. More important, if he always intended to leave it behind to allow the suicide theory, it's a brand-new weapon which is not traceable to him and thus the ideal one to leave in Ketley's grasp. We may have to take that Ruger up later with Mr French. I'll make some discreet enquiries with Manchester CID about where those weapons went to once they were in the country.'

The findings from the forensic laboratories arrived shortly after the PM report. There was no startling clue as to the perpetrator of this crime, but from what they had seen when they visited the scene, neither Peach nor Northcott had expected much. There was a smear on the carpet in the rear of the

Bentley – hardly a soil sample, but enough to provide a match with the soles of the trainers that had left it, if they should ever be located. If this was a professional killer, disposing ruthlessly of his clothing after the completion of a job, those trainers were probably already under tons of rubbish on a waste disposal site.

A single hair had been retrieved from the back of the front passenger seat. It would not lead them to anyone directly, but it might eventually provide a match when a suspect was arrested and charged and compelled to provide a DNA sample. Material to clinch a case for the prosecution months from now, perhaps, but not a direct line to their killer.

This material, like everything found within the car during the minute examination by the forensic team, might be unconnected with whoever had killed Ketley, because there was no way anyone could prove it had not been there before that fatal final trip on Saturday night. According to staff at Thorley Grange, the Bentley had been valeted internally eight days earlier, so anyone who had ridden in the car during those eight days might have left behind the material which had been retrieved and analysed by the forensic team.

Janey Johnson was more comfortable in the office near the front door of Thorley Grange than most of the other people interviewed by the CID.

Most of the others had never been in there before, save for the few minutes when they had been interviewed before they were appointed. Janey had cleaned the room several times, and in recent days had come in to see to the pot plants which were kept on the window-sill of the west-facing window. The primulas were doing well, she was pleased to notice as she came in now; the vivid yellow and the red brightened a dull room considerably and reminded people that in another week it would be March, with the days stretching out and the grass beginning to grow on the long lawns by the front entrance.

Peach looked up from his chair behind the big desk and delivered the mantra he had issued to most of the staff. 'It's just routine, this. Nothing to be afraid of.'

'Yes. I've already seen you once. With Mrs Ketley.'

'Of course you have. You won't need to be introduced to DS Northcott, then.'

Janey smiled cautiously at the formidable black man on Peach's right. Clyde nodded watchfully in return.

Peach said, 'Most of the staff here have been interviewed and have signed statements for junior members of our team. You've got Clyde and me because you're one of the recent arrivals at the Grange.'

Despite his bland smile, he contrived to make the words sound like a threat. Janey settled herself with her knees primly together and said, 'Yes. I've worked here since before the owners moved in, but I've only recently become a resident. I'll tell you whatever I can, which won't be much. I don't think I'll be able to add much to what you heard yesterday from Mrs Ketley.'

'Really? I was hoping you'd have a different perspective and different information to give us. I was hoping you'd tell us things you didn't like to raise when the mistress of the house was present.'

His tone was light, but he was watching her closely. She realized in that moment that he would pick up any mistake she made, that he would notice any unnatural hesitations or evasions. But if you'd nothing to hide, you couldn't suffer, could you? She wondered with a shaft of sympathy how Chung Lee had fared with these two. He'd been struggling with a second language, as she was not. Even though his English was good, he wouldn't pick up every nuance, as she would – and as Peach would on the other side. She said, 'I like Mrs Ketley and she's been a model employer. I wouldn't wish to say anything against her.'

He still had his smile, as if he recognized and was enjoying the preliminaries to something more serious. 'I should remind you at this stage that we have now embarked upon a full-scale murder enquiry. Whatever your personal feelings, you must hold back nothing about Mrs Ketley or anyone else.'

'I understand that. But I do not intend to conceal anything. As far as I am concerned, Mrs Ketley had nothing to do with her husband's death. But I do not know that. If I hear anything which alters my opinion, I shall not cover it up. I realize I would be very foolish if I attempted to deceive the police.'

'I wish everyone would realize that. People who don't realize it get themselves into all sorts of trouble. For our part, I can assure you that you speak to us in the strictest confidence. Nothing you say in here will be revealed to your fellow-workers or the management – unless it becomes evidence in a murder investigation, of course.'

'I don't think there's much danger of that, Chief Inspector.' Her small, serious face relaxed into a smile and her dark eyes sparkled beneath the short-cut dark hair, making them realize what an attractive woman she was. 'As you said, in terms of residence, I'm a recent arrival here. In my view, it will be the people who've lived here for much longer who might have definite views on who killed Mr Ketley.'

'I see. Well, you'll be happy to hear that one of those people, the housekeeper Mrs Frobisher, speaks highly of you and the work you have done since you came here.'

'That is good to hear, because it's Mrs Frobisher to whom I am directly responsible. She has been very good to me; she extended my duties as soon as she decided I was competent. I think she was also widowed early in life, which no doubt gives her a certain sympathy for me.'

'Yes. How did your husband die, Janey?'

The first intimate question, the first use of her forename. She wondered if he had been planning to dart this at her from the start. 'Sam died suddenly. He was – he was involved in an accident.'

'Really? It wasn't from some awful disease, then. One always tends to presume heart disease or some sort of cancer, when a man dies early, nowadays.'

'No, it wasn't either of those. It was . . .' Suddenly she was in tears, throwing up her hands, trying to apologize, fighting for words which would not come.

The formidable Northcott was immediately at her side, thrusting a carefully pressed white handkerchief towards her. It looked even more immaculate as it passed from his large black hands into hers, which looked pale and tiny beside his.

Janey looked up, surprised by his solicitude, then nodded

her gratitude, not trusting herself to speak. She was still shaken by a sob as she eventually managed to say, 'I'm sorry. But this isn't relevant, is it?'

Peach had not moved an inch as he observed the little cameo of emotion between the two. But now he seemed genuinely shaken by his gaffe. 'Probably not. I suppose I was trying to put you at your ease – mistakenly, as it turns out. It's a CID habit to find out as much as possible about everyone we speak to.'

'I should be able to talk about Sam's death, shouldn't I? It's five years ago now. But it was a complete shock at the time, and it still catches me out when people raise it unexpectedly.'

'That's quite understandable – rather to your credit, I'd say. You don't have any children, Janey?'

Another crass enquiry. It seemed for a moment as if she would lapse into tears again as she shook her head, not trusting herself with words. Northcott looked at his chief curiously, then accusingly. Peach's tone was quiet and sympathetic, but did he need to pry into obviously sensitive areas like this? The DCI didn't attempt to break the silence as it stretched through long seconds. Janey eventually composed herself enough to say, 'We didn't have children, no. We were planning them at the time of Sam's death. Now I wish we'd done it much earlier.'

'I see.' He shifted his position, glanced for a moment at Northcott. 'Well, you've settled in well here, according to what everyone tells us.'

'Yes.' She wondered if this was to remind her again that they had spoken to others and taken their opinions, that it would be unwise for her in turn to hold anything back. 'The people I work closely with, like Mrs Frobisher, have been very kind to me. I've only lived in at the Grange for a short time and I don't know everyone.'

'But people seem to trust you. Rely on you, even. You must have taken it as quite a compliment that Mrs Ketley herself chose to have you beside her when she spoke to us.'

'I suppose it was. I'd rather she hadn't done that, as a matter of fact. It didn't make things easy for me with the rest of the staff.'

'I expect some of them were jealous of you.'

A tiny shrug of the slim shoulders. 'It's a small, rather closed world when you're a resident member of staff in a big house like this. Things can easily get out of proportion. I'm learning things like that as I go along.'

'I'm sure you are. I'm sure you're an intelligent and resourceful woman. As I said, it's because you're a recent resident at the Grange that DS Northcott and I are speaking to you today. You must get to know some of the staff pretty well, when you're a resident.'

'Only the ones I work closely with, at present. I see people like gardeners and the business employees sometimes at meal times, but there are still people whom I've never spoken to.'

'I expect you know the residents well, though. You're bound to see them outside working hours.'

She looked full at him for a moment, trying to divine whether this was a serious query or merely a routine comment. Then her features slipped unexpectedly into a rueful smile. 'I'm rather cautious with new friendships, to tell you the truth. Especially with men: some of them think that a youngish widow is fair game. "Gagging for it" was the term I heard on TV the other night. I'm fairly self-sufficient; I've had to be, over the last five years. I suppose I prefer to establish friend-ships on my own terms.'

It was a glimpse into a life which the two men in the room with her could only imagine. But this sturdy woman was merely explaining her conduct, not asking for sympathy. Peach accorded her sympathy, but that did not affect his persistence. He said with a hint of irony, 'And have you made any attempts at friendship on your own terms in the last few weeks?'

Janey reflected for a moment, as the question invited her to do. It would have been easy and natural to say no, not as yet. But she had already been reminded twice that they had talked to lots of other people, who must have given their thoughts about her. She wanted to be finished with the CID and their questions, so she mustn't leave these men with the idea that she was holding anything back. 'I've become quite friendly with Mr Lee – probably more in the days since Mr Ketley was killed than before that, I think. Chung moved into the

Grange only a few days before I did and his room is just down
the corridor from mine. He's keen to become a chef and works
in the kitchen mostly, so we don't see each other much during
working hours.'

'But you've got to know each other quite well, nevertheless.'
She immediately bridled at that. 'I didn't say that. We have
in common the facts that we're resident and that we're alone.
I didn't find him sexually threatening and you'd probably find
he'd say the same about me.' She gave again that small smile,
which was the more attractive for being unexpected and at her
own expense. 'Chung must feel very much alone at times.
He's a long way from home and I think he's a natural loner.'

'Yes. Mr Lee has friends in Brunton, though. He met one
of them on the night when Mr Ketley died.'

'Did he? I'm glad he's kept up with his friends. Still, he
must find it strange here, operating all the time in a foreign
language, even though his English seems very good. And now
he's involved in a big murder enquiry. Whatever he'd antici-
pated when he moved in here, it couldn't have included that.'

'Mr Lee seems pleased with his decision to come here,
though. He told us he's getting the experience he wanted in
the kitchen.'

'Yes. Chung's very determined. I'm sure he'll end up as a
chef with his own restaurant, one day. And I for one would
be happy to eat there.'

Clyde Northcott decided that she would make a good friend,
this quiet, contained, effortlessly pretty woman. Far too old
for him, of course, but a good friend to have. He said, 'Mr
Lee was pleased with the financial aspects of working here,
when we spoke to him. He found he lived cheaply and could
save most of his wage.'

She looked at him for a moment, then gave him a smile
which conveyed that she knew much more of life than he did.
'And you'd like to know if I too am doing well for myself?
Yes, I can confirm everything you say about the benefits of
residence. We exist very cheaply here. And unlike the Victorian
servants who lived here when the older part of the house was
built, we have comfortable, well-heated rooms and we are paid
a decent wage. Would you like to see my room?'

Peach smiled back at her, as if in appreciation of the way she had handled Northcott's suggestion. 'That won't be necessary at this stage, Janey. We must be on our way in a moment.'

She didn't like that phrase 'at this stage'. She was sure he'd thrown it in deliberately to intimidate her. 'I don't think there's anything else I can tell you.'

'Except who you think killed Oliver Ketley,' he said quietly.

She was getting used to the way this bouncy little man suddenly flung unexpected and important questions at her. She said calmly, 'I've thought about it, of course. I expect everyone here has. But I haven't come up with any theories. And as I've indicated, I tend to keep myself to myself, most of the time. So I haven't heard any interesting theories from anyone else.'

Peach handed her a card, 'When you do, please phone this number immediately.'

'When', not 'if', she noticed. She took the card, looked at it for a moment, and nodded.

As the police car wound its way back to Brunton station, Peach said happily, 'You rather fell for little Mrs Johnson, didn't you, Clyde?'

'Not at all, sir. I try to remain objective at all times, as you've taught me to do. I do think she's making the best of life in trying circumstances. I think she'd make a good witness in court, if it ever came to it.'

'As it may do, Clyde, as it may do. Never rule these things out. There's something we need to do when we get back to the nick and the computers, DS Northcott. Can you think what that might be?'

Clyde thought for a moment, then reluctantly shook his head.

Peach smiled happily at such naivety. 'We need to find out exactly how Sam Johnson, Janey's late husband, died.'

There was a much more pressing and intriguing task waiting for Clyde Northcott at the station.

'A woman rang in. Wants to speak to you and only you. She wouldn't give me any idea what it was about.' The young uniformed officer didn't make any joking remark about his relationship with this woman, because she was secretly attracted to Clyde herself. She found his tallness, his hardness, his smooth ebony face which might have come from an Egyptian temple, an intriguing combination.

Northcott's past gave him an extra dimension. There were all sorts of rumours around the station of how he was now in the process of redeeming the violent and lurid years he had lived before becoming a copper – rumours invariably gather size and glamour in the telling. And now this mysterious figure was a detective sergeant, one of the youngest in the Brunton establishment. PC Jones had not been long in the force herself; she was still at what her anxious mother called an impressionable age.

If DS Northcott had any inkling of her secret passion for him, he gave no sign of it. He thanked her for the message, gave her no idea who the caller might be, and went away to ring the number in private. He didn't even use the station phones. He went out to the car park, sat astride his Yamaha R1, and dialled the number into his mobile.

He was prepared to convince the woman of his identity, but she recognized his distinctive deep, dark-brown voice immediately. 'I've got something for you.'

'How big, Joey? Can it wait? I'm on a big case at the moment.'

'It's big. Maybe the biggest.'

Snouts always wanted to say that, always wanted to stress the importance of what they had to give. That was important to the price; this was a buyer's market, with the price always in the hands of the copper who was paying for the information. Clyde hissed, 'Don't piss me about, Joey! How big?'

'The biggest, Bonzo.' The name she had called him when she wanted to taunt him, in the old days. Her voice dropped lower still. 'Could be very big, this. It's connected with this Ketley killing. You buying?'

He gave it a couple of seconds of thought. But you couldn't work out the value of this in a phone conversation. It might be vital, as she claimed, or it might be nothing at all. 'I might be buying, Joey. But only if it's as big as you claim it is. Only if you're not pissing me about!'

'I wouldn't do that, would I, Bonzo? You wouldn't want to miss this. That's all I'm saying, on the phone.'

'You in the same place?'

'Same place. Place where I turned over my new leaf.'

He didn't comment on that. 'Seven thirty tonight.'

'Come the back way. I don't want anyone round here seeing me talking to the filth.'

'I hope it's as good as you say it is, Joey.'

Clyde Northcott stared at his mobile for a moment, not feeling the February cold of the car park as he should have done. It still might be nothing, as he'd said. But he felt the excitement pulsing through him. He wished he could roar away at that moment on the powerful machine beneath him.

FIFTEEN

F our o'clock was the time. That was the arrangement they'd made, and Greta Ketley knew he would stick to it. She wasn't to phone him. He would ring her; if she didn't answer the first two rings, that would mean that she wasn't alone. He'd put his phone down and not try again. They'd spoken on Sunday, when she'd rung him. Just over two days ago. It seemed much longer.

She listened to the pips announcing the hour on Radio 4. On the last and longest one, which announced the hour exactly, her mobile rang. Bang on time as usual. She placed the tiny box against her ear and rapped out the formula they had always used to confirm that it was safe to go ahead. 'Greta Ketley here. To whom am I speaking?'

'Martin Price here,' he said, echoing her formality. And then, in his normal voice, 'How's it going, my darling?'

'I can't believe I'm speaking to you! It seems ages. I know it isn't.' Her English was normally so flawless that many took her for a native speaker. Now her attractive Swedish accent came out, as it always did when she was excited, so that Price in his flat felt excited in turn and much closer to her. 'Have you done the identification?'

'Yes. I did it yesterday morning.'

'Was it horrid?'

'It wasn't pleasant. But I didn't break down. I thought it would take me back to my early days with Oliver, when things had been better, but it didn't. I didn't feel anything, really, except glad that it was over.'

Martin didn't know whether she meant the marriage and her years with Ketley or merely the ordeal of the identification, but he had the sense not to ask. 'He was shot through the head. Was that very obvious?'

It sounded almost like a professional interest. Martin had seen many dead men in his time, some of them much more gory than the one she had stared at so briefly at the mortuary. Some of them had been his friends, some of them had been enemies killed by his own hand. Greta felt a sharp, guilty thrill in these images of death and violence. 'I'd expected it to be much worse. They presented the corpse so that the point where the bullet had entered was on the far side from me. They'd brushed his hair over the exit point on his forehead, so that you couldn't see much of it. You told me how they do their best to tidy up the body for identification, didn't you?'

She sounded detached, almost disappointed. Martin said, 'You'll be relieved that it's over. And I am, on your behalf. I feel guilty sitting here quietly doing nothing, whilst you have all the strain to endure.'

'Thank you for that. But we agreed it was best this way, didn't we? If we can keep you out of it altogether, that will be best for both of us.' She mouthed the right reassuring phrases, but she resented him sitting quiet and safe whilst she was in the spotlight. She was worried and isolated, despite the knowledge that they were doing the right thing.

'How did you get on with the CID people?'

'It went all right, I think. No, I'm sure it did. I got Janey Johnson to sit in with me, as you suggested. The man in charge is very sharp, but he didn't catch me out in anything. He had a big black sergeant with him. He looked ready for a fight, but I think he was quite a softy, really. Perhaps he hasn't dealt much with women before.'

After a single short interview, she had put her finger on one of the few weaknesses in DS Northcott's armoury. Martin Price grinned affectionately: this hard man he had never met would surely be no match for Greta's wiles. 'Do they suspect you have a lover?' He had meant to be diplomatic. He had intended to wrap up his single great concern in softer phrases than this, but in the end the question had burst out in stark simplicity.

'No, I'm sure they don't. They didn't even suggest it. We're in the clear, my darling!'

She sounded so sure, so content, that it alarmed him. He said tersely, 'They'll be back, Greta. They'll talk to everyone around the place, in a murder enquiry. If anyone has the slightest idea that we've been meeting, the police will pick it up. People talk to protect themselves; they're afraid of concealing things.'

'No one knows about us, my love. If Oliver Ketley didn't find out, rest assured that no one else in this house knows about us.'

That was the best guarantee that they were safe, as she said. If Ketley had known about him, he'd have had a bullet through the back of his head the next day. 'That sounds good. But don't drop your guard. The police aren't as stupid as people like Oliver claim they are. They're hamstrung by regulations, as he never was. But once they're on a murder hunt, they're efficient and very thorough. Don't underestimate them.'

'All right, I won't. When can we meet?' The single question she had been dying to ask since the first shrill of her phone.

'I don't know. It's early days yet. Perhaps at the end of the week, if everything goes well.'

'If they've arrested someone else by then, you mean?'

'I don't know quite what I mean, Greta. I just want the heat to be off us before we meet. Once the police discover an eternal triangle, it's the two left standing who become their prime suspects. That's only natural – most of the time, they're right!'

'I want to feel you against me, my darling. I want to be with you in that bed of yours, running my hands over your back, then clasping you tight as you do whatever you wish to me!'

'And I want to do that too, my darling! I think about it all the time. Even at the most inconvenient moments!'

He was trying to bring in a little levity, but she scarcely heard him. 'I want to do everything we've ever done together. And most of all, I want to cling on as hard as I can whilst your whole body goes hard and you come inside me!'

'Oh, Greta, I need you! More than you can ever imagine. But we shall have the rest of our lives to do these things. We shall be able to show everyone openly what we think of each other, instead of stealing hole-in-the-corner meetings and wondering all the time we're together when they must end. But we must be careful, for just a little while longer. I'll ring again, whenever I think it's safe. Same arrangement.'

She flung more intimate, passionate phrases at him before the call ended, and he loved her for it. But he feared as he sat in his empty, luxurious flat that passion might lead to indiscretion, that some slip would bring the police into his life as well as to hers, with much more dangerous consequences.

Martin Price didn't even consider that he and not Greta might be the source of revelations.

Clyde Northcott's motorcycle gear was an effective disguise. No one could say what his occupation was once he had leathers and helmet on.

He roared ten miles through countryside to the house he had to visit in Chorley. He enjoyed riding at night, when all you could see was the long beam of your headlight ahead and the dipped headlights of vehicles coming the other way. It concentrated your attention on this narrow corridor of action and excluded the rest of the world. He always thought of himself at night as a racehorse with blinkers, blind to all the world save for this brilliantly lit tunnel where the action took place.

He went much more slowly when he reached the small town, easing the big Yamaha quietly through the narrowing streets until he reached the place he wanted. He eased himself from the bike and stood quite still for a moment in the shadow of the brick wall, waiting for the adrenalin and excitement he always got from a ride to seep through his veins. He had never taken his blood pressure; he imagined it would be high for a while after the bike. He could feel the pulse in his head slowing, even in the minute or so he allowed himself to remove his helmet and gauntlets.

He was an impressive figure in his close-fitting black leathers, which seemed to increase his already huge height. But there was no way anyone could identify him as a policeman. He was merely a formidable biker who rode a formidable machine.

He moved a few yards to the back of a row of council houses. They were not part of a large and noisy estate, but a mere two streets of older buildings from the fifties. No doubt most of them had by now been purchased by sitting tenants and become private residences. There was no sign of life or movement at the rear.

Human movement, that is. The dark shape of a cat flashed across his vision as he stealthily opened the gate at the end of the garden. The darkness and the suddenness of its flight made the movement seem unnaturally swift, so that he was left with the impression of lightning movement, rather than any image of the animal itself. His first reaction was shock. His second one was relief that it wasn't a rat. Clyde didn't like rats, and where there was one rat there were usually others. Cats were infinitely preferable.

As if to reinforce that view, a dog barked, three times in rapid succession. Not a large dog, Clyde judged, and at least four houses away. Nothing to worry about, especially when you had your leathers as additional protection. He moved cautiously up the concrete path which his adjusted vision could now clearly distinguish. When he felt his way to the handle of the back door, he found it locked as he had expected.

To the right of the door, where the path ran away round the periphery of the house, a single light showed, dim amber behind thick curtains. He tapped gently on the window. Three shorts, three longs, three shorts again. The SOS sign in Morse code, though he doubted whether the woman behind the curtain would recognize it.

He was back at the door when he heard the bolts being drawn back and the key turned. The woman inside gasped alarm at the silhouette of this black giant, but Clyde said quietly, 'It's me, Joey. As arranged.'

She drew back and let him past her, sticking her head out like an anxious bird in the nest to look down the garden and from side to side before she shut the door and followed him into the house. Clyde Northcott stood above her and smiled down at her in the living room. He set his helmet carefully beside his gauntlets on the table, then glanced round the room. Shabby but tidy, the room of someone poor but respectable. 'You've done well for yourself, Joey.'

The thin, angular face smiled at him, very briefly. 'Not as well as you, Bonzo. But I started later. I've got my kid out of care and at the school round the corner. I'm lucky: it's a good school. And they've given me work as a dinner lady. No more than I get on the social, but it's proper work. The head said there might be a job in the office some time in the future, if everything works out.'

She spoke quickly, as if it was important to give him this summary and have him on his way. Old habits died hard: you didn't take any more risks than you had to, when you were giving stuff to the filth. And surely Bonzo Northcott wouldn't want to spend any more time in her house than he had to.

But Clyde seemed in no hurry. He reached out his hand and took her wrist, slowing the movement so as not to threaten her. He eased back the sleeve of her jumper and the shirt beneath it, turned her arm gently so that he could study it under the light. The needle marks and the damaged veins were visible enough; they would always be visible. But the scars were not recent. He looked down into the small dark eyes, but they were quite clear as they stared back at him. No signs of drug usage here.

She said quietly, 'I haven't used for two years, now. Not since I came out of rehab. And I never will. I'm not going to risk losing Kate, am I?'

'Good on yer, Joey!' He took her small right hand between his huge ones and pumped it so hard that she almost lost balance. His pleasure was genuine. Five years ago, he had supplied drugs to the girl she had been then, and set her on the path which had led so many to dependence, squalor and death. Now he could feel a shade less guilty. One of his customers at least was going to be a success story, like him.

She slid away her hand. 'Thanks, Bonzo. But you're DS Northcott now. And DS Northcott isn't here for this. He wants information.'

He nodded quickly, trying not to look at the innocent face of the child in the photograph on the sideboard. 'What you got for me, Joey?'

She should tell him it was good, vital even, upping the value of what she had to give him to its maximum. Instead, she said, 'It might be nothing, but you need to know. I'm not looking for work as a snout. This will be the last thing I ever give you.'

He believed her. But she'd given him one thing before, the name of someone well up the chain in the supply of class A drugs, and it had given him an arrest. Joey Harrison, reformed junkie, was a good judge of what was valuable. He didn't give her his usual stuff about this being of dubious value to him, as you normally did with a snout. He'd treated her like that on the phone, but old times, old guilts and old loyalties came back to you, when you were in this humble room, face to face with a woman winning the war to retrieve herself and her life.

All he said was, 'Best tell me what you've got for me now, Joey.'

'He wasn't straight, was he, this man Ketley? He wasn't the man the newspapers would have us believe he was?'

'He was a murdering bastard, Joey. There'll be lots rejoicing that he's gone and willing to dance on his grave. But it was murder, and we can't let murder go. We have to find who killed him – probably some villain with a soul as black as his.'

'What about his wife?'

He hesitated. You didn't reveal things to the public, even when you were fishing for information. But he wasn't trading anything here; you could surely say complimentary things about people. 'She's as pure as the driven snow, Greta Ketley. So far, anyway. DCI Peach and I saw her on the day after the murder and she didn't seem to know anything about it.'

He couldn't resist letting her know that he had a high profile in this already hugely publicized case. She caught that and said, 'DCI, eh? You're doing well for yourself, Bonzo Northcott, and no mistake! But your lilywhite lady is playing away, love. Banging away like a boxer bitch, I shouldn't wonder!' Joey had no idea whether boxer dogs were more lustful than others, but she had always relished alliteration.

'Mrs Ketley has a lover?' Clyde tried not to sound too excited. He failed.

Joey Harrison smiled happily and sat down at the table, motioning her visitor towards the chair beside her. 'She's been to his flat near Chorley, I've seen her leaving and I've seen her going in.'

'How do you know it was her?'

'I didn't, until I saw her picture in the paper yesterday. I was sure it was her. So I checked in the *Northern Evening Telegraph*. There were two pictures in there; one was full face. It's her all right.'

'Who's the man?'

'Don't know his name. He's quite a looker, though. Short blond hair. Fortyish, I'd say. I can give you his exact address. You'll get his name from the electoral register.'

He saw now the intelligent and resourceful woman he had never seen when he was supplying her with drugs. 'Doesn't necessarily mean anything, of course. You'd probably think of taking a lover, if you were married to a sod like Ketley.'

'I'd think twice though, wouldn't I, if Ketley was as big a villain as you say he was? Dangerous business, taking a lover. And even more dangerous for the lover. I'd say they must both be pretty keen.'

He fumbled beneath his leathers and produced five twenty pound notes. 'Normally I'd say we need to check this out before I can pay. But I'm trusting what you say. If it leads to anything, there'll be another hundred to follow.'

'For old times' sake?'

He smiled grimly. 'Let's forget old times, shall we, Joey? This is for the future. Yours and Kate's.'

'You're a good man, Clyde Northcott.' She'd dropped the 'Bonzo', and both of them knew in that moment that she would never use it again.

'And you're a good woman, Joey Harrison. I had people fighting for me. And I didn't have to go through rehab. You've fought your own fights, and come through. But it's going to be worth it.'

'It's already worth it. Take care of yourself, Clyde. You could always do that, but you're mixing it with some right bastards, by the sound of it.'

Joey stood on tiptoe and placed a brief kiss on his lips. He hugged her tightly for a moment. Then he was out the way he had come, sending the cat flying from the dustbin again with a resentful yowl, watching the lightning black shadow clear the fence and disappear into the night.

* * *

'How're you getting on with Clyde Northcott as your bagman?'
Lucy Peach called from the kitchen.

Percy continued stacking the plates on the tray, then carried
them into the kitchen, where she already had the water running
at the sink, waiting for it to come hot. 'All right. He's a good
lad, Clyde.'

She felt an unexpectedly sharp shaft of jealousy, a sadness
for times gone that could never be repeated. 'I know he is.
I'm glad you made him your DS when I had to move on.'

'Do you want to wash or dry?'

'I'll wash. I've already got these glamorous rubber gloves
on.' She clattered the dirty dishes noisily into the bowl, stealing
a sideways glance at her husband's impassive face. 'He's got
different virtues from me, has Clive.'

'I'll say.' Percy took advantage of her position at the sink
to slide his hands over her generous rear. 'I promise familiarity
will never breed contempt!' he breathed into her ear.

'Behave yourself!' She spun quickly, flicking hot water
over his face before she ran both rubber gloves down the
sides of it.

Percy sighed the elaborate sigh of the downtrodden male.
'He's a hard bastard, Clive. A man you'd want beside you in
a punch-up. When there's knives flashing and fists flying, I'd
rather have him beside me than you.'

'No competition, in that situation. You'd be thinking of me,
I hope, if there was physical danger about – which is presum-
ably why the rules say we can no longer work together. But
how often do DCIs put their lives in danger?'

'Not often, outside detective novels and television series.
They send young lads like DS Northcott and DC Murphy
out to do the dirty work. Mind you, I do get out and about,
leaving Tommy Bloody Tucker to mastermind the strategy
from his penthouse hideaway.'

Lucy gazed steadily at the suds on top of the washing-up
water. 'And when you're out and about, is Clyde better or
worse than I used to be?'

He knew that he should say that Clyde didn't come near
her, that he missed her acumen and insights, that they had
made a near-perfect team together. As indeed they had. But

that was not Percy Peach's way and both of them knew it. 'Clyde's not better or worse. He's different.'

'Of course he is. That's just an evasion. Take your hands off my belly, please, Percy.'

Percy removed them reluctantly and took up his tea towel again. 'There's an example, you see. I don't even know what Clyde's belly feels like. Whereas I should be confident of passing the most rigorous exam on yours. From your belly button right down to—'

'Be serious, please. Is he a big help to you in interviews?'

'He's coming on. At present, he probably asks me more questions afterwards than he asks people in interviews, but it's much better to say nothing than to ask things just to remind people you're there. He'll be all right, Clive. He's a quick learner.'

Lucy was absurdly pleased that the big man wasn't yet as effective as she had been when face to face with suspects. That was a defensive reaction, she told herself; nevertheless, she smiled quietly into the saucepan before she tackled it vigorously with the pan scrub.

Behind her head, Percy grinned a secret, invisible, affec- tionate smile. 'He's got better snouts than you ever had, has Clive Northcott.'

He felt her stiffen, begin to bridle, than carefully relax. 'It's easier for male officers to get snouts. They're more in touch with low life.'

'As you have to be, my darling, to pick up valuable contacts. But I make an exception for you. I'm the lowest life I shall ever expect you to touch.' He polished a teacup reflectively with his towel, then, as she turned face-to-face with him, gave her the most innocent of his vast range of smiles.

She said quietly, 'How's the Ketley case going?'

'Early days, as T.B. Tucker would say under pressure. We're fully stretched, because there are a lot of people who are delighted to be rid of the bugger. You busy at present?'

'Not particularly.' Lucy was working with Asian officers and the national network on anti-terrorist action. We're aware of certain things. Waiting for them to develop. That sounds ridiculous when people are plotting mass murder, but it's what you have to do to get worthwhile evidence to present to a court.'

'I might be able to use you on the Ketley case. Maybe even let you see Clive's strengths for yourself.'

Neither of them knew it, but it was at exactly that moment that Northcott was with Joey Harrison, gathering the information which would open up a new strand of the enquiry. One where Lucy Peach would shortly join him.

SIXTEEN

On Wednesday morning, Clyde Northcott was using the CID computers at eight o'clock. After Peach had briefed the murder team on progress and allotted tasks for the day, he reported his sensational news to his DCI.

The grieving widow had a lover. His name was Martin Price.

Percy Peach was not unduly surprised. Oliver Ketley had not been a man to inspire loyalty. The immediate thought was that Greta Ketley and her lover must have both spirit and cool nerve to risk the consequences of discovery. If, that is, their liaison was fact, rather than gossipy speculation. 'How reliable is your snout?' was the first question he addressed to Northcott.

'Very reliable,' said Clyde sturdily.

'You've had stuff from him before?'

'It's a she. And I've had one tip-off from her before, which led to an arrest and a conviction. I don't anticipate any more after this one.'

Peach glanced at him sharply, but didn't question what he said. It was part of the bond between DCI and bagman that you trusted his judgement and used whatever he brought you. Northcott wouldn't be working beside him if he wasn't prepared to rely on him. 'How significant do you think this is?'

'It could be very significant. I've looked up the resident at this address on the electoral register and done some work on his background. He's ex-SAS. He made captain, then left suddenly.'

A man used to violence then, who wouldn't shrink from it if he thought it necessary. A man trained to kill, in fact. 'You've been busy. How long since he was SAS?'

'Around eight years, as far as I could tell from the conversation. You know what army records people are like: they protect their information like bank managers and they're not as easy to convince. I think we should confront Price as soon as possible and see what he has to say for himself.'

'I agree. But I'd like to find out as much as I can about the bloke before I confront him. With his background, he won't be an easy nut to crack, if he did see off Ketley. We're over-stretched on the Ketley case, so I've arranged for Lucy to help us out. Take her with you and try to see him this morning. Depending on what you find and what you think, I'll interview him at a later stage; hopefully by then we'll have a few more bricks ready to throw at him. You happy with that?'

It was a surprising development for Clyde, but he didn't show that. His dark features cracked into a rare smile. 'Very happy. Be like old times, working with Lucy again.' Clyde had known and admired Lucy Blake, as she had been then, from the moment he entered the police service. He had been Peach's best man at their wedding, an impressive modern figure in the centuries-old village church.

Peach growled, 'Don't relax too much. I'll be back on your tail very soon. And there's one thing you should remember.'

'Sir?'

'DS Lucy Peach is senior to you in terms of service, but you're in charge. This is your case and you've been on it from the beginning. She's helping out because our resources are stretched. Understood?'

'Yes, sir. Thank you. I don't think there'll be any problems.'

'Neither do I. But I don't want you hesitating to take the initiative.'

Typical of Percy to make support seem like a reprimand, thought Clyde. He collected Lucy and she drove the police Mondeo through the traffic to Chorley almost as quickly as he could have moved on the Yamaha. As the old Georgian house which was their target came into view, she said, 'This is your case, Clyde. You lead, I'll follow. I'll take a few notes on what he has to say. Use me as you think necessary.'

DS Northcott didn't tell her that her husband had already indicated the pecking order. He was learning lots of things as his career developed. Tact was a quality he had rarely needed before he entered the police service.

The grounds behind the house had been used for new building, but the original Georgian mansion had been converted into four handsome flats, two on each floor. They had private garaging and a spacious car park for visitors. At ten forty in the morning, this was empty save for their police vehicle. There was no sign of life in the flats, but each of the pair had the feeling that their arrival had been witnessed.

They turned left in the small entrance hall and knocked at the handsome oak door of Number One. It opened immediately and they stood looking at a man whom Clyde recognized from Joey Harrison's description. He was just under six feet, lean and alert. His fair hair was cut short, but not shaven; it was nearer to an old-fashioned crew cut of the sixties. His keen blue eyes appraised them as they announced who they were. Two detective sergeants: an unusual combination. He didn't voice the expected, 'You'd better come in,' but merely turned and led them into a large sitting room, where the minimalist modern furnishing sat unexpectedly well beneath the long Georgian windows, which the 'listed building' status had preserved intact.

Northcott sat down carefully on the elegant settee indicated by Price: he was pleased to find it much more robust than its appearance had implied. The exquisite tidiness of the room combined with his own nervousness to make him resort to the most formal of openings. 'We're here in connection with the death in suspicious circumstances of Oliver Ketley last Saturday evening.'

'I thought you might be.' There was a trace of a smile at the edge of the thin-lipped mouth, as if Price had been awaiting this moment since the news broke upon the world. He certainly didn't seem apprehensive.

'Yet you chose not to come forward. You hid yourself away, in fact.' Clyde was pleased to discover the note of aggression Peach would have favoured.

'As I had no connection with the death and can contribute nothing to its investigation, that seemed appropriate.'

'We decide what matters, not you. We take statements from everyone. That way we can decide where you fit into the full picture.'

Price nodded, looking faintly amused. 'I gather you're not yet near an arrest. You wouldn't be here otherwise.'

'We may be nearer to an arrest when we leave here, Mr Price.' Clyde tried to put conviction into the thought, but he couldn't capture Peach's air of quiet menace, nor the relish with which he delivered thoughts like this.

'Who told you about me?'

This was easier. Northcott gave his man a small smile as he said, 'You wouldn't expect us to reveal that, Mr Price.' He noticed the man nodding his acceptance as he went on, 'You've been seen here with Mrs Ketley, on more than one occasion. Are you denying that there is a serious relationship between the two of you?'

Martin had a sudden, disturbing picture of Greta, admitting their liaison, trumpeting it, telling them she was proud of it, announcing that they could do whatever they liked about that. He loved her for that defiance, even as he saw the extravagance of it. 'Isn't it up to you to prove things like that?'

'It's up to the public to give us every help, when we're investigating a serious crime.'

'Even when we know that we have nothing to do with that crime?'

Clyde found it easier to deal with this resistance than with cooperation. 'With a background such as yours, Mr Price, you should not pretend naivety. I am sure that you are aware that the spouse of any murder victim is always an immediate focus for police attention. In cold statistical terms, the widow or widower is the person most likely either to be involved in the crime or to know who committed it. Any relationship she has is therefore bound to interest the investigating officers.'

Martin nodded his head. He was still trying to work out how they had discovered him. If Greta had let anything out, she would surely have rung to warn him. 'All right, I accept that. It's just that when you know you have no connection with a murder, you don't feel like parading your private life in front of a lot of curious policemen. And women.' He gave a sardonic smile to the woman with the striking chestnut hair, who in dark blue trousers and a lighter blue sweater looked nothing like his mental image of an officer of the law.

Clyde leant forward a little towards his man. 'You admit that you have a close sexual relationship with Mrs Ketley?'

Martin volunteered a sardonic smile, emphasizing that he was still in control, even though he now chose to volunteer information to them. 'Sexual. You people are always interested in that, aren't you? Well, that's understandable; sex is important. I'll make life easy for you. I've known Greta for around ten years now – perhaps I should say rather that I first met her ten years ago. It was just under a year ago that we began what you just called "a close sexual relationship". That has continued and developed. You could call us lovers, in the fullest sense of that word.' He could almost hear Greta applauding him in the background, as he watched DS Peach making a note with the small gold ballpoint she held above her pad.

It was Northcott who said, 'Thank you. Who else knows about this relationship?'

'You tell me. No one, as far as we were aware. But some bugger saw fit to run to you with the information.'

'You had told no one about it?'

Again that sardonic smile, asserting that Price knew more about life and death than either of the other people in the room. 'I suspect that as police officers you knew what sort of man Ketley was before his death. You'll know a hell of a lot more now. He wasn't a man you took risks with. If he'd known anything about me and Greta, I wouldn't be sitting here talking to you. I'd be under tons of concrete or on the bed of the ocean.'

'Yet you chose to work for him.' Lucy Peach's calm statement was more cool and cutting because it was the first time she had spoken.

Martin Price had been determined from the outset to give them as little as he could, feeling his way until he had found out how much they knew about him. They knew more than he had hoped they would. He said coolly, 'That was years ago. That was when I first met Greta, but only briefly. I did a little work for Ketley, yes. Nothing illegal. Frightened a few people, but didn't implement any threats. I got out when I discovered exactly what sort of man he was.'

He was putting the best interpretation on that period, no doubt. Lucy would have liked to press him on exactly what sort of work he'd done, but he wouldn't give them anything

he didn't have to. In any case, she couldn't see much relevance
to the present investigation. She said quietly, 'You did eight
years in the SAS. Made the rank of captain, with a promising
career beckoning. Why did you leave so abruptly?'

He didn't think she could know. Closing ranks was one
thing the army in general and the SAS in particular were good
at. They kept things within house; that was the phrase used at
his last meeting with his CO. 'A career shift. I'd enjoyed my
time with the SAS, but it's a young man's game. I decided to
get out whilst I could still do other things.'

'So you ended up with Ketley, doing work you've just told
us was pretty dubious.'

'That was a stopgap. I've just told you that it was a mistake.'

'So you got out. And then went to Africa, to lead the
dangerous life and gather the tainted money available to a
mercenary. Not so different from life in the SAS, was it?'

'It was a bloody sight worse!' The phrase was out before
he could prevent it, a protest against the cards he had been
dealt, a burst of the resentment he thought had long been
dispelled.

Lucy said quietly, 'You've killed people, Mr Price.'

'Of course I have. It was my job to do that, at different
times. In Iraq, with the SAS. In Africa, when – when there
was no alternative.' The last phrase came lamely, but he stopped
himself in time. There was no way they could know about
Africa, no way he had to tell them. He hadn't even told Greta
about those deaths.

His words were nevertheless revealing, exposing parts of
the man he would rather have left hidden. Clyde Northcott let
them hang in the big, low-ceilinged sitting room for a moment
before he said, 'Of all the people we have spoken to, you were
the man best equipped to kill Oliver Ketley.'

'Better than a contract killer? I doubt that. Better than some
of the thugs he paid himself? Better than the muscle employed
by his rivals in prostitution and drugs? I doubt I'm as well
equipped as any of those, DS Northcott.'

Just when he was channelling his resistance towards the
black man, the cool female voice beside him took up
the dialogue again. 'And no doubt you could find us motives

for some of these people, given time. But you have the clearest and most compelling motive of all. One of the oldest, but still one of the clearest, Mr Price.'

'It's a big step from motive to a conviction in court, as you well know. In this case, you won't be able to take that step.'

Clyde rapped out, 'Where were you last Saturday night, Mr Price?'

Martin had known from the start that this question would come. It was almost reassuring to hear it voiced at last. He said evenly, 'I was here, DS Northcott.'

'Is there anyone who can confirm that for us?'

'No, I don't think so.' He watched the small gold ballpoint make the note in the neat female hand and then added, 'The innocent often don't have convenient alibis. We don't see the need for them, you see.'

'Have you been in contact with Mrs Ketley since this death?'

He thought about it, not troubling to dissemble. 'Yes. There's no law against a man offering his sympathy after a bereavement, as far as I'm aware. There isn't even any law against two people exulting in a death, so long as they didn't contrive it. Damned bad form and all that, but not illegal.'

'So who do you think contrived this death which is so convenient for you?'

'Do you know, I think I'd be tempted to withhold that name, even if I knew it. For the record, I don't.'

Northcott nodded to Lucy and stood up. 'If we don't get that name quickly, I've no doubt we shall be back with more questions for you. Please don't leave the area without telling Brunton CID exactly where we can find you, Mr Price.'

'We need something we can give to the press and the television, Peach. This is a high-profile case. Don't forget that as far as they're concerned Oliver Ketley was a public benefactor.'

Percy sighed. He had more urgent things to do than brief Tommy Bloody Tucker, but life had never been perfect and never would be. 'Perhaps you could begin to educate the public, sir. Perhaps let drop the odd hint that Ketley wasn't the philanthropic giant he made himself out to be.'

'That would be very difficult. We have to accept that—'

'Or you could try the more direct approach, sir. Release me to the press. Let me tell them what a right bastard the man was!'

'Good heavens, Peach! You've really no idea of good public relations, have you?'

'No, sir. I tend to tell it as it is, in my blundering, old-fashioned way.'

'Don't say a word to press, radio or television. Is that clear?'

'Perfectly, sir.' Percy had no intention of speaking to anyone. He shunned all journalists save one aged crime reporter who now worked part-time for the local evening paper. 'If anyone from the media approaches me, I'll say you've gagged me, sir. That should stop 'em in their tracks.'

Lurid headlines of censorship by a chief superintendent blazed in Tucker's cloudy imagination. 'Just say nothing at all. Don't mention anything about gagging. Now, bring me up to date on your progress, or lack of it.' He leaned forward and jutted his chin towards his junior. This was his no-nonsense Churchillian pose.

'Much work, little progress, sir. I'd say we are nowhere near to an arrest. Partly owing to the fact that Ketley was a right bastard with lots of enemies. Or an angel who showered his gifts around, if I'm speaking to the press.'

'This really isn't good enough, you know. You've a big team on this. We're entitled to expect results by now.'

'We' would be the Chief Constable and Tommy Bloody Tucker. And possibly that dangerous and blundering jellyfish known as Joe Public. Peach fell back on the one ploy which never failed. 'Would you like to take over the administration of this one yourself, sir? Drive it forward with your usual verve? Perhaps it needs the Tucker dynamism.'

Tucker shied away from direct involvement as usual. 'It is my task to have the overview, Peach. I have to retain the perspective on crime in our area, not chase about pursuing individuals. I have every confidence in the team I have allotted to this case.'

'Really, sir? That's most gratifying. I'd somehow acquired the impression that you were less than satisfied with our efforts.'

Tucker gave him the glare which signified that he had gone far enough. 'Tell me about your leading suspects – assuming that is that you've managed to get as far as suspects.'

Percy allowed himself the sudden cackle which was one of his most disturbing effects. Tucker started violently behind his desk and continued to tremble for three or four seconds. Peach seated himself carefully on the chair in front of that desk and embarked on what promised to be a lengthy address. 'There's the widow, sir. Greta Ketley.'

Tucker sighed heavily. 'There is usually a widow when a man is killed.'

'What? Oh, very good, sir. Very droll. Greta Ketley is younger than her husband. Forty-two against his fifty-six, to be precise.'

'Ah! She may have another man, then. Have you considered that possibility, Peach?'

'You display your usual percipience, sir. As a result of persistent enquiries and the extensive network of informers maintained by our vigilant CID officers, we have indeed unearthed a lover.'

Tucker rocked himself back and forth in his leather admiral's chair, a movement designed to convey to lesser brains that he was thinking. 'This could be the lead we were looking for, you know.'

'Yes sir.' Percy raised his wrist dramatically and glanced at his watch. 'It seems that this man has worked for eight years in the SAS and latterly as a mercenary soldier, so he is well acquainted with weapons and with violence. Hopefully, DS Northcott and DS Peach are interviewing the man in question at this very moment, sir.'

'DS Peach?' Tucker relapsed into his bewildered goldfish look.

'My wife, sir. The former DS Lucy Blake. Promoted and assigned to me by your good self four years ago. No longer works directly with me because of our marriage. She is supplementing our team on this occasion because we are using all our resources to secure a swift result. You approved that yesterday, sir.'

'Eh? Oh, of course I did! That just shows how urgent I think it is for us to have a result on this one, Peach.'

'Yes, sir. The resident staff who've moved into Thorley Grange most recently obviously attracted our attention, in a case like this.'

'Eh? Oh, obviously, yes. They'd have the opportunity, wouldn't they? Good thinking, Peach. What have you turned up?'

'Nothing very promising so far, sir. There's a Vietnamese man who wants to become a chef and is learning the trade. Chung Lee. All we've discovered so far is that he's given every satisfaction with his work in the kitchens.'

'Vietnamese, eh? You'd better give him close attention, Peach. You never know what these foreigners are up to. They have different standards from us.'

Percy reflected that in this case that might be a good thing. He said patiently, 'We're checking him out, sir. The other recent arrival is a single woman of thirty-five, Janey Johnson.' He waited for Tucker to add sexism to his racism, but the man remained silent. 'She's a widow, not divorced. Her husband was Sam Johnson; no evidence he was a man of letters, however.'

Tucker did not pick up the reference. 'Have you reason to suspect this woman?'

'None whatsoever, at present, sir. She excited our interest only because she's a recent arrival among the resident staff. She seems like Lee to be giving every satisfaction in her work. She is already highly rated not only by the housekeeper at the Grange but by Mrs Ketley herself.'

'Not promising, then. Scarcely a suspect at all, from your account. Have you nothing more likely to offer me?'

'I have indeed, sir. It may be that I have left our prime suspect until the last. Oliver Ketley's death may well have been a contract killing.'

Tucker's face rose for a moment, then fell dramatically. Even he realized that the chances of bringing a contract killer to justice were slim. 'Do you know which one?'

'Chap named George French, sir. Lives in Oldham. I've already been to see him. Took DS Northcott with me, in case things turned ugly.'

'And did they?'

'No. sir. But we didn't make much progress. French simply denied any connection with the shooting of Ketley and challenged us to place him at the scene.'

'Which you've not been able to do?'

'Not as yet, sir. However, we do have evidence of a first payment made to French for the killing, delivered some ten days before Ketley was shot. The final instalment is normally made when the liquidation has been successfully completed. We have not so far been able to find the details of that second payment.'

Tucker pursed his lips, removed his glasses, and polished them slowly; these were the mannerisms he used to convey deep Chief Superintendental deliberation. Eventually he said, 'This French fellow could well be your man, you know. What you need to bring him to court is further evidence.'

Percy Peach left the enchanted world of Tucker's penthouse eyrie and slowly descended the staircase towards real life. He tried to console himself with the thought that, in a world of bewildering change, there were still things which did not alter. One of these was the head of Brunton CID's capacity for the blindin' bleedin' obvious.

'This is a private matter, Mrs Ketley. I think you would find it less embarrassing if you spoke to us alone.'

'I want Mrs Johnson to remain with us. She will be a witness to what is said here this afternoon.' Greta made the words sound as insulting as she could, but Peach was not at all discomforted. He was used to much worse police insults, could if necessary deliver much more cutting thoughts himself.

'That is your choice, Mrs Ketley. I hope you will be more cooperative than when we spoke to you on Sunday.'

Greta flashed them a look of pure hostility. For an instant, she was transformed from cool Scandinavian beauty into dangerous cat. Her blue eyes, which for some years she had striven to make as cold as her husband's, glittered with hate. It was an instant only, but a revealing one. Both Peach and Northcott knew in that moment that this was a woman who could envisage murder as a solution and perhaps execute it, if someone stood between her and her desires. 'I cooperated fully with you on Sunday. I identified Oliver's body as you requested. I answered your questions and I told you no lies.'

'Concealing information can be as harmful as direct lies, when we are pursuing a murder investigation. You are an intelligent woman; you must be able to see that.'

Janey Johnson, who was sitting protectively beside her mistress on the sofa as she had been bidden to do, said, 'None of us likes to reveal the innocent details of our private life unless it is strictly necessary. Our instinct is to keep close relationships secret from the world at large.'

Peach wondered how much had been agreed between these two before the CID arrived; they would have had no more than half an hour, but that was enough to arrange simple tactics. 'I can see that argument: I could even sympathize with it, in ordinary circumstances. But serious crime is extraordinary, and murder is the most serious crime of all. Murder makes its own rules. You must see that anyone who conceals information invites us to treat him or her as a suspect. Deceit is a sort of disease; it corrupts the person who practises it.'

Greta Ketley's eyes shone with passion. 'I love a man who was not my husband. I cannot help that. I deny that it is corrupt.'

'And your husband has been brutally murdered. You must see that you and Martin Price have to be suspects, the more so since you have attempted to conceal your relationship.'

There was a gasp with the first mention of Price's name, as if she had been struck a physical blow. 'As far as I was aware, no one here knew I was seeing Martin. I wished to keep it that way when my husband was shot through the head. That was surely understandable.'

'Understandable it may have been. Mistaken it certainly was. It now appears that Oliver Ketley was shot between nine and ten last Saturday night. Where were you at that time?'

Greta swallowed hard. They were not going to treat her sympathetically any more. The pose of grieving widow was gone and that of scheming and unscrupulous lover now accorded to her by her questioners. 'I was here, watching a DVD. The television is rubbish on a Saturday night.'

'Can anyone confirm your presence here?'

'I wouldn't think so. The staff are off duty and concerned with their own pleasures on a Saturday night.' She glanced automatically at the woman beside her and received a comforting smile and a tiny nod of assent.

'Did Mr Ketley say where he was going?'

'No, and I didn't ask him. I knew better than that.'

Her face had set grimly, but Peach said, 'Could you explain that, please?'

For a moment they thought she would refuse to answer, but the DCI ignored her clear-eyed hostility and waited. Eventually she said harshly, 'Saturday night was his night for women. He sought out whoever he had persuaded to meet him. If no one was so stupid, he went to prostitutes, I think. I can give you no details because I'd long since ceased to care.' She delivered this in a weary monotone. Then she added with angry irony, 'I'd got my own lover, you see, as you've so cleverly discovered. I'd no interest in Oliver. I merely wished to be rid of him!'

There was an electric moment whilst the damning words hung in the quiet room. Then Peach said, 'And how exactly did you contrive that, Mrs Ketley?'

'I didn't. As I've just told you, I was here on Saturday night.'

'You're an intelligent and resourceful woman, Mrs Ketley. You're as aware as I am that you didn't need to be in that car to commit murder. If I'd been in your position, I should have employed a contract killer.'

She looked at him steadily. 'I know they exist. I have no idea how to contact such a person.'

'I described you as resourceful. I'm sure you could have made a few discreet enquiries and discovered how to contact a professional killer. Your friend Martin Price could certainly have helped you.'

'Martin had nothing to do with this!' With the mention of her lover, her fury against this persistent, determined little man redoubled. Her blue eyes flashed not just defiance but hatred. 'Neither he nor I had anything to do with this. Please get that into your stupid head!'

Beside her, Janey Johnson reached out a hand and put it on top of Greta's, stilling the increasingly undisciplined movement of the older woman's arms. Greta flung it aside angrily, then glanced apologetically at Janey and nodded.

Peach watched every movement, as if he was learning things that mere words could not reveal to him. Then he said, 'I'm not going to give you the old line about everyone being a suspect, mainly because it isn't true. I shall merely point out that by concealing your association with Mr Price when we saw you on Sunday, you forfeited any right to be automatically believed. You played the grieving widow then, when you must have been exulting in a death which cleared the way for you and Martin Price. We have to ask ourselves what other deceptions you were perpetrating.'

'All right!' She glared at an unrepentant Peach as if she wished him in the mortuary with her husband, causing Janey Johnson to put a warning hand across hers again. This time Greta did not shrug her aside, but nodded a small smile towards her, reassuring her that she was in control and not about to implicate herself further. 'I can see that if I put myself in your position, the fact that I tried to conceal Martin from you is suspicious. But if you could in turn look at things from my point of view, you might understand – not approve, I'm not expecting you to do that – but understand. We've spent a year concealing what we felt for each other from everyone around us, friend as well as foe. You know by now what sort of man Oliver was; if he'd had the slightest suspicions about Martin, he'd have been a dead man. Secrecy had become a habit for me, one on which life and death depended. Every instinct forbade me to abandon secrecy, even with Oliver dead.'

She spoke with real passion and there was logic in what she said. But Peach wasn't going to admit that. Without turning to the man at his side, he said by way of introduction, 'DS Northcott spoke to Martin Price this morning, as you already know.'

Clyde eased himself forward a few inches and asked the question he had agreed on their way here. 'You say you were here when your husband was being murdered on Saturday night. Was it Martin Price who was shooting your husband through the head at that time?'

Greta gave a little gasp of astonishment. It was a long time since anyone had spoken to her in such blunt and dramatic terms. Even Oliver had chosen to leave his threats unspoken as they had grown further apart. 'Of course he wasn't.'

'There's no "of course" about it, Mrs Ketley. We have to look at things objectively. Martin Price has so far no alibi for Saturday night. He is a man whose background, experience and skills fit him ideally as a man able and willing to plan and execute violent death.'

She gazed into the challenging black face and wondered if there was something personal in this. She had assumed Northcott's background was Caribbean. Was it in fact African? Did the fact that Martin had organized men like him into killing bands in Africa motivate his present hostility? She told herself firmly that she was being fanciful and melodramatic, even racist. This was a policeman following his trade, looking for a conviction. His question had logic and needed answering. She admitted to herself now that it was Martin's capacity to live violently and survive, his air of latent menace, which was part of his attraction for her. She said with all the conviction she could force into her words, 'Martin didn't shoot Oliver. I know that, because I know Martin, but I can't prove it to you. Don't they say that it's always difficult to prove a negative?'

Peach had at that moment no idea who had killed Oliver Ketley; he still rather favoured George French for the crime, though he knew how difficult it would be to pin it upon him. But if the killer was Martin Price, he had a doughty ally in his lover; Peach would much rather have Greta Ketley on his side than against him. With one of his quick switches, he said quietly, 'Did your husband carry a personal weapon, Mrs Ketley?'

Greta switched her attention from the long, menacing black face to the round white one beside it. 'A personal weapon?'

'A firearm for his own use. A pistol or a revolver. Most people involved in the activities in which he made his money carry some form of personal protection.'

'He had bodyguards to protect him, when he went into dangerous places. You should be asking James Hardwick about this. He organizes that side of things.'

'I know he does and I've already spoken to him. Now I'm speaking to you, I'm asking you for a second time, did your husband carry a firearm on his person?'

'He had a handgun of his own.'

'I see. Was he carrying it on the night he died?'

They'd questioned others; Peach had already told her that. She needed to be very careful what she said now. 'He had a pistol. I don't know, any details. I never let him tell me. I hate things like that.' She was making every effort to convince them, but her voice sounded to her very flat as she spoke.

'How did he carry this pistol?'

She glanced sideways at Janey, then down at the hand which lay still on top of hers. 'I don't think he carried it all the time. But as I say, I'm not really sure about that – we haven't been very close in the last few years, and certainly not since I began to see Martin.' She spat the last phrase at him vehemently, as if it were an assertion of integrity. 'He had some sort of harness which fitted the pistol beneath his arm.'

'Yes. A shoulder holster. He was wearing it when he died. Do you know the make of his pistol?'

'No. I hate weapons and bullets, as I said, because they frighten me. I – I think he might have changed it recently, because I saw him loading it and examining it carefully.'

'How long ago was this?'

'A few weeks back. I can't be precise. I hate the things and try to avoid them.'

The third time she had asserted that. It was probably true, but Peach wondered whether the lady did protest too much. 'Where did he keep this handgun and its ammunition?'

'Not in the bedroom. I wouldn't have that. Probably in his office somewhere.' She looked from one to the other of the police faces. 'He was shot with this pistol, wasn't he?'

'We believe he was, yes. There was a rather clumsy attempt to make it look like suicide.'

She flinched on that, which made them wonder if she took it as an insult to her or her lover's handiwork in the Bentley.

Peach asked, 'Would you be able to identify the weapon, if it was indeed the one he carried?'

She said dully. 'No, I wouldn't. I've never wanted to know one weapon from another. I don't know who did this. It wasn't me and it wasn't Martin. I've told you all I can.'

Greta turned to look at Janey Johnson and answered her encouraging smile with a small one of her own. She looked exhausted, almost as if she had been confronting the detail and the reality of her husband's murder for the first time.

SEVENTEEN

George French didn't feel the cold. A raw wind was swirling between the high buildings, making most people hurry about their business. But when he was on a job, George never felt the cold. Afterwards, perhaps, when the business was done and the man dead, he would notice the temperature, would feel the cold biting suddenly in fingers which had been warm and supple minutes earlier when they were working.

He had never lived here. Birmingham always felt an alien city to him. He felt no glow of recognition as the multiple towers of high-rise flats came into view and he turned his car off the M6 and towards the city centre. Yet he knew the small section of the city which was his goal, near the old canals and a mile away from the redeveloped Bullring, almost as well as if he had grown up in the place. He had killed here before. He had a map of the terrain around him committed to his memory. He was familiar with the labyrinth of streets and their buildings, old and new, almost as if he had been raised among them.

He parked the dark blue Ford Focus very near the corner, where it was at the head of the row of parked cars and no one could park in front of it. Ready for a quick getaway. But not so quick that it would excite attention, he hoped. That would mean that things hadn't gone to plan. The Focus was deceptively powerful, with a two-litre engine which could accelerate swiftly to well over a hundred, if necessary. But that too was only a precaution, so that speed was there if needed. He had accelerated hard in the Focus only twice in the three years he had driven the car. Speed excited attention; if you killed people for money, it was much better not to draw attention to yourself.

He could see everything he needed to from here. His car commanded a view of the crossroads, with the high warehouse on his right and the thirties cinema which was now a nightclub with lap-dancing club on his left. He picked up the *Daily Telegraph* from beside him and pretended to read, his eyes not on the print but on the comings and goings of the vehicles and pedestrians in front of him. He liked to use the *Telegraph,* that organ of the conservative middle classes, when he was preparing to kill.

Twenty minutes passed slowly. He didn't mind that; it was what he had expected. He could feel the tension rising as the moment came nearer, like an actor fighting stage fright as his entry approached. He felt his pulse pounding a little faster in his temple as he watched the door of the club. His mouth was dry now; good. He ticked off the symptoms as the time approached, registering them as old friends who guaranteed his efficiency.

The big maroon Jaguar arrived within five minutes of the time he had calculated. They set themselves up for trouble, these people, driving big, flashy, noticeable cars like that. French was out of his car as the Jag eased into its parking place, walking swiftly towards the driver. He was thin, wiry, easily missed in his shabby blue anorak. The Jaguar driver was a heavy man, overweight as many of his like became around fifty, the result of a lifestyle which was too easy and too affluent. He blew out his cheeks as the cold wind hit him after the warmth of the car, then moved towards the door of the club.

George French had timed it right. His quarry was within two yards of the door when he brushed against him. There was a silencer on the pistol, but he also had it against the man's chest when he fired it. The sound was minimal. The only witness was a hundred yards away; he thought at first that the man had just slipped and fallen. The target was dead or dying, but French put a second bullet through his temple to make absolutely sure.

He was back in the Focus before anyone appeared from the club, easing away from the kerb, then departing quietly in the opposite direction from that which the Jaguar had arrived. This time the high blocks of council flats which heralded the motorway were a welcome sight. French observed the fifty

limit carefully, then eased the car up to over seventy when it
ended. Early afternoon was the quietest time on the busy M6;
he was back in his anonymous bungalow in Oldham within a
hundred minutes.

He changed swiftly into his gardening clothes and completed
the digging of the vegetable plot at the bottom of his patch.
His neighbour came in when he had been there for two minutes
and complimented him on his industry on this raw day.

'Good temperature for digging!' said George with a smile.
'You don't feel the cold, once you get going. I shall be finished
soon – I've been at it for two hours. And enough is enough!'
No harm in encouraging the odd witness to your whereabouts
at the time of the latest gangland killing in Birmingham.

Three hours later, he rang Jack Burgess in Alderley Edge.
'Market day Wednesday,' he said. He didn't need to give his
name; it was the code they had agreed to signify the successful
conclusion of an assignment.

'Excellent. No stall this week.' As expected, Burgess had
no further work for him at the moment.

Before he could put the phone down, French said, 'The
Brunton market. The Ketley job. Someone blabbed about
the down-payment. Someone at your end. The police knew.'

A pause, so long that he wondered if the man was going
to react at all. Gangster bosses didn't like being told there
were flaws in their organization. Then Burgess's heavy voice
said, 'Thanks for the information. I'll make enquiries.'

Chung Lee had every reason to be pleased with his accommodation at Thorley Grange. The room was fourteen feet long
and nine feet wide. Chung, with his fascination for figures and
precision, had measured the place as one of his first actions
after moving in.

That did not include the en suite, with its lavatory and
washbasin and shower, which was a further seven feet by six
feet; at one time he would have used metric figures, but the
British preferred feet and yards, so that was good enough for
Chung, who believed that he should fit unobtrusively into his
adopted country.

He liked England. He was learning things he had never

thought he would learn. Perhaps he would stay here. Perhaps he would indeed open up his own restaurant eventually, as he told everyone he wanted to do. But he wasn't looking too far ahead; these things might be outside his control.

It was the first time the CID men had seen his quarters. They looked unhurriedly around them, as was their wont in new surroundings, and decided as he had that Lee was fortunate in the living quarters allotted to him. When you were a single man operating as a full-time residential employee, the room you were given was a highly important factor in your life. It was the place where you lived and slept, where you spent more than half of your existence. Job satisfaction was important during your hours in the kitchen, but for resident staff, accommodation almost merged with job satisfaction. If you found where you lived depressing and claustrophobic, you were hardly going to give full value in the kitchens, or to get much joy out of life in general.

Peach had seen all kinds of rooms where single people had to exist; this was one of the best. It was neither depressing nor claustrophobic. It had a large, west-facing window with a view over the kitchen garden at the rear of the Grange to the woods beyond the wall of the estate. There was a close-fitting blind which would shut out the evening light when the setting sun threatened to dazzle. There was a picture on each of the long walls, one a Lakeland view of Blea Tarn and the Langdale Pikes, the other a still life of fruit in a bowl. Both, he judged, had been provided by the anonymous furnishers of the Grange rather than by Lee himself. There was a television on a stand, with a remote control beside it, a single wardrobe, a chest of drawers, two easy chairs and a bed, all sitting upon a fitted carpet. Everything was scrupulously neat and clean.

There were no photographs, no ornaments which seemed personal. There was nothing to identify this pleasant, comfortable room with its occupant. That might be no more than a reminder that Chung Lee had only occupied it for a few weeks. It might on the other hand mean that he was a man who habitually travelled light and did not put down roots.

As if he felt no sense of ownership, Chung stood awkwardly waiting whilst the CID men inspected his quarters. It was left to them to decide the positions for the trio in this mini-drama. 'Cosy, this!' said Percy Peach, as if he came habitually into the quarters of domestic staff at places like Thorley Grange. 'I think I shall sit here.' He moved one of the easy chairs a yard, so that it had its back to the window. 'And Detective Sergeant Northcott will be perfectly comfortable sitting on the edge of your bed.'

Chung watched them dispose themselves, then sat uneasily in the second armchair, aware that his vision could not take in the man on his left at the same time as Peach sitting opposite him. The DCI smiled blandly at him. Those who knew Peach, as Lee did not, would have expected this to be a prelude to aggression. He said quietly, 'We needed to see you again, as I think I warned you we might when we spoke on Monday. There are certain omissions in the account of yourself and your movements which you gave to us then.'

'Omissions?'

'Things you did not tell us, Mr Lee. A less charitable man than me might have used the term deceptions.'

'I did not deceive you, Mr Peach.'

Peach's eyebrows hoped skywards alarmingly. 'Really? I think you did, Mr Lee. Well, we shall perhaps be able to establish just what you did and why in the next half hour or so.' He stretched his legs in front of him and crossed his ankles, well aware that half an hour seemed an impossibly long time for an interviewee with things to conceal.

The DCI nodded a couple of times, then said, 'Your brother, Mr Lee. The one who plays for Norwich City.'

'The soccer player, yes. I have not spoken to—'

'He doesn't exist, does he? It is an entirely different Lee who plays football in Norwich. He'd never heard of you.'

Chung looked at Peach's shoes. They seemed very black and extraordinarily shiny. 'It's – it's not important. It has nothing to do with Mr Ketley's death.'

'It's always important when you tell lies to the police. Why did you do it?'

'I don't know. Really I don't. Someone asked me quite a long time ago if this man was my brother and I said yes. I was new in the country then and it seemed to make me – well, less of a foreigner, I suppose. It had that effect on the man who asked me. So I built it into my background, when I talked to other people, and it helped me. The English people seemed to find it easier to accept me into their midst as a working colleague with a brother who played football. Your soccer is very important to you, is it not?'

Peach thought of the agonies and ecstasies he had endured during thirty years of following Brunton Rovers and smiled. 'It is, yes. But that does not excuse your lying to CID officers in a murder investigation.'

'No. I am sorry for that. It had become a habit for me to claim this Lee as a brother. I have never been to Norwich.'

'I see. Do you have your passport here?'

He did not reply, but walked across to the small dressing table and opened the top drawer. 'Here it is. You will find it is quite in order.'

Peach took it and studied it for a moment. It seemed to be absolutely in order. It might of course be a forgery, but he did not know what to look for to establish that. He handed it back to the anxious-looking man and motioned him to sit down. He thought the olive face was a little paler, but that was probably imagination or wishful thinking. 'You have been in this country for five years.'

Chung wasn't sure whether it was a statement or a question. 'Yes.'

'Why did you come here?'

'It seemed that there would be more opportunities for me here.'

'There is no work in Vietnam?'

'There is work, yes, but more chance here. More chance to develop yourself. Perhaps I shall eventually return. If I do, what I have learned here and the experiences I have had will help me to get a better position in my home country.'

'I see. What did you do there, before you decided to try your luck over here?' Peach had no idea what the racial relations mafia would make of this line of questioning, but he would pursue it as long as the man did not object to his questions.

'I was a teacher. I had not taught very much. I had not long been qualified.'

'I see. Forgive me, but it does not seem a very logical progression, this. You are a teacher, in your own country, at the outset of a career. You are an intelligent man, with a facility for languages – I say that because of your excellent English. Yet you come here and apparently take whatever work is available. Even this desire to embark on a career in catering seems to have come upon you only in the last couple of years.'

'Yes. I agree it is unexpected.' He hesitated a little over the clumsy, four-syllabled word, as if asserting that his English was not after all so perfect. 'But I wanted to broaden my horizons by travelling, the way the books and the brochures tell you to do. I wanted to sample western civilization.'

He stopped as if he expected to be interrupted, so that Peach was reminded of Gandhi's remark that western civilisation would be a very good idea; the villainies you saw from people like Oliver Ketley tempted you towards thoughts like that. He switched his ground now, in the manner which had outwitted more experienced deceivers than Chung Lee. 'Why did you lie to us about where you were last Saturday night, Mr Lee?'

'What? You're talking about when Mr Ketley was murdered, aren't you? I told you on Monday, I was with my friend Fam Chinh at the restaurant in Market Street. We had a green curry. I had ice cream to follow.' He rattled the list off quickly, as if he could convince them with the detail.

'No, Mr Lee, you were not.'

'There is some mistake I think.' But he did not think that. He knew now that it had been a foolish plan.

'Our detective constables interviewed Mr Chinh. He tried to support you, but they could see that he wasn't happy. When they challenged him, he admitted that this was just a story you had asked him to tell for you. He did not see you at all on Saturday night. Instead, he admitted that he had eaten with you on Sunday evening and that you had asked him to tell this tale for you then.'

Chung's brown eyes stared steadily, unblinkingly, at the carpet between his feet and Peach's. His voice was a monotone as he said, 'I should not have asked Fam Chinh to lie for me. I do not know him as well as I said I did. We worked together for a few months, that is all. We looked out for each other, as you English say. He is a good man, who fears for his family in a foreign country.'

'He has nothing to fear from us. Unless he makes a habit of lying for possible murderers.'

'I am not a murderer. I did not kill Ketley. I was scared, that was all.'

It was the first time he had not accorded Ketley his title. From beside him, out of his vision, Clyde Northcott said, 'Then where were you on Saturday night, Mr Lee?'

'I was here. But because no one can say that to support me, I was afraid that you would suspect me. In my land the police are not as honest as here. They want convictions. They fasten on the weakest story.'

Clyde had no knowledge of the police in Vietnam. The situation Lee had described wasn't unknown in Britain, but this wasn't the moment to acknowledge that. He said calmly, 'You have made the situation much worse by lying to us. We now cannot trust anything else you have told us without checking it out.'

Chung didn't turn to look at him. He ran a hand briefly through his dark straight hair and said. 'I am sorry. What you say is true. But I was very afraid, being questioned by the police in a strange land. I made a mistake.'

Peach said quietly, 'When did you come to England, Chung?'

It was the first use of his forename. They were strange, the English and their little rituals. It might denote some sudden switch in the senior policeman's attitude, but he had no idea what that might be. 'I came here in 2005.'

'And what kind of work did you do?'

A long pause. 'I took whatever I could get, at first.'

'You worked on a building site, did you not?'

'Yes. It was the only work I could get.' He wondered just how much these people knew. This quiet, persistent, apparently sympathetic man was releasing his knowledge in scraps, as it suited him.

'It was the only work you could get in a particular area. In Lancashire.'

'In Liverpool, yes.' Chung looked down at his soft hands, as if wondering how they could ever have done that work with bricks and the cement.

'Between Liverpool and Southport, to be precise.'

'Yes.' They did know, then. But he must be careful, nonetheless. They would have to prove things, in this country, before they could lock him away. There was no reason why he should confess everything.

'Strange work for a teacher to undertake.'

'I told you, I wanted travel and experience. You can't pick and choose what you do. The type of work didn't matter much, so long as I could support myself.'

A pause again; Chung wondered whether they were weighing the merits of what he'd said. Then Peach said quietly, 'I suggest the type of work didn't matter, Chung, so long as it was in the right part of the country. I suggest you wanted to work as near to Southport as possible.'

'No. I took work where I could get it.'

'We have your employment records, Chung. Why did you begin work in that particular part of Lancashire?'

'Anywhere in the country would have been all right. I had a contact near Liverpool who helped me to get work.'

'Name?'

'I do not remember his name. He is no longer in this country.'

'Let me make a suggestion, Chung. In my opinion, you wished to work as near Southport as possible and you took whatever work you could get to be there. You wished to get as near to Oliver Ketley as you could.'

Lee was an undemonstrative man, adept in concealing his feelings behind an inscrutable exterior. There was no sound from him now, but the mention of the dead man's name brought a sharp twitch of the shoulders and a stiffening of the neck above them. He said nothing, continuing to stare at the carpet, so Peach was forced to venture a little further with his conjecture. 'I believe you lost someone very close to you and blamed Oliver Ketley for his death.'

'Ketley was a very bad man.'

It should have been banal, but his sincerity in the quiet room carried them with him. Peach said softly, persuasively, 'He was indeed a very bad man, Chung. We can agree on that. I can see why you would want to kill him.'

'I did not shoot Ketley.' He repeated it doggedly, as if that was necessary to convince them.

Peach, watching him keenly, decided that this was the moment when he had to move from the certainties he had used so far to speculation. 'Fifth of February, 2004. The night of the cockle-pickers, when at least twenty-three illegally employed workers died on Southport sands. You lost someone that night, didn't you, Chung? Someone very close to you.'

'My brother. Ketley took him on, put him in charge of the Chinese labour. I know that now. He was the only man from Vietnam who died that night.' It was an immense relief to have it out at last, when he had concealed it for so long, from others as well as the police. 'His body was never found. He shouted for help on his mobile phone, but those were his last words. No one could find him. He must have been washed out to sea.' His voice broke on the last, hopeless statement.

'But you found you couldn't get near Oliver Ketley.'

This quiet man with the round white face and the bald head seemed to Chung to know everything, even to understand everything. 'No. I couldn't even get to see him. And I realized that he must never know that I was here or that I even existed. He would wipe me from the earth as he might swat a fly. But I had time; I did not need to hurry.'

'So you moved into catering, and eventually into Thorley Grange.'

'Yes.' There was suddenly a small smile on the small, perfectly formed lips. 'I found I was quite good in the kitchen. I might even make a career of it.'

They smiled with him, grateful for any small relaxation of the tension which had dominated the last few minutes. Then Peach said with deadly seriousness, 'And on Saturday night your chance came. You shot Oliver Ketley through the head and avenged your brother.'

Chung summoned his resolution for a last denial. Against all the odds, they seemed reasonable people, these British policemen. They seemed to see the justice of his case. They would surely not wish to put him away for this, if he could

convince them he hadn't done it. 'I should have liked to kill
that man, yes. That would have given me great satisfaction.
But in the end I did not need to. Someone else got there before
me. I hope you never find out who it was.'

There was no moon visible as Greta Ketley drove into the
visitors' car park. The Georgian house which had been
converted to luxury flats rose like a dark cliff above her as
she climbed out of the Audi.

There was no reason why she should not see Martin quite
openly now. Oliver couldn't harm them. The police had discovered Martin and their relationship. There was really no need
for concealment. But old habits die hard; a week ago, discovery
would have meant death for Martin and something worse than
death for her. When the stakes had been as high as that, you
didn't readily abandon the habit of caution.

As usual, the flat door opened without her ringing the bell.
She liked the fact that he had been waiting for her, but she
knew she would have liked anything about him tonight. He
put a hand on each of her shoulders, held her at arm's length
to look into her face, as if seeing her and loving her for the
first time all over again. Both of them understood that: they
had never needed many words.

Martin Price said, 'I'd almost forgotten how beautiful you
are. It isn't long – under a week. But it feels as if it's been
months.'

'It does to me too, my darling. But now we have the rest
of our lives.'

Lovers speak like that and mean it. To outsiders it sounds
fatuous, but what matters is that they mean it. Even if many
love affairs do not last the years they should, the lovers need
to believe these wide, sometimes absurd, claims they make
about the rest of their lives.

As if they recognized that words were unreliable, this pair
did not use many of them. They smiled at each other for a
moment, almost shyly. Then he hugged her hard, kissed her
tenderly, and led her not into the sitting room but the bedroom,
as she wished him to do. She eased off his jacket and he slid
her sweater tenderly over her shoulders and her head. They

kissed again, his right hand holding her breast and squeezing it softly. Then they undressed without a word and slid between the silk sheets, hands searching for each other as carefully as if this was the first time.

Greta was surprised by how long they took over the preliminaries, using their hands to explore each other's bodies, gently at first and then with deliciously increasing urgency. When she spoke at last, it was only to reinforce what their limbs were saying to each other. 'This is our honeymoon!' she whispered. 'This is Martin and Greta beginning a new life together.'

And then at last their bodies stiffened and he stroked the soft symmetry of her shoulder blades, then the small of her back and the pleasures below it. They had complete confidence in each other, as lovers should. The whole exchange became more hectic and urgent as urge answered urge and they climaxed exquisitely together.

They lay for a long time without words afterwards, staring up at the ceiling they could scarcely see. Each revelled in the nearness of the other, in the fact that they were so happy without the need of words. Eventually his hand found hers and squeezed gently. 'Do you want a drink?'

'Tea would be nice. Nothing alcoholic – we don't need stimulants.'

He brought them tea in bone china beakers. She liked the quality he seemed to seek out, even in beakers. But then she would have considered it tasteful tonight if he had served it in chipped earthenware, she thought, with that secret smile he found so attractive.

Martin drained his beaker and said, 'How are the police getting on?'

It should have been an intrusion upon their magic, private world, but tonight nothing could spoil things. She said, 'They seemed very pleased to have found out about us. Made quite a big thing of how I'd played the grieving widow and tried to deceive them. But they don't seem to have much idea about who killed Oliver. They don't like him any more than we did. He's a bigger villain than I ever knew he was when he was alive. Perhaps they're not going to bother too much about who removed him.'

'We mustn't rely on that. Murder is murder to the police, whoever the victim is. And we've got the most obvious of all the motives.'

Neither of them wanted to talk more about the death which had freed them. They made love again, more slowly and with more caresses this time. It was different but equally delicious. Quite a long time later, he said, 'You could stay the night, couldn't you?'

'I could. I don't think I should, though. I think I should get back to the Grange and keep an eye on things there. We don't want to draw attention to ourselves.'

She meant it, but a tiny part of her was disappointed when he agreed with her so readily. She was fully dressed and putting on her shoes when she said, 'You told me you'd had two detective sergeants to see you. You haven't seen the main man, then? Detective Chief Inspector Peach?'

'No. They said he might want to speak to me later.'

'You need to watch out for him. He's a clever devil. Don't give him anything, or he'll be like a dog with a bone.'

It was a cliché that stayed with Martin Price all through the night.

EIGHTEEN

George French decided that a little righteous indignation would probably be in order for the model citizen he claimed to be. 'I don't think I wish to speak with you again. I said everything I had to say when you were here on Monday.'

He had only half-opened the door of his bungalow and now he threatened to close it in their faces. Peach smiled sadly at Clyde Northcott, then shrugged. 'We can have a nice friendly chat here, or we can take you to the station and question you under caution as a contract killer. I prefer friendly chats, but the choice is yours, George.'

French knew there was no choice at all. He stared at them malevolently for a moment, then turned and led them into his comfortable living room. 'Your idea of friendly isn't mine. Say what you have to say and then be on your way.'

Peach had not been invited to sit, but he now disposed himself carefully on the sofa and gestured to Northcott to join him. He stretched his short, grey-suited legs and examined the high polish on his black toecaps. When you dealt with the young yobboes of Brunton on a regular basis, you became an expert in dumb insolence. It was several seconds before he said, 'Further information has come to light, sir.'

French sighed elaborately. 'Further information about what?'

Peach used the opportunity to stretch his eyebrows high towards the whiteness of his bald pate. 'Why, about the murder of Oliver Ketley, of course. Did you have some other crime in mind that you wished to help us with?'

George French realized he had almost made a mistake, that in displaying his contempt for these men he should also be careful. Because it was still fresh in his own mind, he had suspected for a moment that they knew about the killing in

Birmingham on the previous day. 'I had nothing to do with Ketley's death. I told you that on Monday.'

'Indeed you did, sir. But you will remember that we had information which caused us to doubt your assurances. We now know rather more and are even less confident of your innocence.' He beamed as if that was entirely to his satisfaction.

'I didn't kill Ketley and I don't know who did. That is what I said on Monday and that remains the situation today, however much baffled plods might wish it otherwise.'

This was definitely one up from the inarticulate yobboes of Brunton. Peach continued to smile whilst he nodded appreciatively, as if every new denial that French made was merely sealing his fate. 'Whenever it becomes necessary, we can prove in court that you received the first payment of twenty-five thousand pounds for this killing.' Though he spoke with impressive confidence to shake his man, he doubted if that was actually the case. 'In due course, we shall no doubt secure the details of the final payment, made after Ketley's dispatch.'

'You won't, because no such payment was ever made.'

'You're admitting the preliminary payment, then, are you, Mr French? Well, I suppose that's progress, of a sort. Make a note of it, please, DS Northcott.'

'I'm admitting no such thing. Make a note of that, please, DS Northcott.' French, who had remained standing when his visitors seated themselves, now reluctantly sat in his armchair to face them. 'You plainly have me confused with some other person, DCI Peach. I've been very patient, but you should know that my patience is not inexhaustible.'

'I'm pleased to hear that, because we haven't got all day to waste here. Pleasant and respectable though it is, of course.' Peach looked down the garden to the newly dug vegetable plot. 'Your neighbours would have a hell of a shock if they knew what you did for a living.'

French, who frequently had the same thought himself, did not welcome it from this source. 'Have you come here for any other reason than to offer me insults? I have work to get on with. I'm expecting a call from the MD of a firm which has just retained me for a site in Newcastle.'

'Work? Ah, the famed engineering consultancy! Do you know, I'd almost forgotten about that, George? Good thing you reminded me – and reminded yourself, I expect. Have you equipped yourself with any new weapons in the last few months?'

'No. Just the ones I use at the shooting club. Both fully licensed.'

'So you wouldn't know anything about a Ruger SR9 pistol?'

'Nothing whatsoever. A powerful and efficient weapon, I'm told, but I've never fired one.'

But Peach had seen a flash of interest in the heavy-lidded eyes, a brief moment of recognition. 'A weapon purchased in America and brought through Manchester airport illegally by one Stephen Greenoe. It would have been a useful addition to the armoury of a contract killer.'

'But not to that of an amateur who shoots very occasionally at a club.'

George French had recovered himself in a flash, but even his momentary lapse upset him, because he knew Peach had seen it. French was amoral, like most people who assess the odds and kill for money. He was a perfectionist who lived alone and prided himself upon his self-sufficiency. Increasingly as his strange life went on, he felt the lack of any close companion to confide in. Perhaps that affected what he did now. He leaned forward and said, 'We're off the record, aren't we?'

'Completely off the record, George. No one is going to re-hear this conversation, unless you have this place bugged.'

'I did hear a whisper about those weapons from America.'

'At your shooting club, no doubt.'

'Eh? Oh, yes, at the shooting club. It must have been there. I heard most of them had gone to Oliver Ketley's organization.'

'Did you, indeed? Interesting. And not impossible, I'd have said.'

'Really? Well, you know about these things and I know nothing.'

'Except where that pistol came from and where it went to. What I have to ask myself is why you would pass on the information to DS Northcott and me.'

'Because I am acting as the good citizen you told me I should be and that you refuse to believe I am. I'm merely passing on a rumour I heard to the authorities.'

'I think you're telling me that if Ketley was killed with Ruger SR9 pistol, it couldn't have been by you, because you would have used your usual handgun.'

'I was saying nothing of the kind. But if it shatters your bizarre theories about me, then I'm happy you think that.'

'Oh, it doesn't do that, French. Try this one for size. All killers are opportunists, and contract killers most of all. You go there equipped to murder with your usual weapon, but find that the victim has his own handgun on his person. So you shoot him through the temple with that, then add a clumsy attempt to fake a suicide by sticking the pistol in his hand. Leaves no chance of the slug from your own firearm being identified and traced back to the weapon which fired it.'

Peach had spoken slowly and deliberately, watching his man's eyes for any further revelation, but George French had been caught out once. He exhibited no further weakness. He said, 'You live in a devious and ingenious world, DCI Peach. I am glad that I have no part of it. From what I hear, the world is well rid of Oliver Ketley, so I don't think I shall wish you success in your investigation.'

'Are you prepared to give us a DNA sample?'

The sudden request did not ruffle him. If anything, there was a trace of amusement now in the deep-set eyes and satisfaction in the sallow face. 'Not voluntarily, no. I have indulged your outlandish theories quite enough by talking to you about the weapon and passing on a rumour I'd picked up. Now I should like you to leave my house.'

They were up on the moors, ten miles along their route back to Brunton, before Peach said, 'Whether that bugger killed Ketley or not, he knows how he died.'

Greta Ketley found that her husband's death brought an enormous release to her. Only with his passing did she realize quite how inhibited she had been in her own household. She had grown used to weighing her every word before she spoke it, as if she were enclosed in a police state, where innocent phrases might be turned against her. Now, after the foetid staleness of life with Oliver, sun and fresh, clear air were sweeping back into her life.

She found Janey Johnson very easy to talk to. It had been an impulsive rather than a considered decision to invite this bright young woman into her life. The more natural confidante would have been Mrs Frobisher. She trusted the housekeeper, who had always displayed an unspoken understanding of her situation and a sympathy for it. But there was a natural reserve about the older woman, a consciousness of the employer-employee relationship which would have made it difficult for her to exchange confidences. Moreover, she had been at Thorley Grange from the start; through no fault of her own, she was identified with the repressive regime and Oliver Ketley.

Janey, though she had worked at the Grange for some time, was a much more recent resident, and she had apparently found the world of Oliver Ketley as strange and constricting as Greta had. She was nearer in age to Greta than Mrs Frobisher, being thirty-five to Greta's forty-two. Within a few days of Oliver Ketley's death, reserve had dropped away from his widow and she was talking freely to Janey about many things.

Janey was the first person in the house she told about Martin Price, and she gave her more than the simple facts of the affair. Once she had begun to talk, Greta found she wanted to convey her own excitement and pleasure. Martin was a good man and she wanted now to spend the rest of her life with him; it was important to her that she convinced Janey that this was a long-term partnership, not a passing sexual fling.

With some prompting from her mistress, Janey spoke a little about her own husband. She had been very close to Sam. As always when a man dies young and unexpectedly, there were regrets for a few of the things they had done and many more for the things they had left undone. The fact that neither of these woman had the children she would have liked was a bond between them. When Janey Johnson was persuaded eventually to speak of the family she had planned with Sam and never achieved, she descended unexpectedly into quiet weeping.

But that too strengthened the bond between them, as the revelation of vulnerability invariably does.

On Thursday, five days after the death which had brought them so unexpectedly close, Greta said, 'How well do you know Chung Lee?'

'Not well. He seems a nice, rather serious young man. But he keeps himself to himself most of the time; I wish all men did the same.'

Greta smiled. Her pretty young companion had had offers, even within the household in the few weeks since she had been here. Even during the last few days, in fact: Oliver's death seemed to have removed other inhibitions as well as her own. Greta looked at her new friend's neat dark hair and large, unexpectedly humorous, brown eyes. Greta was sure that she herself had looked prettier since last Saturday's events had freed her; now she fancied that Janey also looked livelier and more attractive since that death. Greta said, 'Let me know if anyone is being a nuisance to you.'

'It's not a problem. Most men get the message, if you're firm. The problem is that you don't want to humiliate them. Most of them are just following their hormones; they don't push it, once you show you're not interested. Why did you want to know about Chung Lee?'

'He came to see me this morning. He's wondering about his long-term prospects. Basically, he wanted to know about the future of this place. And I couldn't give him any firm answers, except that nothing will happen immediately.'

'I expect he's worried about his own plans. I gather he wants to become a skilled chef and run his own restaurant.'

'That's ambitious. It's a crowded field.'

Janey determined to do her best for Chung. 'I wouldn't put it past him. He seems very hard-working. And I think your chef would tell you that he's made a good start here.'

'I told him that. I tried to assure him that whatever happened I would try to look after him. He said if there was no long-term future here he'd need to make other plans quickly, but I told him not to do anything in a hurry. I said I'd speak to him again when I'd had more time to think. He's worried about the CID men – apparently they've already interviewed him twice.'

'Poor man. He must feel a long way from home. And also threatened, I suppose; most of us trust our police not to fit people up for crimes, but I expect Chung feels more isolated and more under suspicion because he's a foreigner.'

Greta nodded. 'I couldn't get him to talk much. But I gathered that DCI Peach – that's the bouncy little detective with the bald head and the moustache – caught him out in a couple of things. I gather he's no alibi for the time when Oliver was shot, like most of us. He was here on Saturday night, but he's got no one to vouch for that.'

Janey frowned. 'He lives just down the corridor from me. I think I may have seen him at some time on Saturday night. I'll think about it.'

'I wish you would. He seems very anxious. Talk to him, if he'll let you. He might be a bit more open than he was prepared to be with me.'

'I'll speak to him. Our rooms are quite near to each other, but we've hardly exchanged a word since Mr Ketley was killed. We were getting on quite well before that, though we scarcely did more than greet each other. Our work doesn't overlap much. He spends most of his days in the kitchen.'

Greta was struck suddenly by a horrid thought. 'You don't think Chung Lee did kill Oliver, do you?'

Janey laughed. 'No, I'm sure he didn't. I expect the police are equally sure of it, but they don't reveal much of their thinking, do they?'

As she went back to her own room, Janey Johnson considered a different thought. The most capable and certainly the most powerful woman in this place was probably the one she'd just left. And from what she'd said about her boyfriend Martin Price and the work he'd done, they would make a pretty formidable combination. Perhaps that was the line of enquiry the police should be following now.

Martin Price looked like a killer.

Percy Peach, who was rarely assailed by such unscientific thoughts, felt it strongly. Price looked less than his forty years. His blue eyes glittered, alert, watchful, assessing. Even at the end of February, his face was tanned an unexpected brown;

no doubt that came from his years spent in much hotter climes than England's. His fair hair had scarcely receded at all, though it was cut very short, as if he had to be prepared for instant action. He was just under six feet, lean and fit. He looked confident but not overconfident; that was the least promising condition, from an interrogator's point of view.

Peach stepped into the sitting room of the flat, thrust out his hand, and said, 'DCI Peach. You and I haven't met before, but you know DS Northcott.'

Price gave the big black man a guarded smile. 'Yes. We had an interesting exchange of views yesterday morning. He was assisted then by a Detective Sergeant Peach. Any relation, Chief Inspector?'

'My wife, sir.' He was on the ball, this man. Very few people remembered the names of officers who had spoken to them; this one had not only remembered but made the connection with his new opponent.

Martin permitted himself the thin smile of a man who had scored the opening point. 'You're a fortunate man, DCI Peach.'

'Indeed I am, Mr Price. I hope your affair with Mrs Ketley will be equally fortunate. Why did you conceal it from us?'

Martin took his time, remembering how Greta had told him not to underestimate this unimpressive-looking man. 'I think it was your wife who pointed out that it gave us the oldest and one of the strongest motives for murder, so perhaps you could hardly expect us to declare it. Greta hated her husband. I hated him not just because of what I knew of him but because of the way he treated Greta. Frankly, we are delighted to be rid of him. To present you with all this on a plate seemed distinctly unwise.'

Peach decided there was no point in any more preliminary fencing with this man. 'You're not only the man with the best motive, you're also the man best equipped by experience to remove an enemy.'

'Better than a contract killer? I doubt that.'

'You have no cause to defer to my experience in matters of killing, Mr Price. I've met a few murderers, as you would expect. I've never killed a man.'

'And I have? Well, yes, I shan't deny that. Those deaths

have always been in the cause of duty, and I deny that you could call any of my killings a murder.'

'You were acting on orders, no doubt. The old excuse.'

'In eight years of service in the SAS, I usually was. But you are also given more freedom of action in the SAS than in other military units. That is one of the attractions, the scope for initiative. In many situations, it is a necessity.'

'And you obviously thrived on that system. After eight years you'd made the rank of captain, with more promotions and a promising career ahead of you. Why was that career halted so abruptly?'

Price glanced at Clyde Northcott, who had his pen poised expectantly over his notebook. 'I told you this yesterday. I enjoyed my years in the SAS, but it's a young man's game. I decided on a career shift, whilst I was still young enough to do other things.'

'Things like working for Oliver Ketley and fighting as a mercenary soldier in Africa. Scarcely less dangerous or less demanding than SAS service, I'd have thought.'

'We can't always choose the work we undertake, Detective Chief Inspector. Life doesn't proceed as logically and inevitably as it does in the police service.'

Peach smiled grimly. 'The decision wasn't yours. You were slung out of the SAS. Lucky to leave without a court martial.'

Price nodded grimly. 'You've done your homework. I thought the authorities might have made it rather more difficult for you.'

'They had to be persuaded; Army Records are very good at ignorance, when it suits them. I sometimes wish the police had their clout when it comes to concealing things. But murder opens doors, if you push hard enough. The people concerned didn't seem very surprised that you should be the leading suspect in a murder hunt.'

'Leading suspect, am I?

'You have all the qualifications. Efficiently trained in all sorts of combat by the SAS. Subsequent career where violence was positively encouraged and nothing like so controlled. Determination to lie low rather than even reveal your existence after the murder of a man who stood formidably in your path.'

'You make it sound as if I'm parcelled up ready for a jury. The snag for you is that I didn't kill Ketley. In choosing to lie low, I was allowing you to concentrate your formidable police resources on discovering who did.'

'Your army service was terminated because you sanctioned the torturing of a prisoner in Iraq.'

'You did lean hard on the people at records, didn't you? We needed that information in Iraq. We saved British lives by acquiring it.'

His mouth was a hard line and his experienced face set in stone. This was obviously an argument he had conducted and lost at the time and re-lived many times since then. Peach had wanted to open this up, to weaken the man's position in the rest of the interview. But now he could see no point in pursuing it further. He said curtly, 'Tell us about the work you did for Oliver Ketley after your discharge.'

Martin paused for a moment. He mustn't allow himself to be hurried on this dangerous ground. He said grimly, 'There aren't many employment opportunities when you leave the army under the circumstances I did. You don't like starting at the bottom somewhere else and being ordered about by idiots, when you've been SAS. Ketley knew that when he approached me. He said he wanted someone to organize his personal defences. He said he swam in dangerous waters and wanted people who would watch out for sharks.' Price smiled bitterly as he quoted the dead man's phrase.

'So you surrounded him with vicious people.'

He weighed that. 'Not surrounded him. I supplied him with a couple of men who were skilled and not too scrupulous to act as his personal bodyguards.'

'You might have made a new career with him. But you didn't stay long.'

'No. He didn't just want personal protection. What he wanted me to do was to organize a small private army for him, to contest the gangland wars he saw developing. I wasn't up for that.'

Peach wondered about that. There was no knowing at this distance who had dispensed with whom. But again there was nothing to be gained by pursuing that thought. 'So you went off to Africa to be a mercenary soldier.'

Again that bitter smile, which told them he could tell them much more than he was going to do if he chose. 'When you'd worked for Oliver Ketley and you knew a little about his rackets and the way he ran them, it wasn't advisable to stay in the country. I didn't fancy a bullet in the back of my head. It was safest to disappear to another continent for a few years.'

'So you went off to kill Africans.'

Martin knew the provocation was deliberate, so he refused to react. 'I was offered the chance to lead my own unit of eight men, very much on SAS lines, though in a private army. It was dog eat dog – no one out there was going to bring me to book for torturing the odd prisoner, if we secured our objectives.'

'So you killed people for the highest payer.'

'It wasn't like that. In the Congo you did whatever you had to do to survive, but I got out of there as soon as I could and took my men with me. You won't believe me, but elsewhere I was always on what you'd probably call the right side – that is, against petty tyrants who were exploiting their people and milking their countries. It wasn't easy: a lot of the conflicts out there are still tribally based.'

He had spoken for a moment with something like passion. At some time in the future – possibly when the man was locked away in a cell – Peach would like to hear more of these African adventures. But no doubt he never would. 'And then you came home and began an affair with Greta Ketley.'

Again the attempt to provoke. And again it would be resisted. 'You make it sound as if the two things are connected. Soldiering as a mercenary is a young man's game. I was a veteran when I got out at thirty-nine. The last thing I wanted here was anything which would take me anywhere near Oliver Ketley; I'd been close enough to him to realize what a dangerous man he was. But quite by chance I met Greta in Manchester. I was attracted to her and quickly realized that she was unhappy. I love the woman, DCI Peach, whatever that odd word means. It isn't a word I've had any time for in the rest of my life.'

'And Ketley stood in your way.'

Martin knew where he was going with that, but refused to

follow. 'We were very careful. I have grown used to secrecy over the years; it's become a habit and I think I'm rather good at it. I knew better than Greta herself that I must not do anything to put her in danger.'

'So you watched and you waited. And when the opportunity arrived, you shot Ketley with his own weapon. No doubt the irony of that appealed to you.'

Price had again the grim smile of the man who is more expert in these things than his audience. 'You're very naive, DCI Peach, for a man who knows about violence. When you're killing people, you have no time for such things as irony. They are luxuries you cannot afford.'

'Neither you nor Mrs Ketley have an alibi for the time of this death.'

'And I know as well as you do that the absence of an alibi in no way indicates guilt. You will need something much more positive and you are not going to find it.'

Peach's smile as he stood reluctantly acknowledged the man's qualities and experience. 'Don't go away without giving us your new address, please.'

'I shan't do that, DCI Peach. I look forward to the successful conclusion of your case.'

NINETEEN

As Clyde Northcott collected his lunch in the police canteen at Brunton, he saw Lucy Peach's companion leave her at the table in the corner. He went and sat with Lucy as she opened her strawberry yoghurt. The two had always got on well. Now that he had been promoted to the job she used to do with Peach, Clyde also felt a sort of undeclared bond with a fellow detective sergeant.

'We saw Martin Price in Chorley again this morning,' he said.

'And what did my esteemed husband think of the man? Percy was picking my brains last night about our meeting with him yesterday.'

'You know Percy better than anyone. He doesn't say a lot, when he's thinking hard.'

'And he's thinking hard about Price?'

'Very hard, I'd say. One of the things about this case is that the two strongest candidates are going to be the hardest to pin down – assuming one of them has done it, of course. If you take the backgrounds of both the suspects and the victim into account, the two likeliest killers are George French and Martin Price. Contract killers are always elusive, because they're professionals – they're experienced, and they give attention to every detail. Usually it's impossible to place them at the scene of the crime. I know Price isn't a contract killer, but he ticks all those boxes.'

Lucy nodded ruefully. 'From what I saw of Martin Price yesterday, he'll be as slippery as any contract killer. He's got all the skills and all the experience to take on the job. He also has the nerve to kill a big fish like Ketley. I can see why he appealed to Greta Ketley. I've never met her, but there can't be many men who'd risk an affair with Ketley's wife. And I found myself responding yesterday to his coolness and his frankness about his own capacity for violence. Knowing the sort of villain Ketley was, I almost ended up on Price's side.'

That was an interesting insight, thought Clyde. He wouldn't
have gone as far as that. He came back to what the chief had
told the team at the beginning of this. 'Murder's murder and
it's our job to solve it. I feel in my bones that this one is down
to Martin Price. But pinning it on him won't be easy.'

'Could this murder be a joint effort? The two people who've
gained most from this death are Martin Price and Greta Ketley.
Could they have been operating together?'

'They've both got the nerve for it. Greta Ketley played the
grieving widow when we first saw her last Sunday. She was
quite different after we'd discovered her affair with Price. Even
if she wasn't there, she could have set up the time and the
place for Price to dispatch the man they'd decided to
liquidate.'

Lucy nodded. She felt oddly bereft not to be at the centre
of this case, having operated beside Percy Peach during so
many serious crime searches. 'Percy always said that the more
people who are involved in a crime, the easier it is to solve.
When people have to coordinate, they're more likely to make
mistakes during interrogation.'

Clyde saw the logic of this, but he said dolefully, 'They're
a pretty cool pair, as they'd need to be to take on Oliver Ketley.
They don't seem to have made any mistakes in what they've
said to us so far.'

The long dark face looked so baffled that Lucy tried to cheer
him up. 'All the same, two suspects give you a better chance
of a solution than one, Clyde. That's if our surmise is right
and both of them are involved in this.'

Janey Johnson's room was in the new buildings at Thorley
Grange, at the other end of the corridor from Chung Lee's.
This was obviously where the residential members of the staff
were accommodated. There were four other doors and presum-
ably four other, similar rooms behind them.

Mrs Johnson's room was comparable in size and outlook
to Chung Lee's, but it took them a moment or two to realize
that, because it was much more personalized. There was a
large black-and-white photograph of a young couple marching
arm in arm on the promenade at Blackpool, with dozens of

children leaving the sands with buckets and spades in the background and the Tower rearing towards clear sky further on still. They had the carefree look of a couple without worries and with the world unfolding before them. 'My mum and dad in 1964,' said Janey when she saw Clyde Northcott studying it. He thought of telling her the details of the powerful Norton 500 motorcycle on the road alongside the couple, then caught sight of Peach's face and decided against it.

Peach himself picked up a smaller, coloured picture of the same couple some years later. They still looked happy, but older and less carefree – not surprisingly, as they now had three children sitting between them, two girls and a boy. 'That's me in the middle, I was the baby of the family,' said Janey, pointing to a pretty, serious youngster with plaits and her sister's arm around her. 'That must be early eighties, I suppose.'

There were several other photographs of the family, individually as well as in groups, but Peach walked over to look at the paintings on the walls, of which there were four, in various sizes, all landscapes and all originals. He stopped in front of a woodland scene, with autumn hues on the leaves and a stream running briskly across the foreground. 'These are good. By someone in the family?'

Janey felt herself blushing; she couldn't remember when she had last done that. She hoped the blood didn't show in her face; it wasn't the way she had planned to begin what must be an important meeting. 'They're mine, actually. I used to do quite a lot, in – in the old days. I don't get much time now.'

'You should make the time. I'm no expert, but I think these are good.'

The room was a little squarer than Lee's had been, but with the same outlook over the kitchen garden of the old house to the wall of the estate and woods beyond. As if to reflect a more outgoing occupant, it had three small armchairs rather than his two. Janey had arranged them for this meeting as soon as they had announced it to her an hour ago. She now took the smallest of the chairs, with her back to the window, leaving the two larger ones to the men.

When she had heard that they wanted to see her for a second

time, she had nerved herself for a full grilling about her own background, but this surprising man Peach looked round the room and offered only, 'Very similar to Mr Lee's room at the other end of the corridor, this, but you've stamped yourself on it more firmly than he has.'

She glanced round at her personal effects. 'I've never been in his room. He's a long way from home – his real home, I mean. Perhaps he hasn't got the things I've got to display; or perhaps men don't have the same instinct to shape wherever they live into a comfortable nest.'

Perhaps she was sending herself up a little: this capable woman struck Peach as much more than a nest-builder. 'Do you see much of him?'

'Chung Lee? Very little, actually. He works full-time in the kitchen and I work in the residential parts of the house.'

'But you live very near to each other and you have considerable leisure time.'

'Yes, that's true. But neither of us has been here for very long. We've been finding our feet in the place, I suppose.'

'Of course. But I thought the fact that you came here at about the same time might have given you something in common.'

Janey wished they could move on to the stuff she had prepared for them. She hadn't expected to start with this. 'In my limited contacts, I've found Chung a pleasant and polite man. I think we're both rather cautious about new relationships.'

'And perhaps neither of you wanted to become close.'

She smiled. 'That might also be true. From what I hear, Mr Lee is determined to make himself a master-chef and is working very hard to do that. As for me, I've learned to be cautious. Men, or at least a lot of men, take friendliness as an invitation to something more. If you don't want that, you're very cautious about the sort of conversations you get yourself into. I find it easier to be friendly when there are other women around.'

'Let's forget about Mr Lee, then. It's just that we have certain queries about him and another member of staff suggested that you were closer to him than you obviously are.'

She wondered who that might be. But she mustn't think

about it now. 'I wouldn't want you to think that I've anything
against Chung. I rather like the fact that he's quiet and polite.
I feel sorry for him being so isolated, especially now that Mr
Ketley's death has introduced all sorts of uncertainties about
the future of this place.'

Peach, sensing that there was some other thing she wanted
to add, merely helped her onwards. 'You're right about him
feeling isolated, I think. He's also pretty scared of policemen
and what we might do to him. He's very conscious that he
hasn't anyone to vouch for his whereabouts at the time of Mr
Ketley's death. He doesn't realize that he's not the only one
in that position, but it's hardly up to us to tell him that.'

Her forehead furrowed; curiously, that made her look
younger and more attractive. 'I might be able to help you
there.'

'Really?' Peach arched his eyebrows alarmingly high, but
Janey was concentrating on her own thoughts.

'I'm pretty sure he was in his room last Saturday night.'
She saw Northcott preparing to make a note and concentrated
even more fiercely. 'I passed his room, because I went down
to the entrance hall to check on my flower arrangement there.
With Mr and Mrs Ketley both here for the weekend, I wanted
to make sure it was still looking fresh. His television was on
when I passed: I'm sure I heard it, because it was tuned to
the wildlife programme I'd been watching.'

Clyde Northcott made his note, then spoke almost apologetically in his quiet bass voice. 'We CID men are suspicious
creatures, Mrs Johnson. We have to remember that a room is
not necessarily occupied when a television set is switched on.'

'No, I realize that, but I'm sure I saw him come out of his
room as I returned to mine. We almost bumped into each
other.' She frowned again, working fiercely on her memory.
'I can remember the incident, because we both apologized at
the same time and then laughed about it. He said he'd left his
book in the kitchen annexe – that's where the catering staff
go when they take short rests.'

The dark-brown voice said quietly, 'What time was this,
Mrs Johnson?'

'I remember the incident clearly enough, but I couldn't have told you until now exactly what day it was, let alone what time. But that television programme helps. It must have been Saturday. And it must have been about nine, because the programme was just coming to an end when I slipped out to go down to the entrance hall.' She watched Northcott note it. 'Is that any use? I've no idea when Mr Ketley was killed.'

Peach was almost effusive. 'It's very useful, Mrs Johnson. I wish everyone else would go on thinking, as we exhort them to; it's surprising how often people recall significant details. This can only help Mr Lee.'

'Good. I'm sure he had nothing to do with Mr Ketley's death. Chung seems a nice, inoffensive man, from what little I've seen of him.'

Percy knew one or two nice, inoffensive men and women who had committed murder, but he wasn't going to waste time voicing the thought. 'Tell us about your own relationship with Mr Ketley, please.'

It was another of those abrupt switches of ground, but Janey told herself that she was prepared for it, that she wouldn't give him the satisfaction of being shocked. This was an expected question and she had an answer ready for it. 'I scarcely knew him. He appointed me, but after that I hardly spoke to him, or he to me. I met him around the house and the business suite a few times, but it was the housekeeper, Mrs Frobisher, who allotted me my duties. I answer to her.'

'Not to Mrs Ketley?'

'No. It's true I've worked more closely with Mrs Ketley recently, but that's only because she wanted someone from the household close to her over the last few days. I expect that's the blow of her husband's death.'

'And the manner of his dying.'

'And the manner of his dying, as you say. It must have been a great shock to her.'

'Must it?'

'Yes, I'm sure it must.' She stared hard at him, defying him to challenge her.

'Of those who live here, you've been closer than anyone to Greta Ketley since her husband's death. How much of a shock do you think it was?'

'I think you may have an exaggerated idea of how close I am to Mrs Ketley. She has been kind to me and I have tried to be helpful to her in difficult circumstances. But we'd hardly spoken before last Saturday. I like her and I think she likes me. But I'd say that we're still getting to know each other.'

'Did you know that she was conducting an affair outside her marriage?'

How abrupt the man was! How quickly he switched from the mundane to the disturbing! Janey made herself take her time. 'Not until yesterday. Greta told me herself. It's flown round the Grange in the last few hours, as gossip will. I'm quite sure no one even suspected it earlier.'

'No doubt you're right. If Oliver Ketley had known anything about an affair, he would have taken steps to end it very quickly.'

'I expect you're right. You obviously know far more about Mr Ketley than I do.' She got a little pleasure from this prim reply.

'And perhaps you know more about him than you care to admit to.'

She glanced up at him instinctively. He was observing her every reaction, as he had done throughout. She kept her voice very steady. 'What I know is mostly second-hand. I was told early on that he was a womanizer. He gave me the impression when he interviewed me that he would welcome sexual favours. I needed the job, but I didn't give him any encouragement.'

'And once you were living in the house, did he make any advances, welcome or otherwise?'

A little shudder ran through the slim body. 'They would not have been welcome. And I had no real trouble. I took care not to get into situations where he might paw me or suggest private meetings.' She allowed herself a bitter smile. 'When you are a youngish widow, you develop a certain expertise in these things.'

'I imagine you do. What did your husband do for a living, Mrs Johnson?'

She dropped her eyes from his near-black, all-seeing pupils, finding that an aid to concentration. 'Sam ran a general hardware store, in Preston.'

'Ran it and owned it, did he not?'

'We did own it, yes – with the help of a large bank loan. It didn't feel like ours, but no doubt it would have done, with time.'

'A general hardware store with a lucrative sideline. Your husband obtained a licence to sell guns, did he not?'

'You obviously know he did. You've done your research. But the gun trade wasn't very lucrative. Sam believed it would have become so, given time.'

'I see.'

'It was all strictly legal. Most of the trade was shotguns, for country shooting. There were a small number of sales of other weapons, all properly documented – licensed for use in controlled environments such as shooting clubs, I believe. I helped prepare the books for the accountants, but otherwise I know nothing about it. I've never had any interest in guns.'

'How did your husband die, Mrs Johnson?'

She looked up at him on that, then shot at him bitterly, 'Why ask me, when you obviously know all about it?'

Peach said with a sudden, surprising gentleness, 'Not all. I don't think anyone knows as much as you do, Mrs Johnson. I'd be grateful if you'd answer.'

'Suicide, everyone said.'

'Not everyone, Janey. The Coroner's Court jury returned an open verdict. They were advised by the police to do so. The case is still officially open. I think we know that it wasn't suicide. I think we know who killed Sam, but I don't expect us to find convincing evidence at this stage.'

For a moment, she was grateful for his honesty. Then she looked at him bitterly; what was the point in telling her they knew Sam had been murdered, then saying in the next breath that he'd never get justice? She said dully, 'Everyone who lived in the houses around me thought it was suicide. Someone went into court and said Sam had "business worries". He hadn't; we had a big loan, but the shop was a success. We were paying the mortgage off each month, as the terms said we had to.'

'I don't believe Sam committed suicide, either, Janey. But they sealed him in the car with the pipe running from the exhaust to the interior – one of the classic suicide methods.'

'He was unconscious when they put him in there. No one could prove it, but I know he was. Even if he'd been in trouble, suicide would never have been Sam's way out.'

'There was evidence of blows to the head, though nothing to prove conclusively that he was unconscious. Hence the open verdict.'

She was very white now, very determined with the memory of it. 'The police who'd been working on it wanted a suicide verdict. To take a case off their books which they were never going to solve.'

It was possible she was right. Long-term murder enquiries absorbed precious resources, and in this case there would have been little hope of success. 'I can't comment on that, Janey. The car was on the cliffs at Bispham, outside Blackpool. The investigation was by another force. I can only say that I am as convinced as you that Sam was murdered. And as convinced as you who it was who ordered his death.'

'Oliver Ketley.'

Peach nodded and sighed. 'Yes. But you probably think I'd never have been able to prove it, and you're probably right.'

'He wanted our shop in Preston. Apparently it would have been a nice cover for some of his dodgy operations. The licence to sell weapons appealed to him. Sam wouldn't sell. He never saw Ketley; it was all done through his hard men. They threatened Sam, said he had no real choice in the matter. They didn't know my husband.' At this darkest moment of her recollection, pride flashed out. 'Threats made Sam dig his heels in. He said he was developing a good, legitimate business and he wasn't selling out to crooks. So Ketley had him killed.'

'And being Ketley, he got away with it.'

'Because he was too strong. Too strong even for the police. A law unto himself.' She rapped out the phrases she had hugged to herself for five years.

'We'd have got him in the end, Janey. Even gangster bosses overstep the mark. They take on too much, or they get too confident. They begin to think they're above the law and get careless. It may take years, but in the end we get them.'

'And during those years, small men like Sam get killed. They're just part of the game. They get no justice, because there's "insufficient evidence".' She hissed out the last phrase, which some unfortunate copper had probably offered to her in the past.

'So you administered your own justice.'

She looked at him, gathering in the meaning of his quiet phrase, bringing herself slowly back to this time and this place. She looked around the room as if she needed her photographs and her paintings to confirm to her where they were sitting. 'No. I lay awake the other night wishing it had been me that put the bullet into his head. But that's silly; in daylight, I'm just glad Ketley's dead.'

He looked at her, still sympathetically, then said quietly, 'Why did you come here, Janey?'

'To Thorley Grange? To get as near to Ketley as I could. I had a vague idea that I would be able to do him some damage at some time in the future, if I could establish myself here. But someone took the matter out of my hands.' She looked round the room again. 'I don't know what I shall do now. Greta wants me to stay with her permanently, whatever happens to this place. She says she'll have the money to keep me on.'

'Ketley's money.'

She looked as if he had slapped her face. 'I hadn't thought of that. I suppose it is.'

'I don't think you should even consider it. Money's just money, a means to an end. After a few years. It's almost impossible to say where it came from. And Mrs Ketley's new partner is a rich man in his own right.'

'She's going to marry him, you know. It wasn't just a fling.'

'I gathered that. This death is very convenient for both of them.'

She was still and quiet for a few seconds. 'That's a lousy thing to say.'

'Lousy maybe, but a fact. Sooner or later, Oliver Ketley would have found out about Martin Price, however careful the two of them were. And you know better than most what happened to enemies of his.'

'I accept that. I don't know anything about Martin Price, except what little Greta has told me. She says he used to be in the SAS. I didn't even know he existed until yesterday.'

'He was also a mercenary in Africa. He lived by his wits and by the use of violence for many years: that's what mercenaries do.'

'You're saying he has the right background and the right motive to kill Ketley.'

'Both of those are obvious enough. I'm not saying he killed him, though. Do you think he did?'

Another of those sudden key questions, when she had thought they were finished with them. 'I don't even know him. I hope not, for Greta's sake.'

'Your friend and employer is an intelligent and resourceful woman. Do you think she and Martin Price could have done this together?'

'No.' And yet the arguments were persuasive, she thought. 'Ketley must have had many enemies. Have you no one else in mind for this?'

Peach glanced at Northcott, who had been studying her intently whilst she spoke about the mistress of Thorley Grange. Clyde said in his deep, dark-brown voice, 'There is always the possibility with gangland bosses that they are taken out by rivals. That would almost certainly involve the use of a hit-man, a professional killer who makes a living that way. We know that Ketley had a rival who is anxious to take over his rackets in the north-west. We have a certain amount of evidence, but not yet enough to arrest the hit-man we suspect.'

Janey Johnson had recovered from the stress of speaking about Sam's death, but she was still very pale. 'I hope it was this rival. And I'm glad Ketley's been removed from this world, for Sam's sake and mine. I can see that you have to try to arrest his killer, but as far as I'm concerned I shall be quite pleased if you fail.'

It was not the first time they had heard that view expressed. Clyde Northcott, who had seen life from the other side of the law and was not as clear-sighted as DCI Peach, found himself sympathizing with the sentiment.

TWENTY

'I want progress, Peach!' Chief Superintendent Thomas Bulstrode Tucker thumped his desk.

Percy Peach noted that the chief was in his masterful mode. Pride often went before a fall, especially when pride came in the form of Tommy Bloody Tucker. 'This is a complex case, sir. Oliver Ketley was a man with many enemies.' Let the man see that he wasn't the only one with a taste for the blindin' bleedin' obvious. Imitation was the sincerest form of flattery, they said. But even the omniscient 'they' didn't know T.B. Tucker.

'I'm asking for a solution, Peach. And all you give me is more suspects.'

'When a man is shot through the head in his own car and the crime is not observed, there are inevitably many possibilities, sir. We've narrowed the field. One of the problems is that everyone we've questioned closely has a strong motive for wishing Ketley dead. That is probably inevitable.'

'What about the people working at Thorley Grange? Didn't you tell me the place was teeming with foreigners and women?'

There were probably grounds for charges of both racialism and sexism in that simple question, but unfortunately no moral enthusiast was present to bear Tucker from Percy's presence to the appropriate dungeon. 'Not teeming with them, sir. In a house and business headquarters employing as many staff as Thorley Grange, women are inevitable and the odd foreigner highly probable, sir.'

'I don't want your views on the evils of modern society, Peach.' Percy wasn't aware that he'd offered any. 'I want a solution to a serious crime. It's what you're paid to provide.' His mouth set in the single sullen line of a child prepared to defy all logic.

And what you also are paid to provide. Paid more

handsomely than any of us, you bleating balloon of belligerence.' Percy enjoyed his alliteration as much as the next copper. 'We have been working diligently ever since the crime was discovered, sir.'

'Bullshit, Peach. I hope that is not simply an excuse for cutting deep into our overtime budget.'

'One can't make an omelette without breaking eggs, sir.'

It was the cliché that Tucker used whenever his superiors or the press taxed him with improvidence. The chief superintendent had a vague idea that he was being sent up, but as usual he couldn't pinpoint the moment. He moved to what he considered safer ground. 'The wife, Peach. You said she'd been acting in a suspicious manner.'

'Greta Ketley. She'd been conducting an affair for a year before her husband's death. Brave, even foolhardy, with a husband like hers. I believe she will now marry the man concerned.'

'Didn't you say he had a previous history of violence?'

'Martin Price? Yes, sir. Not a criminal record, though. He was in the SAS and reached the rank of captain. He was then forced out and spent several years as a mercenary soldier in Africa. He was in charge of a group you could call guerrilla fighters, I suppose. I put full details of it in my e-mail to you.'

Tucker waved his right hand vaguely over his empty desk. 'Why don't you get on and arrest this man? And the widow too, if she was in it with him.'

'Lack of evidence, sir. Of course, if you'd like to give us the go-ahead for these arrests, we'd be happy to make them.' He stared steadily at his chief; a small, mysterious smile appeared upon the versatile Peach lips.

'You know I don't interfere with my staff. I'm merely trying to GAL-VAN-IZE them.' It was a word Tucker had picked up from a recent management circular; he pronounced each fearful syllable of it in capital letters.

Peach did not seem as impressed as he should have been. 'Martin Price is the man involved. Both he and Greta Ketley say they now intend to get married. Price has the know-how, the background and the motive for this crime, with or without Greta Ketley's assistance.'

The Tucker chin jutted aggressively. 'Then why hasn't he been arrested?'

'Because we haven't yet managed to place him at the scene of the crime, sir.'

'Then get on and do so! Haven't house-to-house enquiries given you anything?'

'Nothing conclusive, sir. Indeed, very little indeed. A woman thought she saw a couple walking away from the spot where the Bentley was parked at around half past nine, but can give no details of them at all, beyond the fact that they appeared to be a man and woman. She thinks they had linked arms or were holding hands, but she's not even sure of that. She was only interested in driving her own car into her garage and getting safely into the warmth of her home on a cold night.'

Tucker sighed extravagantly at this terrible omission by a member of the anonymous masses he was supposed to protect. 'What about your hit-man?'

Percy noted that any unproductive suspect became his, whilst any promising one was 'ours'. Tommy Bloody Tucker was a hopeless golfer, but he had the attributes of an experienced caddie. 'George French? He's certainly a killer and we know he was employed by a rival villain to kill Ketley. But again, we can't place him at the scene. And whilst we know he received the customary advance payment for a contract killing, we haven't so far pinned down the second payment which follows the completion of the assignment.'

Tucker shook his head gloomily. 'I hope it isn't French. If it is, you'll never pin the bastard down. And we need a result!' He leant forward and banged his desk emphatically.

'We're watching Martin Price and Greta Ketley closely and keeping our ears to the ground, sir.' Percy suddenly caught the mixed imagery of this, and cackled high and loud. 'Quite a feat, sir, if you could bring it off, eh?'

Tucker, who had started violently, now rubbed his ears vigorously. 'I do wish you wouldn't do that, Peach. It's a most unseemly noise for a Detective Chief Inspector.'

'Sorry, sir. I won't burden you with any further speculation or unseemly noises. I shall go away and push the enquiry forward vigorously.'

He left a rather dazed Detective Chief Superintendent feeling considerably irritated but very little wiser. Peach was clearly a difficult man to GAL-VAN-IZE.

On the night of Thursday, 24th February, Martin Price drove his car between the high gates of Thorley Grange for the first time in his life. He parked the BMW near the main entrance to the house, where it would be quite obvious to the resident staff. He got out and stood for a moment with a proprietorial air, admiring the impressive front elevation of the original building which was all that was visible here. He glanced round at the parkland through which he had driven, then mounted the steps unhurriedly to the front doors of the Grange.

It was the statement of intent he had agreed upon with Greta. He enjoyed making it.

Greta greeted him, then embraced him warmly in the privacy of her own apartments. Suddenly, they were in bed and making love. This wasn't part of what they had agreed beforehand, but it proved a wholly acceptable diversion. Martin lay back with her head upon his arm and gazed happily at the high ceiling. Then he frowned. 'Is this the bed you used with Oliver?'

'No. He had his own room and his own bed. I used to go to him there when – when it was necessary.'

'Like a king and queen.'

'Yes. Like Henry the Eighth, I used to think. You never knew quite what to expect. And you knew you mustn't step out of line.'

He drew a finger softly down the vein on the inside of her arm. 'That's all over now.'

'Yes. I can hardly believe it. I have to keep reminding myself.' She let him stroke her arm again, then leaned over and ran her hand through his short fair hair, feeling its springiness against her palm. 'Would it have worried you, if this had been Oliver's bed?'

He smiled, his eyes upon the mouldings of the ceiling again. 'Not really, no. I've made love in some very odd places, in my time. So long as I had you with me, the location would soon be forgotten!'

She loved him for that – not for the conventional compliment at the end, but for not disguising that he'd had other women in other places before he met her. She said, 'It's time we were moving. I told them seven thirty for dinner.' When he reached out to restrain her, she levered herself up on her elbows and looked down into his face. 'We've no need to snatch at things now, my love. We'll hold each other again in this bed tonight. We've no need to snatch at things for the rest of our lives.' She spoke wonderingly, as if she could hardly believe it.

They ate in the small annexe which she'd always used when there were no guests to be entertained with pomp and ceremony in the main dining room. She was there exactly at the time she had arranged. She was the mistress of the place and no one could have chided her if she'd been late, but she regarded punctuality as one of her duties. Besides, the food was always at its best if it didn't sit around waiting for you.

They had a good bottle of claret with the beef and chatted like a happily married couple. It was the performance they had planned for the staff, but they found it came naturally enough to them. Indeed, for Greta it came much more easily than the strained charades of closeness she had needed to perform with Oliver in the months that were gone. There was a moment of intimacy, when the main course had been served and there was no one in the room but the couple at the table. They clinked glasses, muttered a toast to the life to come, and touched fingers briefly.

A little later, he tried to discuss their future together and what they would do about the Grange and its staff. But Greta said, 'It's too early for that, my love. And this isn't the place. There are people serving this meal and running this place who have more at stake than either of us.'

'You're right. I should never have raised it. Not here, and not now.' He was a man used to secrecy, a man for whom it had been a necessary fact of life in many a hazardous enterprise. He had no secrets from Greta; they had come a long way together in the last year, and had further still to go.

But elsewhere it would be difficult but necessary to drop the habit of secrecy, with his last great coup achieved.

*   *   *

In the house of Jack Burgess at Alderley Edge, things were nothing like so relaxed. He had summoned his hit-man, and the hit-man had not wanted to come.

The whole essence of being a contract killer was anonymity. George French had lived by that maxim so thoroughly that he was distinctly uncomfortable whenever he was compelled to abandon it. Jack Burgess was a good customer and a good payer, and the customer called the tune. So he had come here when bidden, parking his car a hundred and fifty yards from the gate of the high Edwardian house, as was his wont. But he wasn't easy about his presence here with the gangland boss.

Indeed, he went so far as to offer the opinion that this could have been better done by telephone, from the point of view of both parties.

Jack Burgess smiled. 'You're quite safe here, George. You surely didn't think you'd anything to fear from me?'

'No, of course not.' French had noticed that all these tycoons of crime liked to demonstrate their power, as if they had to remind themselves continually of how far they had come. 'It's just that I like to keep a low profile.'

'And I like to see the people I use face to face occasionally, George. Especially those people whose services I retain for money.'

'Ah! I was going to mention that, as soon as I got the chance.'

Burgess let the words hang in the high, quiet room, as though exposure to the air might somehow diminish them and cast the appropriate doubt upon the speaker. 'Really, George? I thought myself that there'd been a notable absence of contact or information from your quarter.'

'I've been interviewed twice by the CID. They came to my house.'

'Yes, I know that. Cigar, George?' He pushed the open box towards his visitor and began the unhurried process of piercing and lighting a cigar for himself.

'No thanks.'

'No? Well, I suppose anything which might take the edge off the French reflexes has to be avoided, eh?' He blew a long, reflective funnel of blue smoke towards the glass bowl of the light fitting.

'But I didn't deliver on the assignment you offered me.'

'Indeed you didn't George. Pity, that, from your point of view.'

'I didn't fail. My preliminary plans were already in place. But someone got there before me.' Burgess was making him nervous, and nervousness was something this cool and well-organized man wasn't used to.

'Yes. Who was that, George?'

'I don't know. I thought you might know, Mr Burgess.'

'Me? Oh no, I'm an innocent in such things, George.'

It seemed a strange statement from the man who had given him twenty-five thousand as deposit for the killing of Oliver Ketley. 'I don't know either. I'm innocent of this killing.'

'I believe you are, George. Though not quite so innocent of the death of a certain man in Birmingham yesterday, I hear.' Burgess blew another long, leisurely plume of smoke and smiled reflectively as it dissipated around the light. 'The problem is that I don't like paying for services which haven't been rendered. You've just said you didn't deliver on Oliver Ketley. Pity, but there it is. I've made a large preliminary payment, but never received delivery.' He nodded slowly, apparently happy with his phrasing.

'I've every intention of reimbursing, you, Mr Burgess. Always have had.'

'That's good to hear, George. I'm sure my staff will also be glad to hear it.'

French ignored the threat. 'It's just that with the police watching my every move, I didn't want to offer them anything.' A happy thought occurred to him. 'I didn't wish to do anything which might lead them to you.'

'Admirable, George, admirable. But I don't like paying for what hasn't happened, as I said. It's a matter of principle. If I let one person get away with exploiting me, the word might get around and others might be tempted, you see.'

'I've always had every intention of returning your money, Mr Burgess.' The fear he heard in his voice wasn't a good advertisement for a contract killer. But he was an individual operator, and Burgess had a huge criminal organization. In real life, Goliath rarely lost.

'That's why I brought you here tonight, George, you see. To make things simple for you. An old-fashioned cheque will suffice.' He gestured towards the desk and the thirties desk-set upon it.

French had many objections to cheques, but he wasn't going to voice them now, in this room where might was so emphatically right. He slipped a cheque-book from his inside pocket and said, 'To whom do I make it payable?'

'I like that "To whom", George. Shows a well-educated man, that does. Burgess Enterprises will do, for this one. And you must have had certain preliminary expenses.'

'Pardon? Oh, yes, I mentioned that I'd made preparations for the assignment.'

'You did indeed, George. And I shall make allowances for that, being a reasonable man.'

'There's no need for that, Mr Burgess. Luck of the game, as you might say.'

'Might you, indeed?' He blew a valedictory funnel of smoke, then stubbed his cigar into the ashtray. 'But fair's fair, George. I shall allow you five thousand for preliminary preparations and the expenses involved. I know you plan carefully, and I know that time is money, for a professional man like you. Make out your cheque for twenty thousand only – assuming that is acceptable for you.'

'Very fair, Mr Burgess.'

'Good. I like to be fair. I should like to think you would be glad to oblige if I should require your services in the future.'

'Always willing, Mr Burgess. And always discreet.' French tried too late to recover equilibrium and standing.

'Good to hear, George, good to hear. And now I expect you'd like to be on your way.'

George French had to prevent himself from scurrying down the drive. In the road outside, he found himself wishing that his car was rather nearer. He kept a wary eye on the straggling rhododendrons and cedars in the gardens of the big houses beside him as he hurried back to his car. He wasn't used to being scared. But then he was used to controlling the places where he went and the plans of action he followed.

He drove fast down the M56 towards the haven of his anonymous bungalow in Oldham.

TWENTY-ONE

Percy Peach was normally a good sleeper. It was one of the reasons why he arrived at the station bouncing with the energy of a March hare, a quality much regretted by his fellow officers in the CID section.

But in the early hours of Friday the 26th February he was much disturbed. He woke at one a.m. with an idea in his mind which refused to be dismissed. He slept but fitfully for the rest of the night. Like all people in such circumstances, he resented the serene sleeping of the person beside him. Lucy lay still and breathed evenly through the wildest of his speculations. That seemed to him insensitive. He was, he was sure, quite right to be irritated.

He would like to have tested his ideas against his wife's sturdy common sense, but she slept on regardless until the clock shrilled beside them. Then she stretched her arms extravagantly, slid from the bed, and showered quickly. 'Time you were moving!' she called breezily to the mound beneath the bedclothes.

Percy had suffered the usual fate of the deprived sleeper. He had fallen into an exhausted sleep half an hour before the alarm summoned him back to the harsh realities of the day. 'Who rattled your cage?' he growled at Lucy, who was already almost dressed.

'And a bright good morning to you too.' She slipped into a New York accent for the phrase she knew he hated. 'Have a nice day now!'

Percy groaned and levered himself to a sitting position on the edge of the bed. He scratched his head, as he remembered his father doing when he was a boy. But his father had possessed hair, which he did not. He felt better by the time he had washed and shaved. The ideas which had disturbed his night were still with him. He would run them past Lucy at breakfast and get her professional opinion as to the best way to proceed.

But Lucy was ready for the off as he poured his cereal from the packet. 'We've got militant Muslims to question,' she explained casually, as if this was run-of-the-mill stuff for her. Unfortunately, that was very nearly the true situation. Brunton, with its large Asian population, was a centre for the fanatical minority who plotted terrorist acts. The CID section where DS Lucy Peach now worked was aware of several embryo plots against the state. They observed and waited, hamstrung by the necessary restrictions of a democracy. You couldn't arrest and charge anyone until you had enough evidence to mount a convincing case in court. Yet if you let the action move beyond a certain point you endangered innocent human lives.

'Good luck, then. And for God's sake take care!'

She smiled at him from the door, blew a silent kiss at the figure hunched at the breakfast table, and was gone. It was a useless phrase he had flung at her as she left – like that of an anxious parent. But wasn't that appropriate, for a newly married man bidding farewell to the woman he loved? Percy went back to his thoughts of the small hours and his plans to take account of them. He knew quite well what he was going to do, but it would have been heartening to run it past Lucy, his companion on many previous and similar occasions.

Instead, he voiced his thoughts to that very different figure, DS Clyde Northcott. The tall and powerful black man could hardly have been more different in appearance from the fair-skinned, chestnut-haired and voluptuous Lucy Peach. Yet they had one thing in common which was more important than any physical feature. Both of them were detective sergeants, experienced not only in the many manifestations of crime but in what was possible and what was not for those whose duty it was to uphold the law.

Clyde Northcott listened, at first doubtingly, then with increasing excitement. He asked a number of questions as Peach outlined his thinking, then sought directions about the way he should play his own part in this unfolding drama. 'By ear,' said Percy rather grimly. 'We haven't a lot of firm evidence yet. We'll get it over the next couple of weeks, if we have to. My feeling is that there won't be much resistance, if we blend accusation with understanding and a little bluff.'

Clyde weighed this judgement as he drove the police Mondeo towards Thorley Grange. Percy Peach was very good at understanding and bluff. He also had judgement, an appreciation of when to move and of what was possible. As his still quite new DS, Clyde was quite prepared to follow the master. He was also unexpectedly nervous about it. Playing it by ear was all very well, but if you misjudged the moment, you made mistakes. And Percy had that determined look which indicated that he wouldn't allow mistakes.

They'd given no notice of their arrival, since Peach wanted the two people concerned to have no warning and no chance to confer. Mrs Frobisher allotted them the office by the front entrance, which had been little used since Ketley's death, and promised to locate and deliver the two employees concerned without delay. It was a test of her professional bearing, but the housekeeper passed it easily enough. She showed neither the surprise nor the curiosity she felt with the announcement of these names.

Chung Lee came to them within two minutes. He was clad in his white kitchen overalls, which seemed to Clyde Northcott to make him more defenceless and vulnerable. Lee had grown used to being inscrutable; it had been a great help throughout his time in Britain. Even now, his pleasant, olive-skinned face and watchful brown eyes gave nothing away, though he plainly wondered what was in store for him.

Peach examined him from head to toe, then said, 'Sit down, please, Mr Lee. We are waiting for someone else.'

With the mention of this unnamed other party, Chung Lee's sphinx-like control showed its first cracks. He glanced at the door, then swiftly from one to the other of the two contrasting faces in front of him. He sat down very cautiously, as if he feared that the chair beneath him might explode if he treated it roughly.

It was a full two minutes before their other suspect arrived. Peach continued to study Lee throughout this time, offering neither smile nor frown, uttering not a word to break the tension of a period which seemed to the man in whites to stretch interminably. When Janey Johnson knocked softly at the door and came wonderingly into the room, he leaped immediately to his feet, as much from shock as from natural courtesy it seemed.

'Sit down, Mr Lee,' said Peach calmly. He too had risen when the woman came into the room. He gave her the smallest of smiles, then said, 'Sit here, please, Mrs Johnson,' and installed her in the chair beside Lee. She seated herself watchfully on the edge of the chair, finding that she and the man from the kitchens could not look at each other without a deliberate turn of the head.

It was to her that Peach addressed his first words. 'A well-known fact, attested by you and by others, Mrs Johnson: Oliver Ketley was a womanizer. You realized that this could be useful to you.'

'I couldn't stand the man anywhere near me. I told you why yesterday.'

'You also told us that he had your husband killed. That he had got away with that, for a variety of reasons. That you were determined on retribution for that crime.'

'I don't think I said I was determined on retribution. I believe I said that I was glad Ketley was dead and that I hoped you wouldn't manage to arrest whoever killed him.'

She was very cool, very determined. Defiance had given her colour and made her small, neat face even more attractive beneath her short-cut black hair. She had taken off her apron before she came here; she sat with knees together beneath her modest dark blue skirt. Her brown eyes bold and watchful. Peach said quietly, it seemed almost apologetically, 'I believe you conquered your revulsion for Oliver Ketley long enough to sit in the passenger seat of his car and lure him to his death.'

She gasped. 'I couldn't stand being near the man. And much as I'd like to have shot him to avenge Sam, I could never have done that. I hate guns of all kinds. I've never handled one in my life.'

'We can accept all that. But you had assistance.' He glanced at the man beside her.

'Chung was here on Saturday night. I saw him coming out of his room to collect a book from the rest room by the kitchen. I told you that yesterday.'

'You did indeed. And thus gave yourself an alibi for the

time of the murder as well as Mr Lee. But it was rather a shaky story. The notion that you would leave your room at nine o'clock on a Saturday night to check on your flower arrangements in the hall seemed at best unlikely. So did the possibility that Mr Lee should emerge from his room to collect his book from the kitchen refreshment area at precisely the moment when you were returning to your room. Perhaps that is what set me thinking.'

'This is preposterous. You've nothing to support your outrageous accusations.'

Peach continued to study her face for a moment, then nodded to Northcott beside him. The dark-brown voice said quietly, almost melodically, 'Are you willing to give us a DNA sample, Mrs Johnson?'

A pause, whilst she considered the implications of this. Janey found herself desperately wanting to look at the man in whites beside her, to take his counsel in this. 'What would be the purpose of that, when I know that I had nothing to do with this crime?'

'The forensic examination of the Bentley has revealed hair from a human head, Mrs Johnson. Dark hair. If you have never been in that car as you claim, a DNA test could eliminate you from the enquiry.'

'It's tempting. But as I was never there, I see no need to account for myself.'

Peach said softly, 'When you are arrested, Mrs Johnson, we shall be able to take a DNA test with or without your permission.'

Janey noticed that 'when'. She said stubbornly, 'I didn't shoot Oliver Ketley. I've told you that. I wish I could have done it, but I didn't.'

'No. You made him think he could have sex with you.' He watched the involuntary shudder shake her small, shapely body. 'You distracted him so ably that Mr Lee was able to put the bullet through his head without resistance from the victim. I doubt whether Ketley ever knew he was there.'

Her brown eyes stared fixedly ahead of her. 'I've told you. Chung was here on Saturday night at the time of the murder. I saw him.'

'Yes. It's interesting that you were able to pinpoint the right time for that alibi when we spoke yesterday. The time of the death has never been revealed in our press releases.' He switched his attention suddenly to the man beside her. 'Our forensic laboratories have analysed fibres found in the rear of the car, Mr Lee. Green woollen fibres, which I believe in due course will be found to have come from the sweater you were wearing at the time of our first interview on Monday. That was when you told us a fabricated story about eating Thai green curry with a friend in Brunton at the time of Ketley's death.'

The detail of that lie, which he had admitted yesterday and which was thus irrelevant now, was what finally undid Chung. Suddenly everything seemed hopeless. They would arrest him, take his DNA, pin the crime on him once and for all. All this shabby deceit seemed suddenly unworthy of him, an insult to the brother he had worked for years in this foreign land to avenge. He glanced wildly at Janey, and each of them knew in that moment that it was over.

Janey nodded at him, reached across and put her small hand on top of his, as if for those few seconds they were the only people in the room. Then she turned back to face the two CID men. She was silent for a moment, forcing herself to accept that the lying was over and the final brief act of confession was all that was left. She burst into a sudden smile which showed how near she was to hysteria.

She said, dully, as if speaking only for herself, 'I'm glad it was such a big car. Ketley tried to paw me for a moment when he got into it, but I told him to wait.'

It was Northcott's deep, reassuring voice which said, 'Isn't it time you told us all about it, Janey? That will make it easier for you, as well as for us.'

She glanced again at Lee Chung, who nodded and gave her his own smile, resigned but fearful. She said, 'Ketley had already made a couple of passes at me. It was only a question of time before he cornered me somewhere in the house. I saw the way Chung looked at him one night after we'd served a meal – with the same accumulated hatred I felt for the man.'

She turned and grinned at Lee, who said, 'Janey told me

she could see how I hated him and told me how he had killed
her Sam. I told her about my brother on the night of the
cockle-pickers in 2004. I told her how I had been scheming
to get near him for years. We saw that it was possible we
could work together.'

Janey took up the tale again, it seemed almost eagerly. 'I
let Ketley lure me to one of his Saturday night assignations.
He offered me big money.' Her mouth curled in contempt at
the memory, at the thought that any amount of money could
have induced her to sleep with that monster. 'He specified an
exact time. He told me to go to the Bentley in the garage and
wait for him in the front passenger seat. He'd make sure the
car was left open. What he didn't realize was that I wouldn't
be the only one in that car.'

Lee spoke up; he seemed quite determined to assert his part
in this. 'I am very small man, when I need to be. I curled up
very small behind the driving seat, on the floor of the car.
Janey she very good. Very good indeed. She keep all his attention. She make sure Ketley don't see me behind him.' His
normally near-perfect English was suffering a little, becoming
jerky under the stress of confession.

Janey said. 'I had a short skirt. That was enough to get all
of the man's attention. He tried to stroke me, but I said I was
nervous that someone would see us. He must wait for the
hotel. He managed to paw my thigh just once as he started
the engine.'

She looked down at the offending limb as if she had washed
it many times and still found it soiled. 'I was glad when we
moved out of the Grange and on to the roads. He had to give
his attention to driving then. But he apparently still wanted a
preliminary snog. He pulled up the car in a quiet place when
I suggested it and reached out for me. He was trying to put
my hand on his penis when Chung shot him.' She stopped
abruptly, still aghast at that final action of Ketley's.

Chung Lee asserted sturdily, 'It was I who shot that man.
Janey had nothing to do with it. Except that she gave me the
opportunity to do what we both wanted to do.'

Peach shook his head and smiled grimly. 'You will both be
charged with murder.'

Janey had the fixed smile of the fanatic. 'And I wouldn't have it any other way.'

Clyde Northcott stepped forward and delivered the formal words of the arrest. It might have been done much earlier, with its warning that anything said would be recorded and might be used in evidence, but all four people in the room knew that neither of the accused was going to go back on anything they'd said.

Peach looked from one to the other of the two contrasting faces. 'A second police car arrived here ten minutes ago. You will both be handcuffed until you are delivered to the station, where formal charges will be made. Mr Lee will ride with the two uniformed officers. Mrs Johnson will be in our vehicle.'

As they followed the police car back to Brunton, Peach and Northcott could see the small figure of Chung Lee sitting very upright in the rear seat of the car ahead of them. Peach drove this time, leaving his large assistant beside the still composed woman on the back seat. They were within a mile of the station when he spoke over his shoulder, apparently to his DS. 'I can't condone murder and the law must take its course. But the punishment should take account of the character of the victim and the motives of his killers. I am glad that the world is rid of Oliver Ketley. It is already a much better place without him.'

Many months later, a judge would utter more guarded but surprisingly similar sentiments as he prepared to deliver his sentences.